They saw me! All of them. ... upon me, avid and victorious, not moving, not needing to move, for there were other things swarming around me, binding me while the smoke held me fast. The words came as though in a dream, from some distantly echoing place. "Let me have her," begged Dedrina. "No," the Oracle said, looking in my direction. "Such is not what the Great Ones prefer." I said nothing. Lips and tongue did not obey. No part of me would move.

They went into the darkness then and Jinian Footseer was forced to follow. Into darkness and pain.

Then only darkness.

Also by Sheri S. Tepper

THE TRUE GAME
THE CHRONICLES OF MAVIN MANYSHAPED
JINIAN FOOTSEER
THE REVENANTS
BLOOD HERITAGE
THE BONES

and published by Corgi Books

THE AWAKENERS

published by Bantam Press

DERVISH
DAUGHTER

Sheri S. Tepper

CORGI BOOKS

DERVISH DAUGHTER
A CORGI BOOK   0 552   13190 3

First publication in Great Britain

PRINTING HISTORY

Corgi edition published 1988

Copyright © 1986 by Sheri S. Tepper

This book is set in 10/11 Joanna

Corgi Books are published by Transworld Publishers Ltd., 61-63 Uxbridge Road, Ealing, London W5 5SA, in Australia by Transworld Publishers (Australia) Pty. Ltd., 15-23 Helles Avenue, Moorebank, NSW 2170, and in New Zealand by Transworld Publishers (N.Z.) Ltd., Cnr. Moselle and Waipareira Avenues, Henderson, Auckland.

Reproduced, printed and bound in Great Britain by
Hazell Watson & Viney Limited
Member of BPCC plc
Aylesbury Bucks

CHAPTER ONE

Just across the chasm from the town of Zog a bunch of wild brats with crossbows – and poisoned arrows, to add to the general sense of fun – had given us quite a run. We'd barely gotten away from them with our skins whole.

There had been constant storm damage blocking the roads, continuous sullen clouds, and a threatening mutter of sentient-seeming thunder.

I had a huge, aching lump on my forehead from not being quick enough ducking into the wagon during the hail storm four days before. Hail the size of goose eggs!

Add to that the remains we kept finding along the way, more and more of them as we went farther north. Human remains, mostly, and the yellow dream crystals that had killed them.

Throw in the fact we'd been driving two days and nights without sleep, dodging shadow, which seemed to be everywhere.

Then season the whole horrid mess with a harsh scream as a night bird plummeted across the moonlit sky screeching, *'Lovely dead meat, not even rotten yet!'*

I understood it as easily as though it had been shouted at me by some old dame in the underbrush. The bird's cry said 'human meat,' not some luckless zeller killed by a pombi's claws. I put my hand over Queynt's where they lay on the reins.

He snapped out of his doze, immediately alert, as I reached beneath the wagon seat for my bow. 'More trouble ahead,' I said wearily, nocking an arrow.

Queynt yawned, giving my bow a doubtful look. Though he had been teaching me to shoot with the stated intention of providing for the pot, my inability to hit anything smaller than a gnarlibar had become a joke. They had begun to call natural landmarks that were suitably huge a 'good target for Jinian.' The problem was that I couldn't shoot anything that talked to me. Oh, if someone else shot it, I could eat it, and if something came at me with unpleasant intent, I was able to kill it readily enough no matter what it was saying. Bunwits and zeller and tree rats, however, were safe from my arrows so long as they said good morning politely. I hadn't discussed this with Queynt, though I thought he suspected it.

He glanced down, then back into the wagon where his Wizard's kit was. I knew he was considering getting out his own bow or taking time to set a protection spell, evidently deciding against it. We'd learned to trust the instincts of Yittleby and Yattleby in times of danger, and neither of the two tall krylobos pulling the wagon seemed overly disturbed. Their beaks were forward, their eyes watchful as we came around a curve at the crest of a hill, but neither of them showed any agitation. We came out of the jungle at the top of a long, sloping savannah, dotted with dark, crouching bushes and half-lit by a gibbous moon. I could see all the way to the bottom of the hill where the forest started again and two twinkling lanterns, amber and red, moved among the trees near the ground. That had to be Peter and Chance. They'd been riding ahead and had evidently found something, disturbing the bird at the time. Queynt clucked to the krylobos, and we began the slow descent toward the lanterns with him looking remarkably alert for such an old man.

Vitior Vulpas Queynt is over a thousand years old. Everything I have learned about him indicates this is really true and not some mere bit of rodomontade. He hadn't made a special point of claiming to be that old, mind you; it simply came out as we went along. Peter and I had met him a couple of years before, or rather, he had picked us up on the road – he and his remarkable tall-wheeled wagon and the two huge birds that pulled it. He had picked us up and made use of us and we of him, all in a fit of mutual suspicion, and when it was over we found ourselves quite fond of one another. And the birds, too, of course. Krylobos are very large – tailless, as are all native creatures of this world, with plumy topknots and somewhat irascible tempers. They like me since I can talk to them, and I like them because they dislike the same things I do. Bathing in very cold water, for example. Or eating fruit that isn't quite ripe. They don't have teeth to set on edge, but the expression around their beaks is quite sufficient to evoke sympathy.

Which is beside the point. Queynt has a fondness for fantastical dress and ornamental speech and enjoys being thought a fool. He says he learns a great deal that way. He is an explorer at heart, so he has said, and exploring is what he and Peter and Chance and I had been doing for some time. He is the only person to whom Chance has ever given unstinting admiration. So Peter says, who has known Chance far longer than I.

This admiration is more understandable in that Vitior Vulpas Queynt and Chance much resemble each other. Both are brown, muscular men who look a little soft without being so at all. Both are jolly-appearing men who seem a little stupid and aren't. And both have quantities of common sense. As for the rest of it, Queynt is a Wizard of vast experience and education, while Chance is an ex-sailor with a fondness for gambling who was hired to bring Peter up safely and did so – more or less. Both of them have had a certain tutelary role in our lives. Peter's and mine, and truth to tell, I like them both mightily. Even on an occasion like this, when weariness made it hard to be fond of anyone.

We approached the lanterns. A faint sweetish smell told me everything I wanted to know about it before we got there. More dream crystal deaths.

Before we ever started on this trip – after the Battle of the Bones on the Wastes of Bleer it was, when we were all remarkably glad merely to be alive – I had known about dream crystals. My un-mother (the woman who bore me but did not conceive me, if that makes sense) had had at least one. It had led her into ruin and ended, I supposed, by killing her. My much hated enemy, Porvius Bloster, had had one, and it had done him no good at all except to make him exceed his limitations and bring destruction upon his Demesne. Even girls at school had had dream crystals, assortments of them, like candies. I had known what they were in a casual way, known enough to stay away from them and mistrust those who used them, but it was not until this trip that I had seen them in general use. Misuse. Whatever. It was not until this trip I had seen them killing people by the dozens. There, that's plain enough.

The current situation was a case in point. It was another of those pathetic encampments we had seen entirely too many of during the past season.

One couldn't dignify the structures even as huts. They were the kind of shelter a bored child might build in a few careless moments; a few branches leaned against a fallen tree – its trunk loaded with epiphytes and fogged by a dense cloud of ghost moths – and a circle of rocks rimming a pool of ash. And the corpses. Three of them this time; man, woman, and baby. Starved to death, from the look of them, and with food all round for the picking or digging – furry, thick-skinned pocket-bushes full of edible nuts, a northern thrilp bush – smaller fruit, and sweeter than the southern variety – table roots just beside the tiny stream.

'Hell,' I said to Queynt, disgusted. 'I suppose they've got those yellow crystals in their mouths, like all the rest.'

Half-right. In the lantern light we could see the male corpse had one on a thong around his neck; the female had one in her mouth, having sucked herself to death on it. Their bodies were still warm. The baby was cold, probably dead of dehydration after screaming his lungs out for several days trying to tell someone he was hungry and thirsty and wet.

Chance and Peter were dismounted by the corpses. Peter gave me a troubled look, knowing I'd be upset by the baby. Chance eased his wide belt and mused, 'I suppose we could dig them in, though there seems little sense to bother.'

At first we'd stopped to bury the human dead along the road, but they had become more and more numerous as we came farther north. There had soon been too many to bury, but it still bothered me to let the babies lie. 'I'll bury the baby,' I said in a voice that sounded angry even to me. 'Let the others alone.'

Queynt shook his head, but he didn't argue. All the babies reminded me of one I'd taken care of in a class back in Xammer. The one in Xammer had the same baffled look when he fell asleep that many of the dead babies did, as though it had all been too much for him and he was glad to be out of it. I wrapped this one in our last towel, reminding myself to buy towels the next time we got to any place civilized – if there were any place civilized in these northlands. I'd used up our supply burying babies and children.

Queynt said, 'Jinian, if you're going to go on like this, I'll lay in a supply of shrouds. It would be cheaper than good toweling.'

I flushed, getting on with the half-druggled grave I was digging with the shovel we used for latrine ditches. 'I know it doesn't make sense, Queynt, but otherwise I get bad dreams.' He already knew that; we'd discussed it before.

'There's a city somewhere ahead,' said Peter, trying to change the subject. 'I can hear it.'

It wasn't surprising. He had Shifted himself a pair of ears which stood out like batwings on either side of his head. Probably hadn't even realized he was doing it. I turned away to hide the expression on my face – he did look silly – only to see Queynt touching his tongue to the crystal the dead man had had around his neck. Even though Queynt had told us over and over he was immune, seeing him do that made me shudder. I was going to find out about that alleged immunity sooner or later, but so far he hadn't explained it. Now he saw me shiver and shook his head at me.

'We have to know, girl!'

Well, he was right. We did have to know. Those louts outside Zog had had crystals hanging around their necks, too. Reddish ones. Queynt hadn't had a chance to taste one of those, but then he hadn't needed to. It was evident what dreams of violence and rapine they were breeding in the brats. Along with everything else, they had been chanting a litany to Storm Grower while they tried to kill us. We'd been hunting Storm Grower for some seasons now, and hearing the name in this context made the hunt seem even more ominous than we'd already decided it was.

Queynt nodded at me about this yellow crystal, telling me it was like the others we'd found beside the dead bodies along the road. Anyone touching it to his tongue would be utterly at peace, in a place of perfect contentment with no hunger, no thirst, no desires. Someone sucking a crystal like that wouldn't hear a baby crying or the sound of their own stomach screaming for food. Someone sucking on that dream would lie there and die. And there were hundreds along the road who had done just that – families, singletons, even whole mounted troops, dead on the ground with the horses still saddled and wandering. We'd found one pile of small furry things which Queynt believed were Shadowpeople, though the carrion birds had left little enough to identify. All with yellow crystals in their mouths, their hands, or on thongs around their necks. We hadn't found a single one on anyone still living.

When the grave was filled in, I pulled myself up on the wagon seat again. Queynt nodded sympathetically as we started off into the gray light of early dawn. 'Someone's getting rid of excess population,' he mumbled. 'Dribs and drabs of it.'

'What I can't figure out is how and why certain ones are so all of a sudden excess! We've found dead

Gamesmen and dead pawns, young and old, male and female. All with these same damn yellow things. The crystals are all alike, same color, same size. Someone has to be making them!'

'You've mentioned that before, Jinian. Several times, as I recall.' He sighed, yawned, scratched himself. 'You know, girl,' he drawled, going into one of his ponderous perorations, 'though we may conjecture until we have worn imagination to shreds, theorize until our brains are numb with it, baffle our knowledge with mystery and our logic with the futility of it all, until we find out where they're coming from, anything we guess is only hot air and worth about as much.' He fell into a brooding silence as we rattled on with the krylobos talking nonsense to one another and Peter and Chance riding just ahead. So we had ridden, league on league, hundreds and hundreds of them, ever since leaving the lands of the True Game. Some days it seemed we'd been riding like this forever.

I could see Peter's animated profile from time to time as he turned to speak to Chance. His face was bronze from the sun. He'd grown up, too, in the last few seasons. The bones in his cheeks and jaw were bold, no longer child-like, and there was a strong breadth to his forehead. It was his mouth that got to me, though, the way his upper lip curved down in the center, a funny little dip, as though someone had pinched it. Every time I saw that, I wanted to touch it with my tongue. Like a sweet. No. Not like a sweet. Well, I needed comforting, and seeing him there within reach, within touching distance, made me want to yell or run or go hide in the wagon.

Sometimes I wished that the way I felt about Peter was an illness. If it were an illness, a Healer could cure it. As it was, it went on all the time with no hope of a cure. Every morning when the early light made sensuous wraiths of the mists, every evening when the dusk ghosts crept into erotic tangles around the foliage (see, even my language was getting lubricious), I found myself thinking unhelpful thoughts that made me blush and breathe as though I'd been running. I furnished every grove with likely spots for dalliance, and lately I'd taken to crossing off every day that passed, counting the ones that remained until the season my oath of celibacy would be done.

Queynt had been watching me; I caught his kindly stare and blushed. 'Troubled about your oath?' he asked me sympathetically.

He caught me unaware. One of the things that bothered me about Queynt was his habit of knowing what I was thinking. He wasn't a Demon. He had no business just knowing that way. 'Yes.' I turned red again. It wasn't any of his business, and yet . . . 'By the Hundred Devils and all their pointy ears, Queynt, I can't understand the sense of it. They said it was to let me study the art without distractions, but I'm not studying the art! I'm traveling. Trying to keep my skin whole. Trying to locate Dream Miner and Storm Grower and find out why they want me dead. Praying Peter keeps on being fond of me at least until the oath runs out. Celibacy doesn't seem to make a lot of sense!'

'Oh,' he said mildly, 'it does, you know. If you examine it. For example, you've been doing summons, haven't you?'

Well, I had, of course. A few. I might have called up an occasional water dweller to provide a fish dinner. Or maybe a few flood-chucks, just to help us get through some timber piles on the road. I admitted as much, wondering what he was getting at.

'Well, if you've been doing summons, have you ever stopped to think what an unconsidered pregnancy might do to the practice of the art?'

An unconsidered pregnancy – or even a considered one – was about the furthest thing from my mind at the moment. But this was something not one of the dams had mentioned to me, not even the midwife, Tess Tinder-my-hand, who would have been the logical one to do so. My jaw dropped and I gave him an idiot look.

12

'Well, let's say you're pregnant and you summon up something obstreperous in the way of a water dweller. Then you go through the constraints and dismissal, but the water dweller considers the child in your belly was part of the summons. That child has neither constrained nor dismissed. So, time comes you give birth to something that looks rather more like a fish than you might think appropriate. Recent research would indicate a good many of the magical races are the results of just such Wize-ardly accidents.'

'Mermaids? Dryads?'

'Among others, and not the most strange, either. Have you ever called up a deep dweller?'

I had heard them laugh a few times during bridge magic but had never called them. Murzy had told me to be careful, very careful, with them. I shook my head again.

'I have. Pesky, mischievous creatures, but more than half-manlike, for all that. If it weren't for their fangy mouths, you'd think them children. I shouldn't wonder if that race came from some magical accident during pregnancy. Not that deep dwellers are common.'

All of which was something to think about. I snapped my mouth shut and thought about it.

I'd never really understood the reason for the oath – three years of celibacy (virginity in my case) sworn when I was just fifteen. I'd done it, of course, because they wouldn't let me be in the seven otherwise, and if I weren't in the seven, I couldn't go on studying the art. At that time, the art was just about all I had to care about except for the seven old dams themselves. Well, six and me.

So, I took the oath, and got initiated, and learned some fascinating things, all a good bit of time before Peter came along. When he did come along, however, the oath began to feel like a suit of tight armor. There was it, all hard and smooth outside, and there was me, all sweaty and passionate inside. And that's the way this trip had gone, with me being hard and cold half the

13

time and hiding in the wagon the rest of the time, afraid of what might happen if I came out. I didn't wonder that Queynt could see it. No one could have missed it.

Peter came galloping back, head down, looking thoroughly tired and irritable. 'More trees down. A real swath cut up ahead. We'll need to find a way around. No possible way of getting through it.'

When we arrived at the tumble, it was obvious he was right. Seven or eight really big trees, fallen into a kind of jackstraw mess, their branches all tangled together. Lesser trees were fallen in the forest, the whole making a deadfall that we could have scrambled through if we'd had a few extra hours with nothing better to do and hadn't minded leaving the wagon behind.

Off to the right the forest thinned out a little. There were wide-enough spaces between the trees to get down into a meadow, and the meadow looked as though it stretched past the obstruction and back to the road. Chance was at the edge of the open space, beckoning.

Queynt krerked a few syllables to Yittleby and Yattleby, they turning their great beaks in reply. He had said, 'Can you handle this?' and they had replied, 'Why even ask?' He had picked up a few words of the krylobos' language over the years. I wasn't always sure that he knew what he was saying.

It was first light, still very dim. I got off to walk beside the wagon as it tilted from side to side over the road banks and through the scattered trees. Watching where I was walking had become a habit, and when I saw it I stopped without conscious effort, hollering to Queynt, 'Shadow! Stop. Look there.'

Unlike the rivers of dark we had seen flowing along the road farther south, this patch was a small one, the size of an outspread cape. It lay under a willow copse, directly in my path, easy to miss in this half-light.

When we'd started this adventure, traveling along

the shores of the Glistening Sea among the towns of the Bight, we'd seen shadow piled on shadow. We'd taken refuge in the wagon more than once when we'd encountered great swatches of it creeping and crawling about us in the forests and chasms. In comparison to that, this little patch was almost innocent looking.

'What's holding you?' asked Peter, riding down behind us.

'Shadow.' Queynt was laconic about it. Though he claimed to have seen it seldom before we started our northern trip, he had accustomed himself to the sight better than I. Shadow never failed to give me a sick emptiness inside, a fading feeling, as though I had become unreal. I had been shadow bit once, in Chimmerdong. As they say, once bit, twice sore.

'Well.' He sat there for a moment, staring at it, shifting from haunch to haunch, looking cross the way he does when he's hungry. 'It doesn't look any different from any other we've seen. Are you going to sit here all morning looking at it, or can we go around it and get back to the road?' Peter was, as usual, impatient.

There was no reason to watch it. Shadow seldom did anything. When it was angered, and as far as I knew no one knew what made it angry, it attacked. Otherwise, it simply lay. Anything that stepped into shadow, of course, would be better off dead sooner than it died. Moved by a fleeting curiosity, I took off one boot and set my bare foot on the ground. There was a tingle there, very slight, which meant there was a remnant of the Old Road buried deep beneath us. I'd had the suspicion for some time that the shadow gathered mostly where there were remnants of the Ancient Roads, though I had no idea what it meant. Seeing Queynt's curious gaze focused on me, I flushed and put my boot back on.

We led the birds around the shadow patch, though I think they were fully capable of avoiding it on their own, and then back up through the meadow to the road once more, where the stack of shattered trunks was now blocking the way behind us. Since hearing those Zoggian brats chant their litany to Storm Grower, I had a pretty good idea where this kind of damage came from – not that we could verify it. Ever since we'd first seen this random destruction, we'd asked about it. Those we'd asked didn't answer. Since we had no Demon with us to read minds, we had given up asking, but we hadn't given up wondering. We went on, with me still suspiciously looking for shadow as we rattled along the road.

'There's the city Peter heard,' said Queynt.

We had topped a rise and looked down into a green valley, a city cupped at the center. The place was crowned with ostentatious mansions, much carved stone and lancet windows and so prodigious a display of banners – which were either excessively pink or blushed by the sunrise – some festival must have been in progress. I sighed. Towns of any kind seemed to mean trouble recently, and I was too tired even to fight for my life.

'I wonder if there's an inn with a good cook!'

'Burials make you hungry, do they?'

I swallowed my protest. Fact was, they did make me hungry. As did traveling, practicing the wize-art, talking to animals, or virtually anything else one wanted to mention. 'Good appetite, long life,' I said sententiously.

'I suppose you're right.' He sighed, peering down at his own round belly. 'My appetite is very good, and I seem to have lived some time.'

'Which is a story you have promised to tell me, Queynt. About long life, and immunity to crystals, and things.'

'Ah, well, Jinian. Sometime.'

'I'll make you a deal, Queynt. You tell me about you and the crystals after breakfast, and I'll tell you something you don't know.'

'It's a long, dull story.'

I snickered. Queynt didn't tell dull stories. Oh, he could be dull, but if he was, it was for a purpose. At storytelling, he was a master. I said, 'I presume as much, and we haven't time now, anyhow. The city will be all around us shortly. But when we find lodging? Is it a promise?'

'You won't let me alone until I do. You're a presumptuous chit. A nuisance. Still, there's no real reason not to tell you, and it may gain me a little peace.'

I held out my hand to clasp his, making a bargain. I'd wanted to hear that story for a long time, but Queynt always seemed to evade telling me about it.

A difference in the sound of the wagon wheels rang in my ear. Paving. The talons of the krylobos scraped upon cobbles. Beside the wagon a sign. BLOOME WELCOMES YOU. Another, only slightly smaller. SHEBELAC STREET.

CHAPTER TWO

We rode on Shebelac Street, paved as far as the eye could see with glistening cobbles, shiny as turtle backs from the night's rain. At either side were high, carved curbs, and above that, slabs of walk-stone, embellished with an incised serpent's twist, to make them more interesting to walk on, I suppose. On either side of the walks, the houses and shops of the outskirts of Bloome were still quiet against the jungle in the dawn time, not bursting from doors and windows with banners and bells and drums as they would on the morrow.

It took us very little time to learn that five days before had been the procession of Jix-jax-cumbalory and that tomorrow would be Finaggy-Bum. It took us no time at all to learn that today the procession route would be announced, and every house and shop holder attentive in the forum to know whether he would need to spend the night getting ready or might sleep for once. Those along the Forum Road, Tan-tivvy Boulevard and Shebelac Street had given up sleeping long since. All processions came to the Forum along one of those three and left by another of the same. A one-in-three chance of sleeping the night before procession meant less and less as the season picked up speed. Five days hence, we were told, would be Pickel-port-poh, with Shimerzy-waffle three days after. The cloth merchants would rise early. The banner makers not long after. Tent and marquee manufacturers would be in their shops even as we rode. As I say, we were soon to learn all this. And more.

And in the high mansion upon Frommager Hill, reached from the Forum by the twisty peregrinations of Sheel Street, Dream Merchant's man Brombarg –

whom we were shortly to meet – woke in an unusually foul temper. Time had come to make a decision. Time to go on or get out, one or the other, and he couldn't make up his mind. If he decided to retire, he'd need a naif to lay the job off on, and there weren't any strangers in Bloome to choose from.

He rose, fuming, yawning, scratching his crotch with erotic insistence. (I am not certain about this, but it seems in character.) The festivals of Finaggy-Bum and Shimerzy-waffle! Merchants' men were always elected on the one and sworn in on the other. He could wear the pink vertical for the election. No one had seen it yet, and hideously hot and uncomfortable though it was, it was the most stylish thing he possessed. And it was *pink*! It would be at least a season before the fashions would swing back to anything comfortable to wear, and it might be forever before there was any other acceptable color. Damn the machine. Couldn't afford the fine if he was judged to be far out of fashion, either. Being Dream Merchant's man took every coin he could lay hands on. (It did, too. The poor fellow had next to nothing of his own.)

Still scratching, he leaned from the westernmost of his tall, lancet windows. From this tower he could look across the city walls to the jungle, brilliantly, wetly green in the morning light, swarming with birds. From here every street in Bloome was clearly visible. Only the huddle of servitors' huts along the walls themselves could not be seen, they and the prodigious mill that rumbled on the eastern border of the town, shivering the ground in a constant hyogeal vibration.

Sheel Street sinuated down Frommager into the Forum. He followed it with his eyes, imagining himself on a capacious horse riding there. Down Sheel, across the Forum, into Tan-tivvy and along that, titty-tup, titty-tup, all the way to the city edge and away northwest. Leaving it. Dressed in a simple shirt, mayhap, with trousers that fit. A cape to keep off the storm and a hat to shelter his eyes. 'Oh, by all the merchants in Zib,

19

Zog, Chime, and Bloome,' he moaned. 'But I am sick of this.' And he was. He would leave it in a minute – if they would only let him!

A distant movement caught his attention.

There. Entering the city along Shebelac, which ran south, far south, becoming merely a track at the base of the mountains if one went far enough. What in the name of five foul fustigars was that? A wagon drawn by birds? And two riders alongside on great southern horses.

Sweating with sudden excitement, Brombarg moved toward his closet. Day before procession he could get away with something fairly simple. He dressed quickly, knowing he had to get to *them* before anyone else did.

Them, of course, was us, riding down Shebelac in the early morning. Chance and Peter kept their eyes busy looking at the houses and shops while I yawned and struggled to stay awake. The two days without sleep, mostly on the run, was taking its toll.

'Years since I've been here,' Queynt said, looking about him with interest. 'Three, four hundred, maybe. Cloth-manufacturing town, as I remember. It isn't much bigger. They used to have a special kind of wineghost—*Good merciful spirits of the departed.* What's that?'

Queynt drew up the reins, and the tall, dignified birds halted as one, their long necks bent forward to examine the creature that had come into the road at the distant corner and was now plodding toward them.

'Gods,' I murmured sotto voce. 'A madman, perhaps?' At that first instant, I really thought it was, and my hands started for my bow.

But Peter shook his head. 'A player, maybe. The town shows signs of festival. Costume booths on every corner. Banner wires across all the streets.'

'Trust you to notice such a thing.' I gave him a relieved and adoring look – remembering too late to make it merely friendly – and he flushed with pleasure, pushing back the ruddy wave of hair that seemed to be always draped across his forehead. I went on hurriedly, 'I did see the streets were freshly swept. Look at those trews!'

We examined the trousers together, equally interested, unequally appalled. I didn't care that much about dress, quite frankly, and was simply dismayed at the thought of wearing any such thing. As a Shifter, however, Peter was professionally intrigued, busy calculating how the vast protrusions were kept afloat. The man coming toward us seemed to have a huge hemisphere of fabric around each leg, which bulged forward, back, and to either side like halves of a monstrous melon. From the back of his shirt, five vasty wings exploded, their inclined planes just missing the edge of his huge, circular hat brim. Glitter shot from his hands; more glitter from the throat, where some seal of office – a plaque of jet picked out in brilliants – hung on a lengthy chain. Only the boots seemed rational, and even they were topped with a fringe of chain that swung and tinkled as he walked.

'He comes,' intoned Queynt, 'robed in glory.'

Tinsel, I thought. Robed in tinsel. As a student in Vorbold's House I had learned to distinguish quality, and there was no quality in this apparition. The materials were sleazy. The seams were crooked, gaping, shedding frayed thread from the edges.

'I greet you, strangers,' puffed Brombarg, horribly out of breath. The balloon pants were hell to walk in; he had forgotten that. (A perennial optimist, Brom. He did tend to forget unpleasant things.) 'Welcome to Bloome.'

Peter and I bowed politely. Both of us had been school-reared for sufficient time to make courteous behaviour almost second nature. Chance and Queynt were subject to no such disadvantage. In any case, Chance wouldn't have submitted to mere courtesy.

'What in the name of Seven Hundred Devils are you got up as?' he demanded.

Heaven smiles on me, thought Brombarg. A naif has

come to save me. 'Clothing, stranger,' he said. 'We're having a minor festival, and we all dress a bit ... fantastical during it.' (I can tell you what he was thinking. Later it became more than obvious.)

'There,' said Peter. 'I knew it.'

I had seen lies before, and I knew one had just crossed Brombarg's mind, though his lips might have told most of the truth. Still, I smiled with a kindly expression. 'We'll need costume, then, if we decide to stay.'

'Not obligatory.' He waved a coruscating hand, throwing sun-sparkles into my eyes. 'Certainly more *fun*, wouldn't it be? But no need to go to any trouble. I've a wardrobe full of festival dress. You're welcome to it. And to the hospitality of the mansion. Yonder.' He gestured again, upward at the looming bulk of the walls upon Frommager Hill. 'A short way up Sheel Street.'

'Then you are?' I pursued the point, catching Queynt's skeptical look. He was no credulous youth to believe everything he heard. Chance, neither, who was still staring at the apparition before them, breathing heavily through his mouth as though to taste what it might be. 'You didn't tell us your name.'

'Auf!' Dramatic blow to the forehead to illustrate his own stupidity. 'Dream Merchant's man. Brombarg. Everyone calls me Brom.'

'Dream Merchant's man? I don't think I know the title.' Still smiling, though inside every fiber quivered to alertness. A solid lead to the Dream Miner, perhaps? I knew Brom wouldn't take offense at a woman. Queynt was keeping still. He knew what I was trying to find out, though Peter didn't, shifting on his horse impatiently as he was. Well, poor man, he had been riding all night.

'Ah ... why, there used to be a Merchant's man in each town hereabouts. Cloth Merchant's man in Bloome. Pottery Merchant's man in Zib. Metal workers were over in Thorne, and so on. Merchants' men did the job of managing the towns – you know, Zib, Zog, Zinter, Thorpe, Fangel, Woeful, Chime, and Bloome.'

He chanted this last like an incantation, grinning and sweating the while. 'All the towns need someone to see to the garbage, you know, and to the streets and the fire brigade. So, when the Dream Merchant set up in Fangel, he took over all the old Merchants' men and made 'em Dream Merchant's men. Different title but same duty, you know.' The man was a fountain of inconsequential information.

'Dream Merchant?' Queynt was smiling, quiet, non-threatening, helping me out. 'That's one I haven't heard before.'

'Would your invitation include breakfast?' This Peter, breaking our concentration, changing the subject. 'I'm starved.'

Sighs all around. I was peeved at the interruption, thinking it too soon to put ourselves in the man's arena; Queynt likewise; Chance and Peter both hungrier than consonant with good sense and relying, as usual, on Peter's Shifter Talent to get them out of trouble that a little patience might have avoided. Brombarg grinning, turning to lead us up Sheel Street. Windows beginning to open, now, and him in a hurry to get us high above the town before someone said or did the wrong thing.

Yittleby and Yattleby, the two giant krylobos who drew the wagon, turned to one another, then to Queynt. 'Krerk whittle quiss?'

I heard the question conveyed in this wise. *'This man is dishonest, friend-humans. Do we follow him or kick him to death?'*

'Follow,' I said to them in a croaking whisper. They whistled a few choice phrases and nodded plumes at me, argumentative but obedient. Queynt cast me a sidelong look. Perhaps I wasn't fooling him. Perhaps he knew what my Talent was, though I had not told him.

Peter had already dismounted to walk beside Brombarg. 'What is the nature of your festival, Merchant's man? Is that the correct title?'

Brom nodded, puffing. 'We are a festival-ridden city, my friend. I'm sorry, I didn't catch your name?'

'Peter. Just that. We don't much use other titles.'

Brom smiled more widely. In his experience, those who had titles used them, and those who had none said they didn't care for them. So, likely these were insignificant creatures of a certain eccentricity. (He had begun to patronize us.) The birds, for example. Now there was a team worth having. (This was evident from his expression.) He revised his earlier vision to include himself on Queynt's wagon seat, riding titty-tup down Tan-tivvy toward away. (Extrapolation, but not unjustified.)

'The lady's name is Jinian. Beside her is Queynt, and the other one is Chance.'

'And you come from?'

'Far away,' said Queynt firmly. 'To the south.'

Brom smiled more widely yet. No titles, no place of residence. Drifters. Tra-la. He did not notice my eyes fixed upon him from behind, like a gimlet into a hole, no longer smiling. 'As to our festival, it is the festival of Finaggy-Bum, during which are processions, bands, feasting and gaiety, dancing in the streets, and fireworks at dusk. And,' he said with a sidelong, sly look, 'the determining by the Cloth Merchants' Council of who should be Merchant's man for the next year.'

He must have been disappointed that we showed no interest in this topic. Instead, Peter changed the subject once more. 'Are there many Gamesmen hereabout?' We had seen none of the familiar Game garments among those on the streets.

'Gamesmen? From the True Game lands? Oh, no, young sir, indeed not. It seems their Talents are somewhat muted in these Northern Lands. Was a Tragamor came through only a season ago told me he could not Move a filled cup off the table here in Bloome.'

'Krerk,' said the left-hand krylobos, most probably Yittleby. *'Liar.'*

'I know,' I agreed. Still, there were very few Gamesmen about. Either they did not come here, or did not stay here, or ... Or they stayed here in some other guise than their own.

'Keraw whit,' agreed the birds.

The way up Sheel Street was lengthy because of its many turnings as it wound back and forth across the hill. There were wagons everywhere, transporting bolts of cloth, mostly of a vile, organic pink color. There were more costume shops, and here and there a booth blazoned, NEWEST CRYSTALS: NEW FEELINGS; NEW TALENTS: NEW WORLDS OF SENSATION, with a display case of dream crystals glittering inside, green and violet and amber orange. I didn't see any of the reddish ones we'd seen at Zog or any of the piss-yellow ones we'd found on the corpses, but every other color was shown.

Large, ornate houses stood on either hand, most of them in some state of disrepair, sounds of occupancy beginning to be heard in the street, 'Morning, Brom,' said one gatekeeper curiously, leaning on his broom as he spoke. His hat was two armspans tall, with a ruff of feathers at the top, and his trousers were made up of narrow ribbons wound 'round his legs, ending in a kind of obscene pink tassel over his crotch. 'Visitors?'

'Visitors.' Brom waved offhandedly, not stopping. 'Hungry visitors, Philp. Can't stop. Have to offer some breakfast before they fall flat.' Then, as the road turned to come back above the sweeper, 'Nice fella, that. Cloth merchant. 'Course, most of us in Bloome are, come to that.'

We approached the portal and were admitted to the courtyard through a narrow door set in the greater one. Queynt unharnessed the birds, refusing the assistance of a rat-faced stableman, and left them to guard the wagon. We hadn't walked twenty paces down a corridor after Brom when a terrified squeal from the courtyard brought us back. The rat-faced man lay supine beside the wagon, a large bird's foot planted on his belly. 'I was just having a look at the wagon, having a look, that's all.'

'I wouldn't,' said Queynt cheerfully. 'The birds don't like it.'

Brom's face was not quite as cheerful as he led us the rest of the way to the dining room. He left us there while he spoke to certain kitchen people, obtaining enough reassurance from that to regain his grin by the time he returned. 'Breakfast coming,' he said. 'Baths if you want them. Then – why, then I can lend you some clothes to wander about town, if you like.' He seemed almost to be holding his breath as he awaited our response.

'Perhaps after we've eaten,' I said firmly, in a don't-contradict-me voice. 'We'll talk about it then. And we would appreciate a bath, if you don't mind.' Thinking it would be the one way we could get off to ourselves.

Which I, but only I, achieved after refusing an officious offer of service from a chambermaid. Brom accompanied the men to their bath and stayed with them. Peter told me later he thought Brom would probably have washed their backs for them given half an opportunity. They came back for me when they were clean and brushed, and without ceremony I invited Peter and Queynt inside, saying, 'Excuse us a moment, Brom. There are a few things we need to discuss . . .' waving him away with Chance, hearing Chance's voice start up immediately.

'This is a city worth seeing, sure enough, friend Brom, but let me tell you about the city of Cleers. Well, now . . .'

'For heaven's sake, Jinian. What's the matter?' Peter knew from my expression I was bothered.

'I have a notion of trouble, and the man's a liar.'

Queynt was examining the room for hidden panels or grills. 'What do your notions tell you, friend Jinian?'

'Hints only, but worth considering. Whatever the Merchant's man is up to, it isn't what he says he's up to. I suggest we go wary, Peter, wary.'

'Seems a nice-enough fellow.'

'I'm telling you.'

'I hear you. Seems determined to get us to wear his old clothes, doesn't he?'

'That, yes. Among other things.'

'You think he's connected to this Dream Miner nemesis of yours?'

'Could be.'

'A lot of villainy to lay on one strangely dressed fellow.'

'I know. He may not be involved at all, but he's mighty sweaty and eager over something. It's that which bothers me. He's trying to use us for ends of his own, all excited over some possibility or other. Go wary, folk. That's all. Don't eat anything I don't.' I laid down my hairbrush, threw my hair over my shoulder, and led the way to the door. 'I thank him for the bath, at least. It's been a while.'

I scarce knew myself these days, so breezy and casual I'd become. It was the only way I could manage to get along with Peter, I'd found. Intensity itched at him, and since my celibacy oath prevented our being ... well, closer than mere friends, it was better not to itch at him with things he could do little about. So, I'd adopted this manner, this easy loquacity, which sometimes rubbed me raw. Now, for example, all I wanted to do was huddle in the room with the others discussing all the possibilities and deciding what to do next. It's my basic nature to be a long thinker and slow mover; it's more Peter's nature to push at things and see what happens, getting himself out of scrape after scrape by pure intuition and flashes of sudden, inspired fire. Queynt merely watches a lot of the time, humming to himself often, as though he were invulnerable and it didn't matter what we do. He did so now, probably wondering what Brom planned to give us for breakfast.

While in the bath, I had wrought a small spell over my lips, Fire is sparkening, setting them to burn if they touched anything unhealthful. So, I tried the sliced thrilps in syrup, finding them delicious, and the whipped eggs and sliced, smoked zeller, finding them likewise, the menfolk politely letting me eat first. Seemingly, I had worried over nothing. That is, until I raised the teacup

27

and felt more than a natural heat from its steam. I coughed.

'This tea,' I said, allowing my voice to complain a little. 'It has an odd smell, friend Brom. Acrid. Something I've smelt before but don't remember where. I think it must have become spoiled somehow. Here, smell it?' Holding it out to him so that, perforce, he must sniff at it and make up a puzzled face. 'Yes? I thought so. I have some lovely stuff we bought in Zinter, and I'll just whip into your kitchen and brew some for us all.'

Brom did not drink the tea he had sniffed, nor did he insist the others do so, regarding me glumly when I returned with a steaming, well-rinsed pot.

'Your kitchen help seem oddly depressed, Brom. Is it all these festivals? Hard on kitchen people, I've always thought.' Passing clean cups. Seeming to pour it around, filling Brom's cup, chatting the while in that casual, wordy way that cost me so much effort. Peter was looking at me with his face squeezed up, two vertical lines between his eyes. He knew I was up to something. Brom drank. We seemed to drink. Brom's face cleared like a misted window under the caress of the sun.

'Oh, that's very good!' And it was, for that which had gone into his cup, and only into his, was a Wize-ard brew that guaranteed both calm and truth a good deal of the time. Bless herbary. It's so useful.

'Why do you want us to wear your festival clothes?' I asked him in a friendly voice.

'They're out of fashion,' he said, suddenly desirous we should understand. 'Last year's. Last season's. So, if you wore them, the arbiters might pick you up, you know, and sentence you to service for being out of style. They might elect one of you to be Merchant's man. Then you could deal with the garbage and the roads. And the Cloth Merchants' Council, and the festival board. And the distribution of the crystals. More cloth coming every day, all to be made something of before tomorrow. More crystals arriving every day from

Fangel and all to be sold before the next lot comes. I'm tired of it all. I want to ride away, down Tan-tivvy, you know, titty-tup, titty-tup, going north.'

'Oh, I see. You were sentenced to the duty for being unstylish? Well, why haven't you become stylish? Surely they could find someone less stylish than you?'

'Bribes,' he muttered. 'They bribe the costume makers. My outfits are never right. Never. Too big, too small, too red, too green. Whatever.'

'And you can't bribe the costume makers?'

'With what?' he cried, anguished. 'Being Merchant's man takes every coin. Who pays for the street sweepers? Eh? Who pays for the parade horses, the musicians? All of that falls on Merchant's man. And nothing coming in but taxes on cloth, and that never enough!' He put his head between his hands with a gesture of despair.

'What would happen to you if you simply went away?' asked Queynt, tapping his glass with a fork to make a tiny, jingly sound in the room, an obligato to Brom's moans.

'Death. Death sudden and horrible. So they say. Merchant's man who's derelict in his duties or goes without leave is taken by the shadow. So they say. I don't know. So far it hasn't been bad enough to risk it.'

Me, eyebrows halfway to my hair, nostrils narrowed in disbelief. 'So what was in the tea you gave us, Brom? Not healthful stuff, that.'

'Zizzy stuff was all. No worse than a bottle or two of wineghost to make you happy with life. So you'd wear the clothes and not realize how old-style they were. Oh, Devils and dung-lice, I've done it now, done it, and no other naifs coming to town soon enough. Finaggy-Bum tomorrow, and that's the last chance, for after that I've been summoned to Fangel. I've no time. No time.'

'Shhh.' Me once more, sorry for this unfortunate, ineffectual fellow. Poor thing, caught in some trap or other. Well, he bore the name of dream and dream we sought. 'We'll stay a while,' I said. 'Perhaps we can think of a way to help you.'

'You're crazy,' Peter said to me affectionately. I knew I was a sometime enigma to him, the oath standing between us like a perforated screen, half hiding, half disclosing, driving him wild sometimes, wanting to see what was really there. He was not sure of the true shape of me, even now, even after months of traveling together. This was merely one of my new insanities. 'Quite crazy. You go 'round and 'round.'

' 'Round and 'round,' said Chance, making hypnotic circles with his head. ' 'Round and 'round. If the rest of you are as near to sleep as me, you're talkin' through your ears. I'm for findin' a bed.'

'As we all should be.' Peter dabbed his mouth with the napkin and rose from the table. 'We've been riding all night, after all, and lucky to do so. I thought we never would escape those brigands on the slopes above Zog.'

'Children,' said Queynt sleepily. 'Mere children.'

'Children with crossbows,' said Peter. 'And poisoned arrows. Deadly children. Thank you, Jinian, for the whatever-it-was-you-did! I thought we'd die there, late supper for the owls.'

'It was nothing.' I shrugged. It had been the hiding spell, Egg in the Hollow, done masterfully quick in time to save our lives, a good deal more than nothing, but Wize-ards didn't talk about that. 'Come, Brom. Take us to a room we may share for sleeping. We'll keep watch, as we would in any unfriendly territory, but that won't stop us trying to help you.'

The man's face, as he rose, was a study in halfness. Half disappointment we had found him out. Half hope the finding out would come back to his own advantage.

CHAPTER THREE

Brom gave us his own rooms in the tower, trying to court our favor, I suppose, but kindly meant for all that. There was an inner room with a wide bed, which the menfolk allotted to me, and an outer room full of great soft couches, which they took for themselves, barricading the outer door against intrusion with several items of furniture. Perhaps we were overly cautious, but I had no quarrel with the barricade. More than once on this trip we'd been awakened to danger in the middle of the night.

Then Queynt got out one bottle of wineghost and Chance another. Queynt, I knew, would try to give me at least two glasses. He found me very funny when I had had several. 'Serious as an owl when sober, silly as a duck when zizzy,' so he said, pretending to think it a good thing for me to be unserious from time to time.

This time I gave him no room to get started. 'We have a bargain,' I announced. 'You are to tell me about your long life and what you learned from the Eesties.'

'Arum, ah, oh,' he mumbled, 'but that would be a bore for the others.'

'Oh, not a bit of it,' said Chance. 'I've wanted to know about those rolling stars all the years of my life, ever since my own mother told me tales of them at her knee. Wonderful things they are, and a wonderful tale it is, I'm sure. Tell away, Queynt, and I'll keep your glass filled.'

He muttered a bit, but with us all set against him, he couldn't refuse. He settled down with a full glass. The rest of us gathered around, and he began.

'It was shortly after I'd put brother Barish to sleep in that cave along with his Gamesmen, most of a thousand years ago, give a hundred or so. He had arranged to be wakened every hundred years, and I was supposed to meet him – supposing I lived that long, which wasn't at all certain. We'd extended our lives quite a bit by then, but I was doubtful I'd meet him more than once, if that. So, having put all my kith and kin into storage, so you might say, I went looking for something to do with myself.

'There were many stories about the rolling stars. People had seen them, particularly back in certain parts of the Shadowmarches. They were said to be thick there, so thick that the people left their farms. Not just a few people, but many. A veritable flood of people coming out of the north, frightened and hungry.'

His voice lost its usual pompous, theatrical tone and fell into the rhythm of the storyteller, dreamy and possessed. We did not interrupt him, listening with our mouths open and glasses largely untouched at our sides. 'They said that nothing prospered there . . .'

Nothing prospered in the Shadowmarches. Crops withered or were eaten by beasts. Domestic zeller broke the fences and wandered away or went mad and attacked the herdsmen. Rank growths sprang up along the streams, poisoning the water. Noises in the night woke the inhabitants from deep, drugged sleep, and the dawn came through greenish mists with a sharp, chemical smell.

And there were sightings of the rolling stars. Great wheels rolling on the hills, spinning discs down the river valleys, the smell of burned air and hot metal. Vitior Vulpas Queynt heard all this as rumor in the farm town of Betand, a day's travel south from the ancient city of Pfarb Durim and as close to nothing as a town could be, a few implement merchants huddled along one dirt street together with one general merchandiser, one farmstock merchant selling both hybrid and this-world livestock and crops, two inns, and five taverns.

Don't forget the taverns, said Queynt to himself as he

came into the Blue Zeller to stand a moment waiting for his eyes to adjust to the dark. No matter what world one came to rest on, there were always taverns, and those taverns were always dark. A re-creation of the primeval cave, Queynt thought. Smoky, as from campfires, with rituals as old as time. Probably earliest men crouched in a place not unlike a tavern, fortifying themselves with something brewed or distilled, getting ready for the hunt. Man did not seek to return to the womb, as some alleged. He sought to return to the cave. Drier than a womb. More congenial.

Though not always. The Blue Zeller did not look or sound congenial. The place was almost empty except for a depressed-looking couple against the far wall on either side of a sleepy child.

'Got run out of the Marches,' said the barman, Guire, nodding in the direction of the family. 'Lost everything to the rolling stars.'

'I didn't know it was the stars causing the trouble,' Queynt remarked in his usual uninterested voice. The way some people were feeling lately, it didn't do to take any position very strongly.

'If not them, then what?' brayed the woman, thin lips drawn back over stained teeth. 'You never see anything but them! Them and dead stock. Them and dead crops! You never hear anything but their music – singin' wild in the hills.'

Queynt commiserated. 'Things are better in the south. If you're set on farming, why don't you try west of the Gathered Waters. I just came from there.'

'No stock left,' grumbled the man. 'Nothing left. Horses died.'

'Horses don't like it here much anyhow,' Guire remarked, wiping the bar in an immemorial gesture. 'And there's nothing local to cross 'em to. Still, the animal market says they've got a new strain's more likely to make it.'

'My dad's dad said it was a damn fool world didn't have some kind of draft animal on it,' the woman bleated. She did not seem to be able to speak softly. 'Nothing but pombis to eat your stock. Nothing but warnets to run you out of your house.'

'If you decide to try south,' Queynt said, 'I'd be glad to lend you enough to stock up for the trip.'

He did not expect them to thank him, and they did not. Both ignored the statement, peering at each other as though for some confirmation of a closely held suspicion. Queynt did not repeat the offer. They would think it over, and the town was not so large they could lose him in it. He turned back to his beer.

'What about those wild Talents,' the woman shrieked. He wondered if she were deaf, pitching his answer very softly to find out.

'What about them, ma'am?'

'We heard they was profligatin' down south. More all the time. Traggymores. Flickers. Dragons and all that. Freezin' out the common folk.' She had heard him. The shriek was simply a harpy's cry for notice.

'It's not that bad,' he assured her, lying only a little. It wasn't bad, quite, though it was getting worse. At first the Talents had been interesting and, if not benign, at least not overtly harmful. Lately, though, there had been more and more births of Gamesmen, the name they had chosen for themselves. Not exactly a game, he thought. Talents were not easy to handle. Someone needed to start some schools for the youngsters, teach them some rules or something. He made a mental note.

'The towns around the Gathered Waters need food,' he said. 'The Talents leave the farmers pretty much alone.' Which was more or less true. Gamesmen would be fools to meddle with the farms. Though Queynt had yet to see the limit of their foolishness. Some of the things the new race of Gamesmen did were not only unbelievable but childishly silly and cruel. 'There's lots of good land west of the Lake, and plenty of it left. The farmstock market in Laketown sells on credit, too. I'd recommend you go there and give it a try.'

There. He'd given them his best advice. He finished the beer and left, hearing them coming after him before he was halfway down the short street.

'Sir! Sir!' Her voice like a whetstone, he thought, wondering how the man and child could bear it. Maybe they were deaf. 'We'd be mighty grateful for the loan you offered.'

'You'll go south?' He kept his face neutral, still. No loan would help them if they were determined to return to the northlands.

'South,' the man agreed in a toneless mumble. 'We won't need so much, actually. We do have one good milk zeller left.'

He gave them money. 'When you have prospered,' he said, 'you are to make this amount available to someone else in need. It is a trust, you understand?'

The woman turned away, eyes wary as a flitchhawk's, but the man gave him a straight look. 'I take it as such, sir. Don't mind her. We left two children buried there, north.' He put his arm protectively around the woman and they went down the street, the child silent as a shadow at their heels. Queynt stared after them, not the first he had met, not the first he had sent south with enough to buy food and little more. And still he did not know the truth of what was happening there, in the Shadowmarches. He would not know, until he went himself.

He went afoot, trusting no horse – new stock or old – carrying only a few odds and ends and what he needed to eat to supplement stuff taken from the wild. At one time, he thought sardonically, he would have distrusted anything resembling a hunch, but he was in the grip of a hunch when he walked alone up into the Marches. It was the woman's plaint about music in the hills that had set him off, and he thought much about that remark during his travels. When he had come past the farthest reach of the attempted settlements, he found a tall rocky hill and camped himself on it in a half cave with its back to the wind.

It was a high, lonely moor he sat upon, the stones at his back raising themselves like the heads of questing beasts toward the lowering sky. Low, woody plants carpeted the hills, amber and wine, bronze and green. At the bottom of the hill, the forests began, twisted and low in a furry mat like the pelt of some great beast, wide swamps of darkness lying beneath the trees. And over all a shrill, keening wind, coming and going like a visitant ghost.

Queynt smiled, well pleased. He took the bait he had brought out of its careful zellerskin wrappings, an ancient instrument, one brought from the former world, a thin column of old wood with double reeds to blow through and a plaintive, importunate voice, unlike any in this world. The thing made a sorrowful, interlocutory cry, which would, he felt, summon any creature with a grain of curiosity in its bones – or whatever passed for bones with northern creatures.

Waiting for a caesura in the wind, he played. While no great shakes upon the instrument, still he had a feel for it when he stuck to easy things, and the simple melodies winged out from the height like native birds seeking nests. A few quiet elegies and nocturnes were what he knew best. When he had finished, the hills around sank into waiting silence.

It was the third day he was there – playing each day a bit at dawn, noon, and dusk, sitting in the meantime quietly over a steaming pot of grain and broth, mostly native stuff – that he heard a phrase from one of the elegies come fluttering at him out of the shadows along the hill. It was almost the sound of his double reed, but not quite, and the phrase was followed by a tiny spitting sound which could not be other than an expression of artistic annoyance.

In a moment the unknown singer tried again, closer this time, but still not exactly. Queynt set the reeds between his lips, gave a faintly expository warble, then played the melody into the waiting air once more.

A small creature, virtually invisible in the dusk, came

out upon the hillside before him and sang. It had wide ears, huge eyes. From either side of its face soft, flowing whiskers swept back to join its shadowy mane, and needle teeth glimmered in the half-light. It had the flattish star shape of all the tailless, backboneless creatures of this world, yet with legs, arms, and head that parodied humankind. It stood there and sang.

By the time full dark had come they had progressed to the point that Queynt dared assay a contrapuntal arrangement. The shadow voice dropped into silence. Queynt played the first part again, encouragingly, taking up the counterpoint when the singer began again. After several false starts the singer got the idea and they proceeded through the composition, harmonically intertwined. During this concert, Queynt was conscious of a soft gabble, interrupted by fragments of song, as though the audience were explaining to one another the intricacies of this new – obviously new – kind of music.

So, he thought with satisfaction, they are musical but did not know harmony. What an interesting gift to have given them. He set his instrument down, put a few more sticks on the fire, and settled himself to await developments. There were none. There was only a softly retreating murmur interspersed with fragments of melody. After some time, he sighed and settled himself to sleep.

The following night they progressed further. Not only did the singer keep strongly to the melody, but the harmony was picked up by other voices in the woods. By the end of the evening Queynt was sure he heard one flutelike voice in an original harmonic line high above the rest.

On the third night *they* sang and Queynt listened ruefully, wondering if he would ever touch his own instrument again. When they had finished, he felt a small hand tugging at his own to put something in it. There were half a dozen jewels there, bright blue and faceted. He held them, admiring them, surprised when the same tiny hand took one from him and pressed it to his lips. His sucking reflex took it in, fondling it with his tongue.

When he came to himself again, the fire was burnt to ashes, only a few coals blinking at him from slow, basilisk eyes. Nothing was left of the jewel. It had dissolved into him, permeated him. He could feel it moving in his veins, a flow of quiet certainty. Beside the dead fire crouched the singer. When it saw he was awake, it pointed to the pouch at his belt, to his hand. The jewels he had held had been put away. Finger on lips, the creature shushed him. Secret. Secret gift. Not to be mentioned. Then it summoned him with flickering fingers. Queynt packed up his few belongings and followed.

Though he was an experienced woodsman, a good tracker, an excellent navigator,. he was never able to find the place again. Sometimes, remembering it, he felt there had been some large, brilliant curved structure in the background. Other times he remembered only forest and rock. Whatever the setting may have been, he was sure of one thing. The Eesties.

'*The singers call us Eesties or Eeties, which in their language means "bone music" or "bone song" or some other such phrase. Call us something similar if you like.*' The star stood to speak with him, tall upon two of its points, the other three moving as though blown by a harsh wind. Later he recalled it as having had a face painted at its upper end, but the voice spoke as much inside Queynt's head as in his ears. He did not find this surprising. What he did find surprising was the tone of irritation, of an angry contempt that hid something deeper and more vital. '*Why did your like come to this world?*'

Queynt spoke of several ships that had fled to this world in recent centuries, his own group only one among many, and of the wars and destruction they had fled from.

'You have fled from destruction, yet brought it with you? Like a beast which flees from the plague it carries?'

Since this was what Queynt himself had thought many times, he could only agree.

'We try to flee. We, some of us, do not want such violent things, do not want conflict. So we try to run. But I suppose we do bring some of it with us.'

'Like the little singers, the Shadowpeople. They, too, desire holiness. They, too, have little talent for it.' The creature's irritation seemed exacerbated by this, a scarcely veiled hostility that did not at first threaten force, but rather seemed to imply anathema, a casting out. It was as though the Eesty tolerated Queynt's presence at all only with difficulty, and now the mention of his yearnings for peace infuriated it. It was then Queynt thought he identified what lay beneath the anger, beneath the contempt. Guilt. This being, whatever it truly was, was guilty of something, and that guilt ate at it like a cancer. He did not know how he knew this. Later, he realized the crystal he had taken had enlightened him in ways he was scarcely aware of.

'We want you to go hence,' the creature told him. 'Go away, to some other world. This one does not need you. You do an evil thing here.' It moved away in a flutter of ribbons, leaving a stink of hatred behind it.

Queynt could not understand what the evil was they were trying to communicate. The concepts swam in his head, half-formed, vertiginous edges of ideas which touched and darted away, only partly seen. A word. 'Bao.' Or maybe 'Bah-ho.' It had no meaning for him. In it there were Eesties, Shadowpeople, birds, beasts, trees, long white roads under a scarlet sun, stars spinning upon them in a constant glittering flow. Disruption. He tried to explain that the ships were gone, disassembled, that mankind could not leave. The Eesty went angrily away.

It tried again later. 'Badness is being done. (Most desirable of all things) is being destroyed.'

39

Again he struggled with the concept. Humans were doing something wrong. He could not tell what it was. Not a matter of breaking a taboo, not a matter of destroying some holy site. More than that. They were doing this (had done this?) evil by merely existing. Then why did the creature feel guilt? What was it hiding?

Then there were three of the Eesties, not now merely questioning him but examining him as well, looking into him as though digging some root crop, plunging through him to leave disruptive pain behind. One of them had his pouch, was looking through it. They saw the blue gems.

Fury. Anger. Hot, hideous, destructive. The air blazed around him, fire hot, making him fear for his life until a great cry came from somewhere, from some other Eesty, perhaps, a warning, a threat? The creatures were all around him, whirling in a frenzy of hatred, frustrated hostility, desire to kill. Queynt fell to the ground, covered his neck with his hands, curled upon himself knowing he was to die then, there, in the instant. Against that anger was no possibility of reprieve. Even through his fear he heard the cry come again, louder, more impassioned, a kind of agonized command. Another of their kind had come and made them stop. 'Ganver,' someone whispered. 'Ganver.'

Then it was all over and he was alone upon the hillside, unchanged, totally changed. He had failed, but so had the rolling stars; they had exhausted one another in their mutual failure.

He had understood almost nothing. How could he have understood its frustration, its anger, perhaps its fear? The bright images swam in his head like fishes, but he had no hooks with which to catch them. There was an understanding that evaded him, a sense of incompletion.

The singers came back for him, sadly, patting him on his bruised places and offering herbal teas and poultices. He came down out of the hills, sometimes playing for

40

the Shadowpeople, sometimes listening as they sang for him. To accompany their singing they had only drums. When he returned to a town where there were craftsmen, he had bells made, and silver flutes, taking them into the Marches as gifts for the Shadowmen . . .

'And now, a thousand years later, I sit in a tower room,' he said, 'in a strange city telling the story to Jinian Footseer, watching the wrinkle between her eyes deepening like a crevasse. You will be a quizzical oldster, Jinian. What deep thoughts has my story raised in you?'

I was fingering the star-eye that hung about my throat, which had hung there since I had received it from Tess Tinder-my-hand when I was only a child. I had always thought of it as an Eesty sign. Now that Queynt had told me his tale, I was not sure it was an Eesty sign at all. The Eesties he described were not what I had thought then. They were not what Mavin, Peter's mother, had thought them, either. A mystery there. I asked him, 'But if they hated you, why have you lived so long, Queynt?'

'Something to do with the blue crystal, I think. When I left the Marches, I knew I would live a very long life. No. That's not quite right. I was conscious of death being remote, put it that way. The blue gem did that. It imposed a kind of understanding upon the fiber of oneself.

'I said to Peter once they would likely do the same for him. I think they would do so for any of us. If whatever makes the gems could only make enough of them to go around, to make everyone understand what I did . . .' I recoiled at this, but he did not see me. I could not bear the thought of being compelled by some outside force. I rebelled against it. He went on, 'That is why I am immune to other crystals, I suppose. The pattern of the first one, the blue one, is too well set in me to be disrupted.'

He sighed then, taking the pouch from his belt and

pouring the crystals into his palm. 'There are enough here for you to have one, and Peter.'

I thrust out my hands, warding him away. 'No! No, Queynt. Not for me. And I would hope Peter would say no as well. I do not like the thought of compulsion.'

He shook his head at me. 'Not compulsion, Jinian. Information, more like. It is as though I had been given a map which showed both the good roads and the swamps. Is it compulsion to avoid the swamps if one knows they are there?'

I thought he was sincere, but still I would have none of it. Compulsion is always said to be something else. 'Kind of you, Queynt, but no.' Changing the subject, 'It is noon. We have been riding for two days without sleep. If you wish to drink and tell tales, do so, but quietly. I'm going to sleep.'

Which I did, lying awake only a little time thinking about Queynt's story and that strange word or meaning the Eesties had used. Bao. Bah-ho. I knew I would think of it at more length another time.

CHAPTER FOUR

I woke with a start to a cacophony of shouts, thuds, and explosions. Among these louder sounds were Chance's whuffing complaint at being wakened and Queynt's calm voice going on in one of his loquacious monologues.

'. . . when one is having the best rest one has had for ages, something eccentric in the way of barbaric behavior breaks loose outside one's window, and the peace of the evening is disrupted . . .' It was disrupted further by more violent blows on the door and another explosion from the street below.

'Friends, visitors!' Brom's voice, frantic with a mixture of frustration and panic. 'The fireworks shop on Shebelac Street has caught fire and is going up all at once. Let me in. You have the best windows!'

Furniture-moving sounds came from the neighbouring room, the barricade being removed. I rose, albeit reluctantly, leaning out of my own window to watch bouquets of rockets blooming across the darkening sky above a volcano of spouting scarlet. Whistles and sirens competed for attention. Figures as dark and tiny as ants ran to and fro before the leaping light.

It was night. We had slept the day away. I rummaged in my pack for something to wear, taking what was on top, one of the voluminous smocks they wore in the purlieus around Zog. Pulling the soft, bright fabric over my head, I went into the other room.

Brom hung half-out the window, hitting his fist on the sill in an agony of amused apprehension. 'Oh, what a mess! It's funny, you know, but it isn't funny at all. At dawn tomorrow comes Finaggy-Bum – not a major festival, but one that deserves some effort for all that – and there won't be a rocket left. The revelers will be so disappointed.'

'Revelers?' asked Queynt. 'Who *are* the revelers?'

'Why, Queynt, those for whom the festivals are held, surely. Those from the towns of Zib and Zog, Chime and Woeful. Those from the villages and farms around Thorpe. Those travelers from no settled place. We do all we can here in Bloome to attract them, though there are those who say our festivating so to excess has lowered our custom rather than raising it . . .'

'Customers? For?'

'Well, originally for anything at all made of cloth, sir. We're a cloth-weaving town, after all. More recently for the dream crystals as well. What else have we to sell? Why else am I Dream Merchant's man?'

'Would some of these be yellow crystals?' I asked. 'Yellow as piss, about the size of my thumb-tip?'

'They would not,' Brom said in an offended voice. 'They would be green ones, some large, some small. And amber-brown ones as big as my ear. And little red ones. Those yellow crystals were never intended for commerce. Dream Merchant sent a man here from Fangel. He told me to keep an eye out, confiscate any I found. Which I did. Told me to destroy any I found. Which I would have done. Save for that damned Oracle. Took the sack I put them in. Took them all. Stole them.'

'Would this "Oracle" be a strange creature in a fancy robe?' I asked. 'With a painted face, and full of emphatic language?'

Brom assented at once to this description. 'Oh, he came here, all ribboned up like a Festival Horse, wandered around Bloome, full of amusing stories. So, I invited him here to amuse my . . . my friends. When every day is festival it's hard to come by any genuine amusements. He was gone the next day, and so was the whole sack of yellow crystals meant for the disposal pits. And since then I've been hearing troubles from every side. People who should have come to Bloome

44

to take part in festival, who should have come to buy costumes, come to buy good crystals, dead along the road! Dead! What good will that do commerce? I ask you! Bad enough that half the roads are ruined.'

For a moment, when it seemed he knew something about the crystals, I had been almost ready to fly at him, dagger in hand (and no small weapon, but the Dagger of Daggerhawk which needed only to touch in anger to cause death). Now I took my hand out of my pocket. The Dagger was in its holster high upon my thigh. It was seldom far from my reach, but Brom did not seem worth the use of it. Besides, what he had to say was interesting.

I said casually, 'And what has destroyed half the roads, Brom? Come. Tell us.'

He choked. I saw him struggling not to speak. He had been told not to speak? Threatened, perhaps? Whatever it had been that kept him silent was no match for the truth tea we had given him.

'Storm Grower,' he mumbled, making two syllables out of it, the last one a growl.

'Why? Why is that, Brom?'

'Does . . . does that when she's angry. When people don't . . . do what she wants. Oh, don't make me speak. She'll kill me, truly she will. Or Dream Miner will. Or the Merchant. He's their son, you know. So he says. I don't believe it, but so he says.'

'So you are not responsible for ruining roads or distributing yellow crystals. None of it.'

'None of it but doing my job,' he sulked. 'And that's no more than anyone would do. All I really want to do is go away.'

'How was it you had the things in the first place?' asked Peter, watching the man through narrowed eyes. 'Where did you say you got them?'

'They came in a shipment from the Dream Merchant in Fangel, as all of them come. Neatly packed in boxes, a dozen to the box. They come to me from the district headquarters, in Fangel. They come to Fangel from the

45

Dream Miner, I suppose. How these yellow ones got in with the others, no one says. No one tells me anything.'

'And the Miner gets them where?' pressed Queynt, eager to learn something real after our long search.

'Why, I suppose he digs them up! I've seen Dream Mines. Well, no, I saw one. A little one, just outside Fangel. Nice old fella there, him and his wife, they watch the place. He digs them up with a shovel and a pick, just like you'd dig for anything.'

An idea flicked through my head, one of those quick, glittering ones that go before you can grab it. Something to do with mines and crystals. I sighed.

'There for a moment, I thought I had something. By the Hundred Devils, Queynt, but this whole business gets stranger and stranger.'

'There's nothing we can do about it now, Jinian,' said Peter, doing what he too often did, coming close to me, putting his arm around my waist, his hand flat against my side, burning there with an aching heat. I took a deep breath and moved away, choking back a desire to return the caress.

'I suppose you're right. But still, I'd like to know more about these mines.'

'Well, of course,' said Brom. 'If you'd like to come with me to Fangel, you could see the one I saw for yourself. But if you come with me to Fangel, you wouldn't be staying here in Bloome, and I'd still be Merchant's man.'

I returned to the other room as Chance said, 'And why're you goin' up to Fangel, friend Brom? Is it a city worth seein'?'

'There's to be a great reception there for the delegation of the Duke of Betand on his way north,' came the answer in a dull, uncaring voice. 'Him and his new allies. The Ogress, Valearn. The Witch, Huldra. There's another Gameswoman, too, but her name I can't remember. All the Merchants' men have been sent for.'

I turned, suddenly alert, seeing Peter stiffen as well. He had responded to the first name mentioned; I to

46

that of Valearn. Queynt, too, had suddenly grown very quiet. 'Huldra?' he said. 'Peter, I seem to recognize that name from conversations I had with Mavin. Isn't that the twin sister of your old friend Huld?'

'Gamelords,' Peter hissed. 'I thought that family done with. Is there no end to them?' He began to enumerate them, coldly ticking them off with his fingers. 'There was Huld's father, Blourbast the Ghoul. Huld killed Blourbast, and Mavin saw him do it. Then Mavin herself killed Pantiquod the Harpy, Huld's mother, and that other harpy, Foulitter, Huld's half sister. All that was long ago, before I was even born. Then I came along to fall victim to Huld's son-thalan, Mandor. He died by his own act, though Huld held me at least partly responsible. I thought all were gone but Huld, and him we did away with on the Wastes of Bleer. That should have been an end to it! Now we hear there's another one yet alive? That Huld had a twin?'

'That and worse,' I said from the doorway. 'You also did away with King Prionde on the Wastes of Bleer. But he had a sister-wife, Valearn. Their son, Valdon, was killed by the Faces some eighteen or nineteen years ago, so Mavin told me, though it is unlikely they ever knew Mavin's part in that . . .'

'My mother seems to have confided greatly in you both,' said Peter, not altogether pleasantly.

'Peter, before we began this journey, you may recall that you and I and Mavin and Himaggery and a great mob of people all traveled together to Hell's Maw, a trip of some days' duration, during which time I got to know her rather well. She told me her life's story, as she would have been glad to tell you if you'd ever taken time to sit down and listen. I continue: Out of grief, it is said, Valearn turned Ogress and feasted upon the children of our region. Those of us from the lands around the Stonywater in the south were warned to fear her more than her late husband, the King. And now these two are allies with the Duke of Betand? I heard of these dangerous alliances in Xammer!'

(Actually, I had heard of them at the Citadel of the Wize-ards, but that was no one's business but mine.) 'Now, what is going on here? What is the reason for these alliances?'

Brom was looking from one to another of us, his worried face growing more haggard with each word he heard us say. 'It would be more likely for the Cloth Merchants' Council to award you ten thousand bonus points than for me to know anything about that, lady. Do you think the Dream Merchant consults me? Do you think he asks a Merchant's man, "May I take an ally?" He sends us crystals to sell, and sometimes he summons us up to Fangel for some do or other, and that's all I know about the monsters you're talking of. And I'm supposed to go be part of a welcoming deputation!' He sobbed. 'I would as soon walk into a gnarlibar's jaws.'

'Ah, well,' I said comfortingly. 'It is the Merchant's man who is to go, is it not?'

'I. Me. The Merchant's man, yes.'

'And on the festival of Finaggy-Bum, tomorrow, the arbiters of Bloome will select their Merchant's man?'

'From among the least stylish, yes. But you have found me out. You were not naifs at all. My chances of laying the job off on one of you are next to nothing.' So saying, he burst into angry tears, letting them flow down his face and into his beard without bothering to wipe at them at all. The truth tea had this effect of truth telling even upon emotions. Chance patted the fellow on the shoulder, commiserating, while Queynt tried to hide his smile.

'I think we may assure your stylishness tomorrow,' I told him. 'And one of us will wear your old clothes, friend Brom, thus guaranteeing that it will be one of us who goes to Fangel as Merchant's man of Bloome.' Of course, which one of us it would be was another matter.

'One of us, then,' I said to the troupe. 'Whoever wishes to act the part?'

'I,' said Queynt. 'Peter and Chance may be known to Huldra or Valearn. You traveled in the High Demesne, didn't you, my boy? Some three or fours years ago?'

'We did, yes. But I never saw Prionde's wife. Chance, did you?'

'I didn't see any such lady. Oh, there was talk of a wife hiding somewhere in a tower, but I never saw her.'

'Still, she may have seen you. You, Jinian, will be needed for something else. Therefore, it must be me.' Queynt smiled again, posturing. 'I will make a very good Merchant's man.'

'We are not too different in size,' said Brom. 'The old things would fit you. But . . . but no matter what we do, it may be the Cloth Merchants' Council will still hold me to the position. They've said I'm not bad at the job. Or maybe they just hate me. Oh, it may be hopeless!'

'We will see to that,' I promised him. 'Do they meet at any given time and place?'

'They will meet tonight,' he answered. 'In the loft of the weaving mill.' He turned away, his face working, murmuring as he went, 'Think of it. Riding out of Bloome. Titty-tup, titty-tup, along Tan-tivvy Boulevard. Not to Fangel. No. West, I think. Or even south. Titty-tup, titty-tup.' He went down the corridor, galloping as though he had a hobby between his legs, lashing one thigh with an imaginary whip.

'Mad,' said Queynt almost affectionately. 'Quite mad.'

The great mill of Bloome crouched upon the eastern edge of the city, a heaped monstrosity, glaring banefully through a hundred eyes, growling and munching as it ate the provender brought by the citizens, spewing out its cloth in endless lengths to be rolled into bolts and carried away. Day and night those who were not involved in the festivals of Bloome were involved in feeding the mighty machine or carrying its excreta away. Just now all the shoulder-high slots in the courtyard were vomiting fabric of an excruciating pink color into waiting wagons. A bored knife man stood to one side, ready to cut the weave when each cart was full, and around him the drivers sat, some drinking, some playing at dice, some half-asleep.

From this cluttered courtyard, a narrow door opened upon an even narrower iron stair, which twisted its skeletal length upward through roaring, dust-filled spaces to a loft. This space, tall as a church, was lit by grimed windows and a few scattered bulbs whose filaments alternately glowed and dimmed as the mechanicals below grumbled and howled. There, at a broken-legged table, the Cloth Merchants' Council of Bloome sat upon rickety chairs at its interminable meetings. It was here they were assembled while the fireworks shop burned on Shebelac Street, unable to hear the sirens for the endless growling of the looms below.

If one looked out the dirty windows by daylight, one could see the hoppers at the rear of the building where the carts lined up each day to dump weeds and trees, trash and old furniture, last night's costumes and banners and tents into the huge, shaking hoppers. The hoppers emptied into a steel enormity where no man had ever gone alive and from which only fabric emerged at the other end. There were only two rules of life so far as the Cloth Merchants' Council was concerned. Never let the machine run out of stuff to weave. Never run out of ways to use the weaving up.

The machine had run out of raw materials only once. Bloome had learned then that the machine had its own ways of collecting materials if it was not sufficiently fed. Babies, geese, fustigars, tame zeller, houses, people – the machine did not discriminate. Since that time (called 'The Exemplary Episode' in the minutes of the council) the machine had not been allowed to run dry.

That was practical politics, that rule.

The other rule was religious.

Bloome had been a cloth-making town as long as

anyone remembered. The mill had always been there. It was assumed to have been put there by a god or by the ancestors, either to be equally revered. Since neither god nor the ancestors did things without purpose, the cloth, arriving in quantities ever greater and always far more than could be used in Bloome, must have a purpose. It had been up to the people of Bloome to find it.

They had found it at last, after many trials. Festivals.

At first only once or twice a season, later six or eight times a season, most recently every few days. Every few days a new festival, to deck the city with new banners. Every few days a new festival, requiring new costumes for residents and visitors alike. Every few days a new festival, with new tents and marquees to be sewn. And in the quiet times between, weary cleanup crews laboured to gather the materials to take to the hoppers again. A precarious balance, but better than another 'Exemplary Episode'.

'I'm not selling the pink stuff,' said a banner maker, who, as he often mentioned apropos of nothing, had been a member of the council for fifty years. 'It won't go. They don't want it. Everyone is sick to death of it.'

'Bonus points,' remarked a heavyset, dark-skinned woman, scratching her nose and making notes at the same time. 'We'll award bonus points for pink. The way we had to do with the puce chiffon three years ago. Machine made it for two seasons, and we couldn't give it away.'

'How about lining the streets with it? We did that once, I remember. In my mother's time.'

'Trouble is, the stuff tears so. Shoddy. You'd have half Bloome tripping and rolling around on the cobbles. No, we'll award bonus points and double to tent makers if they'll quilt it in layers. Next?'

'Arahg,' growled the long-faced banner maker, referring to his notes. 'Everyone's running out of thread. Machine hasn't given us any thread for three seasons.

We're going to have to set up to ravel if we don't get some soon.'

'We saved out a thousand bolts of that loose, blue stuff last year,' said the heavy woman. 'The thread pulls right out. No weave to it to speak of. We can put the children on it.'

'Going to look like hell,' growled the banner maker.

'So what else is new?'

The door opened to admit a wizened man in a violently striped cloak, notable for its inclusion of the pink stuff in wide, bias-cut borders. 'Evening,' he said. 'Mergus. Madame Browl. Gentlemen. Sorry I'm late. Stuck around my front door for a little extra time tonight waiting to see if Brom's guests came out. I think he may have found a naif.'

'Evening, Philp. I didn't know anyone came to town today. Why, when there was no festival?'

'Wasn't till early this morning. Don't think they came for festival. Four of 'em. Wagon with birds pulling it. Haven't seen anything like that before. Two older fellows. One young one, one girl. Brom got to 'em before anyone could stop him. They didn't exactly look simple. Brom may have a time with 'em.'

'The problem is,' said Madame Browl, scratching her nose once more, 'whether we want to let Brom off the platter. He's been a good Merchant's man, all things taken into account.'

'Gettin' restless, though.'

'Well, restless is one thing.'

'Mad is the other. Don't want him doing anything silly. We had one once who did, remember?'

'Tried to blow up the machine, by Drarg. Got a hundred or so of us killed.'

'Still, I'd be disinclined to let Brom go. A visitor simple enough to accept the honour might be too simple to do the work!'

'Might have been an honor once,' said Mergus, the droopy cheeks of his long, lined face wobbling as he spoke, one tufty eyebrow up, the other down in a hairy diagonal that seemed to slide off his face near his large left ear. 'Since the Dream Merchant's been in on it, it's less so.'

'Dream Merchant only took advantage of the fact we've flocks of revelers,' said Philp. 'The Merchants' men in Zinter and Thorpe have to distribute crystals, too. We're not the only town with the burden.'

'Not the only town under threat from storm, either. We haven't been hit by wind or hail yet, but there's towns farther north that have!' Madame Browl growled at them, looking from face to face. 'Towns that complain learn to regret it. I say we do whatever's needed to keep things peaceful and running, and Brom's not been bad at that.'

'Still,' said Philp, 'there was a time the Merchant's man of Bloome worked for the Cloth Merchants' Council of Bloome, not for some foreigner. Makes it hard to hold him accountable.'

'Come, come,' huffed Mergus. 'We hold him accountable enough. Except for a day or two a year when he's off to Fangel or a few days when the emissaries from Fangel come here, he's biddable enough. I vote we keep Brom in the job, no matter he's been tryin' to bribe the costume makers to get him off the hook.'

*   *   *

High in one shadowed corner of the room, a slithery shape that had been extended over a roof beam withdrew itself into a ventilation duct, slithering out again some distance down in the building with me in its dusty coils. Peter and I had heard all we needed to hear.

'Well?' asked Queynt.

'They're not inclined to let him off,' said Peter, brushing the dust off his slithery skin even as he Shifted

53

back into a shape closer to his own. 'Funny thing. They don't seem to be in control of the weaving machine. All these festivals? Just to use up fabric.'

'Ah,' Queynt said, scratching his head with one finger. 'What happens if they don't use up the cloth?'

'Two of the oldsters were mumbling about the machine seeking raw materials on its own. The way they figure, they have to use it up so they can feed it back in.'

'It seems to be religion,' I said. 'They're predisposed to believe that the cloth has to be used for something.'

'Ah. Well then, we'll have to take that into account. If the problem has emanated from a religious source, the solution will have to come from some similar source. What do you think, Jinian? If it's me to be the naif, then it's you to be the plenipotentiary. From whom will you say you have been sent, do you think?'

'A god, perhaps. There's less chance of controversy that way. If I represent myself as coming from an ancestor, someone is likely to ask which ancestor, and that might lead to endless conversation. Who do they worship here? What gods are given houseroom?'

'Few or none,' said Chance. 'I trotted up and down half a dozen streets, in and out of a dozen taverns or so. They swear by no gods I know of, though they swear often in a cowardly craven manner by the wind and the hail . . .'

'By Storm Grower?' I asked him.

'Never. They swear by the wind and the hail, and then they spit, thus, to drive the evil away. Oh, and sometimes they swear by Great Drarg, Master of the Hundred Demons.'

'Great Drarg of the Hundred Demons,' I mused. 'There's something I can use. Well. No time like the present.' And I went off that weary climb up those long, metal-echoing stairs to the room where the council met, leaving Peter to scramble into the ventilation ducts once more.

* * *

I could read their faces well enough. The Cloth Merchants' Council of Bloome had probably not been interrupted in living memory. Never by a stranger, certainly. Still, they were impressed by my demeanor, by my hauteur, my poise.

'Good citizens,' I said. 'Council members of the town of Bloome. I have arrived today as plenipotentiary of Drarg, Master of the Hundred Demons, sent to beg your pardon and ask a small boon on Drarg's behalf.'

The voice I used was one learned from my Dervish mother, Bartelmy of the Ban. It was a cold voice, without edges, which left nothing of itself lying about to be picked at by the argumentative. The best Madame Browl could do was stutter, 'We . . . what have we to do with ah . . . Drarg?'

'Nothing, madame, save that his minions have been trifling with you. You have here a certain great machine established by your ancestors. Is that not true?'

They nodded that it was true, very true. Since they were sitting on top of it, it would have been difficult to deny.

'And this machine has a voracious appetite which cannot be stayed? Ah, yes. So we have been informed. Such was the work of the Demons. My master's apologies. He has sent me to rectify matters.'

'You mean . . . you mean the mill isn't supposed to be fed – isn't supposed to run . . . all the time?'

I allowed frost to creep into my words. 'Have I not said as much?'

They nodded, shook their heads. Had this person said as much? Had she? Perhaps she had.

'While my master is unable at the moment to correct the actions of his minions (he is far away on pressing business), he has directed me to take measures to alleviate your troubles. Measures which will allow the citizens of Bloome to sleep, to dream, to cook good food, to make love. Ah' – I changed the voice to one lyrical and romantic, lush as a summer meadow – 'to enjoy all life's pleasures.' It became cold once more. 'Drarg wishes the boon, of course.'

'Boon?' Philp trembled. 'What boon would that be?'

'Simply to release your current Merchant's man from his position. It is not fair that he be kept in his job longer. He has suffered much, as indeed so have you all.' I stared around the table, meeting incomprehension on some faces, distrust on others, hope on a few. 'How do you say, council members?'

Madame Browl found her voice again. 'If you can do as you say, ah ... Your Excellency? Your Worship? If you can relieve us of the constant necessity to feed the mill – oh, yes, we would grant any boon. Provided no blasphemy takes place. No heretical notions?'

'None. On the festival of Finaggy-Bum tomorrow, pick yourselves a new Merchant's man. There is an excellent candidate, one Queynt, among the visitors. As soon as that is done, send carpenters and metal workers to me where I reside at Brombarg's house. They will be given instruction.'

I turned, wishing for some glorious gown and high headdress to punctuate this speech and make a dramatic exit. Well, the smock from Zog would have to do. It was certainly unlike anything being worn in Bloome. I let myself out, not pausing to listen to the babble behind the door. Peter would be hearing it all from the ductwork, anyhow.

'Done?' I asked him when he returned below.

'Done! Half of them don't believe you, but they're all willing to give it a try. There are one or two say they'll hunt Brom down and kill him if you're lying, and another few who talk of putting you into the hopper if you're leading them a fool's track. All told, however, I think they're peaceful enough. For now.'

I nodded, thinking very hard. This put a serious expression on my face, and Peter did what he always did when I got that expression. He reached for me. That particular expression, he had told me, reminded him of Jinian when he had first met her, so serious, so determined, like a belligerent child, set upon knowing everything there was to be known. That particular expression turned his stomach to jelly, so he said, and he could no more stop himself reaching for me than he could have stopped eating ripe thrilps. He flexed an arm to draw me closer there in the dusty, roaring room, me all unprepared for his lips on mine and the warmth of his body pressed tightly to my own.

I trembled, adrift, unable and unwilling to do anything at all except drift there in his arms while the hot throb of my blood built into its own kind of ending. I was saved by an urgent summons from Queynt, a clatter of feet coming down the stairs. Peter tried to hold my hand, but I drew it away, suddenly so distressed I couldn't speak. It wasn't fair of him to do that. Not fair. I had talked to him about it. He knew well enough what gaining the wize-art meant to me. I felt tears beginning to burn, half frustration, half anger. Oh, why couldn't he . . .

Fuming, I slipped down the stairs after the others, reaching the bottom only moments before the council members erupted into the street. Peter was looking for me, but I slipped away from him. He was doing this more and more frequently, as though to make my own body betray me. As though to test whether I would choose between him and my Wize-ardry. He simply wasn't content any more to let patience solve the matter.

My knees were weak. I could hardly breathe. I was angry, and sorry to be angry, and wanted to run after him, and wanted to run away. Things couldn't go on like this. Once we had taken care of the matter of Brom, something would have to be done about it.

CHAPTER FIVE

Early in the morning, Brom was valeted by the three men. They dressed him in pink vertical, lacing and buttoning, rigging the internal bones and stays that held the unlikely garment aloft, trying vainly to keep their faces straight. There was as much of it above his head as there was from head to foot. That part above his head was decked with such unlikely ornamentation as to cast doubt upon the humanity of the wearer, and the part below his head was of sufficient discomfort as to deny whatever humanity existed. It took some time. I watched for a while, disbelieving any of it, then went to the tower room where I could be private and laid two spells upon him.

First I laid Bright the Sun Burning, a beguilement spell. No one looking at Brom that day would consider him any less than stylish. He would gleam like the sun itself, making a warm space in any perception, a suffused glow like a little furnace. And, lest that perception wane as the day passed, I laid Dream Chains to Tie It, a keeping spell – though I had a devil of a time finding a live frog and finally had to summon one from the garden window. There were other and more esoteric uses for Dream Chains, but Murzy had always taught that the tool might be turned to the task if the Wize-ard willed. When it was all done, I tested it by going down and asking Chance how he thought Brom looked.

'I thought it was enough to make a pombi laugh,' Chance said, walking around Brom and looking him over from top to bottom. 'It looked like pure foolishness on the hook. Now – well, it has a kind of majesty to it, don't it?'

I nodded, contented. It was probable the council members would keep their agreement with me, but why have the town buzzing about their reasons for letting Brom go? If the town talked, some rumor might reach Fangel. No. Let the matter be self-evident. Brom had become stylish enough to escape, and a naif was present to take over the job.

At the end, Queynt could not bring himself to wear Brom's cast-off things. Instead he burrowed into the wagon and found those garments he had been wearing when he first met Peter and me, wildly eccentric clothing that was certainly not in fashion. Then Queynt and Brom swaggered into the street, a colorful exercise in contrasts. It would have been difficult to say which of them looked more ridiculous.

Chance disappeared into the town with a few innocuous words. Seeing his compact form disappearing down Sheel Street, I shook my head over the fate of the gamblers of Bloome. Peter dozed in the garden, the warmth of the sun provoking dreams – probably erotic – that made him twitch and mumble in his sleep. Looking down on him from a window, I could almost tell what he was dreaming of, as though I could read his mind. I frowned and bit my lips. There were only two seasons of my oath to run, but while I had kept that oath to the letter, the spirit of it had been lost long since. It was impossible to concentrate on the art – or on anything else – with Peter around. The more casual I tried to be, the closer he came. There were a dozen things one might do; putting a spell on him came first to mind. A distraint. That same spell I had used on Brom, Dream Chains. I still had the frog. It would do Peter no harm. He wouldn't even be aware of it.

No! I couldn't do that. I couldn't compel him to do anything, or not do anything. Not ever. I would rather have lost him, or so I thought then, than do anything to put him under compulsion. No matter how tempting it might be.

And it was very tempting. I could only distrain his

touching me. Nothing else. And only for a short time. I could still allow affectionate speech, companionship. And yet – if he couldn't touch me when he willed, something would have been taken from him. As something must have been taken from Queynt when he was given the blue dream crystal by the Shadowpeople. Though he denied it, I thought it must be so. It was unlikely he had not been changed by it. So he was compelled, whether he knew it or not, by something or someone outside himself.

And yet, being honest about it, I'd met him after he'd tasted the thing, not before. So how could I say whether he was changed by it or not?

I sat upon the windowsill, looking out over the town with its crumbling towers, its moldy roofs, the streets clean swept and shining for festival, the lower walls painted and gleaming, and all above the street level falling to dust and decay. The vibration of the mill shook the stone I was sitting on, a ceaseless quivering, a gentle dust of mortar from between the stones, a constant reminder the mill was there. The people of Bloome had made an uneasy peace with the mill, but I was going to change all that. Compellingly. But that was Game, of a sort. Compulsion was allowed, in Game.

Barish, for example! He had arranged for himself to be put to sleep, to sleep for a thousand years or so. And while he slept, one hundred thousand great Gamesmen were to be abducted and frozen into sleep like his own. Compelled. For some misty idea he had about a better future world. An idea so misty that he and Himaggery had done nothing but argue about it constantly before we left and were probably still arguing about it. Meantime the hundred thousand rested beneath the mountain, still frozen. Compelled.

Everyone else did it! So why did it bother me so? Besides, there were situations when it seemed right.

If I had come upon that man and woman outside Bloome, for instance, sucking upon their piss-yellow crystals and lying there in their own stink. If I had compelled them, even against their wills, to give up the crystals and live again, wouldn't I have been their friend?

A better friend, perhaps, than their own inner spirits, who had let them die? Or was the right to die part of one's own right? If so, was it everyone's right, or only the right of some? A child, for example. If a child risked its life foolishly, without knowing what it was doing, shouldn't one save that child by compelling it to forgo the risk? Or a stupid man, perhaps one besotted? Though if one were to follow that argument, it was probable the besotted one got that way of his own will and had been told often enough the dangers of it. Or true naifs, simpletons, those who would never learn the ways of the world, the eternally surprised, the perpetually astonished? Should they not be compelled, for their own good?

When one played Game, there were rules – oh, often disobeyed, but still acknowledged. If one compelled outside of Game, then what was it one was doing? If one seduced, which was another kind of compulsion?

'Saving one's life, perhaps,' I mumbled, remembering too well what I had had to do to the centipig in the Forest of Chimmerdong. 'Saving someone else's life.'

Or, said some deep voice, saving something more important than life itself.

I remember putting my head down on the stone, wishing Murzy were there to give me some advice. It would be so easy to hold Peter at a comfortable distance, just for a time. Surely there were rules! Surely there were answers!

Well, Murzy wasn't there, so it did no good to wish it. I gave up the whole matter and went to find myself some breakfast.

The delegation from the Cloth Merchants' Council arrived a little after noon bearing Queynt on their shoulders and hailing him as the new Merchant's man. He already wore the sparkling seal of office, the letters 'DM' entwined in gems upon jet. Brom, sneaking along behind so as not to draw any attention to himself, stayed only long enough to divest himself of the pink vertical and get his horse out of the stable. It seemed he had been packed long since, for the merchants had scarcely begun advising Queynt of his future duties before the titty-tup of Brom's horse's hooves was fading down Sheel Street.

'The garbage schedule tomorrow,' Madame Browl was saying in a firm voice. 'First thing tomorrow!'

'Not tomorrow,' said Queynt. 'Tomorrow the Merchant's man is summoned to Fangel. Brom told me so. I leave tonight.'

The council members scowled at one another, robbed of their opportunity to show authority immediately and thus, some seemed to feel, robbed of it perpetually. 'Well then, when you return. As soon as you return.'

Queynt had no more intention of returning than I did, but he agreed amicably and things went on pleasantly thereafter as they discussed the matters of garbage and machine-feeding detail and the maintenance of the fire brigade. In the midafternoon the festival ended – early, because there would be no fireworks – and soon after that, the workmen I had asked for arrived. Peter and I went off with them to the great mill while Chance and Queynt prepared to depart. There was something in my boot, and as I stopped to empty it, I heard the two of them behind me.

'What's she up to, that girl? Lately she's seemed troubled.' Chance was a dear to care like this. Though he never seemed to be taking notice, nothing really escaped him.

'She has power, Chance. Power she may use, if she will. Power she fears using unwisely and thus fears using at all.'

'Looked on Barish, didn't she?'

'Yes. Yes, she looked on my brother, Barish, and what Barish did. Jinian sees the implications of that, I think. She does see things like that.'

'But Barish took the hundred thousand for something greater. So you said.'

'Oh, yes. And now he must try to answer the question I've been trying to answer for these hundreds of years, Chance. The question those hundred thousand will ask when they wake. The question Jinian is trying to answer. Is there anything greater?'

And there it was, of course. That was the thing that had been bothering me, and it didn't help greatly to know that many others had wrestled with it as well.

We went out onto the dusty cobbles of Sheel Street, littered with torn banners and tangled worms of confetti. Birds quarreled in the gutters over spilled confections. Wagons were moving from corner to corner while weary crews filled them with the festival flotsam. Down the hill we went, twisting and turning to arrive at the yard before the mill. We got to work, Peter and me and a dozen carpenters and metal workers, toiling away on the roof.

When Queynt and Chance arrived in the wagon, each endless length of pink cloth that had spewed from the front of the building was drawn up like a great fustigar tongue, licking the nose of the mill.

Chance was astonished. 'Now, by all my grandma's teacups, what're they up to?'

'Rollers, I should imagine,' said Queynt. 'Drawing the stuff up the front, and across the top, and down the back into the hoppers. Saves all that using up in between.'

'Well, why didn't the silly Bloomians think of that?'

'Religion, I imagine, friend Chance. Religion serves to prevent thought in many cases, and I'd say it had done so here. They started with the presumption that anything as complex as the mill must exist for a good reason. Then they spent all their time inventing a good reason – and some god to be responsible for it – rather than looking for a sensible solution to their problem. Jinian has merely substituted Drarg for whatever other deity they had involved.'

'Clever,' mumbled Chance. 'Only I don't think she'll let herself enjoy it. By night she'll be worrying whether it was the right thing to do.' He leaned back to watch the carpenters where they hammered away on high and saw that I'd been listening. He merely winked at me. Chance wasn't at all shy about his opinions.

There was a cheer from the roof as the first of the cloth reached the hoppers in back. Queynt clucked to Yittleby and Yattleby, who strode off around the building to the rear. Wide bands of pink descended in a steady flow to disappear into the huge, shaking hopper. Queynt got down from the wagon and came to meet me as I came down the ladder.

'They're going to have to add some trash now and then, you know,' he told me. 'The cloth alone won't be enough.'

'It won't? I thought if everything that came out went back in . . .' In fact, I had been rather proud of thinking this up, and his corrections made me peevish.

'Not quite. It uses up some, you see. During the weaving. Better tell the workmen, or it may not work right.'

He strode back to the wagon, pausing to take a bow to the group of council members who had just come around the corner of the building. Madame Browl was staring upward, face creased in concentration. Mergus frowned, at first unable to believe what he saw. Others murmured behind them, Philp among them.

'An excellent solution,' said Queynt in a loud, definite voice, winking in my direction. 'Drarg's representative is to be congratulated.'

'But, but . . . ' Madame Browl seemed about to object.

'No longer the endless round of festivals!' cried Peter. 'The people of Bloome may sleep of a morning.'

'No more uncomfortable clothes,' cried Chance, getting into the spirit of the thing. 'No more being bedeviled by the Hundred Demons!'

'No more banners,' someone cried from the rooftop.

'No more pink stuff!' cried someone else.

At the reference to the pink stuff, there was a general cheer, under the sound of which Madame Browl's disapproving voice fell silent.

'Leaving already, are you?' Philp asked Queynt, staring suspiciously at the great birds the while.

'Drarg's ambassador will ride with me to Fangel,' he replied in an innocent tone, bowing in my direction. 'It seemed impolite to delay her. Inasmuch as she has helped Bloome so immeasurably.

'Well. Be sure you get back promptly. This' – he gestured at the mill – 'is going to cause upheaval. Half the people in town won't know what to do with themselves. Do we go ahead and arrange for Pickel-port-poh? I ask you, do we? And Shimerzy-waffle?'

'Oh, I would,' said Queynt. 'Definitely. However, as Merchant's man, I'd suggest Bloome should start looking into handlooms for your weaving. No reason you can't use some of the stuff from the mill, here, if it ever produces anything you want, but for real quality, one wants the handwoven stuff. That will provide jobs for all those ousted as hopper fillers, and it will be better quality than you've had for centuries. That, in turn, should increase custom. No reason you can't still sell costumes, and have processions. And fireworks. The fireworks factory should be half-rebuilt by the time I'm expected back. I'm sure the Cloth Merchants' Council can hold things together while I'm in Fangel.' And thereafter, I thought to myself. And thereafter.

I came to the wagon, walking in my best plenipoten-tiary manner.

'Madame.' Queynt bowed.

I gave them all a haughty look before climbing to the seat. 'When Drarg returns, he will see to turning the mill off for you, though I am bound to tell you he may not return for several hundred years.' Then I waved at them all in an imperious manner while Queynt krerked to the birds and took us off.

Peter and Chance mounted up and plodded behind

the wagon. 'We could've got one night's sleep,' complained Chance. 'Before settin' out again. Those were good beds there in the mansion.'

'I think our Wizards are on the track of something,' said Peter a little sullenly. He was cross and irritable, overtraveled, underslept, underloved. With a sudden clarity I realized that if I was finding our relationship difficult, Peter was finding it damn near impossible, and this threw the whole matter into confusion again. If he felt grumpy and uncivil about it, well, so did I.

We followed on Brom's track for the first part of the way, back up the twists and down the turns of Sheel to the Forum Road, thence northwest on Tan-tivvy until it came to a crossing some way out of the town. Painted signboards pointed the way to a dozen places, east to Omaph and Peeri and beyond them to Smeen. Northeast to Jallywig and the unexplored depths of Boughbound Forest. Northwest to Luxuri and the Great Maze. South, the way we had come, to Zib, Zog, Zinter, Chime, and Thorpe. North to Woeful and Fangel.

The way from Zinter to Bloome had been river bottom, a flat road and an easy one, which went on through Bloome to Luxuri through the warm, moisture-laden airs of the jungle. The northern road to Woeful climbed abruptly out of this basin onto a narrow ridge-back above the trees. We looked down onto a steaming roof of vegetation, where flocks of bright parrots screamed their way toward the setting sun. The road stretched upward, no end to the slope in sight, and after some leagues of it, the krylobos decided abruptly that they had had enough for one day. They communicated this fact by squatting and waiting to be unharnessed.

'They never stop unless there is water near,' commented Peter. 'I'll find it.' He set off down the western slope, listening as he went. In a few moments he called out, returning shortly thereafter with a full bucket. 'A spring,' he said. 'Running into a lovely, cool basin. Supper first, then cold baths if anyone wants.'

'How far to Fangel?' I asked.

'A long day,' replied Chance. 'The fellas I talked to usually make it in two, stopping in Woeful for the night, but that's with a late start. I figure we can make it in one.'

'The fellas?' inquired Peter. 'What were you up to, Chance?'

The round, brown man shrugged elaborately in response.

'Well, we have to know what's goin' on.'

'There wasn't a small game, was there?' Peter asked.

'Might have been,' Chance replied with a complacent expression. 'Looky here.' He squatted at the side of the wagon, spreading the contents of his pouch on a flat rock. Coins, large and small, silver and gold. A piece of worked gold – half of a lacy brooch. And an amethyst dream crystal, larger than others we'd seen, of a curiously muted color, as though a shadow lay across it.

'They gamble with crystals? As though they were coins or gems?'

'This one fella did. I said no to him twice, told him I didn't want it. Fella insisted. Said it was valuable, not like any others we'd ever seen.'

'You won, of course.'

'No reason not to.' He shuffled his loot upon the stone, running it through his fingers. 'Wonder what good it is?'

Before I could move to stop him, Queynt reached for the stone and touched it to his tongue. Truly, I did move to stop him, warned by something, perhaps by the shadow that seemed to lie across the color in the stone. I was too late.

It was as though he had turned to lava, a kind of liquid stone that surged slowly beneath the skin, changing him as one watched, but so slowly one could not see change from moment to moment, could not say, 'See, see what just happened,' for nothing just happened. His face changed, and his body, not as a Shifter changes, but as water in a bucket changes,

67

sloshing to and fro, returning always to the shape of the container. I couldn't keep myself from screaming, a little high-pitched shriek of horror that brought Peter to us at once.

Queynt was weeping, huge tears welling from both eyes to make long dust tracks down his broad face, and he making no effort to stop them or wipe them away, meantime shrieking a high, lifeless sound like a knife upon a whetstone. His eyes were distant, unfocused, his breathing shallow and slow. The hideous shifting under his skin went on for a moment longer, then stopped slowly, like a tide ebbing away as he sagged onto the ground, the thin, shrieking sound going on and on, endlessly. The amethyst crystal dropped into the dust. I seized it and put it away, where it could do no more damage.

He had showed me the blue crystals he carried, those few the Shadowman had given him in the long ago, the ones he had offered to me. They were in his pouch, and I burrowed for it, trying to move his heavy, shrieking body aside, finally dragging it out and pouring the contents into my hand, three of the small blue crystals he had shown us in the tower of Bloome.

I didn't know what to do! Surely these had some curative properties if one of them had kept him alive for a thousand years. There was nothing else to try. No wize-art could be used against the totally unknown, and I could not taste the amethyst crystal to see what horrible thing in it Queynt had encountered. Peter read my terrible doubt and indecision and said, 'Do it, Jinian. Something awful has him. Anything's better than this . . . ' as he helped me get one of the blue stones into Queynt's mouth.

For a time nothing changed. Then the thin, tortured shrieking ended, the tears stopped flowing, and he looked more or less like himself. We held him between us, warming him. After a long time he spoke in a distant, windy voice not like his own.

'I thought I was immune.' The words were said so

slowly I had to recapitulate the sounds to understand them.

'What was it? What did it do?'

He could not or would not answer. He could not or would not say anything. We sat beside him, watching his face. After a time, his eyes closed. After a longer time, he began to breathe as though he were asleep. We wrapped him warmly. After a long time, we left him there. The two krylobos had come nearby during his shrieking, and they sat by him, keeping him warm. We prepared a meal, laid out our blankets, fed the birds, who were up now, striding nervously back and forth, staring at Queynt from the sides of their eyes, muttering bird talk that I could not really understand because they didn't understand it. I took it to be some kind of rote-learned ritual or invocation.

We ate. Chance took a bowl of broth to Queynt and spooned it into his mouth, whispering to him the while. I think Queynt slept then. Later, when we were all almost asleep by the coals of the fire, he began to speak, little more than a whisper, so we had to strain to hear him.

'I thought I was immune.

'The blue crystal I was given so long ago – oh, it does not seem long sometimes, but now it seems an eternity since that happened. The blue crystal – often I tried to tell myself what it had done to me. All I could think of to describe it was to say I had swallowed a map.' He fell silent again, as though thinking what he might say next.

I sat up, seeing the fire reflected from Peter's eyes where he sat half against a wagon wheel.

'Perhaps it was not a map or not only a map, but a set of instructions, a guide in cases of perplexity, a set of consistent directions to be used in all eventualities.' He struggled up on one elbow, reaching for the water jug. I gave him a drink, hushing him. 'No, no. You worry, Jinian, that the crystal took my will from me. It did not. If one has a map which shows two routes going to a place, one a good road, the other through a swamp, does it destroy one's will to know the swamp is there and reject that direction in favor of the better road? You are not sure. You would like all choices to be equal. Only if all choices were equal could one be sure one had free will. Otherwise ... otherwise ... ' He pushed himself up, half-sitting.

'Otherwise one always wonders if someone else is pulling the strings. However ... however, I had swallowed the map and it was part of me. From that time to this I have never felt anyone else pulling the strings. Inside myself the map was clear. Avoiding the swamps was simple good sense. Avoiding accident. Avoiding death. Avoiding pit and dragon, both. So. I wandered the world of my map ...

'Which, like most maps, did not specify a destination.'

I could hear him breathing, deep, fast breaths as though he fought to climb some great height.

'A destination?' I asked at last, prompting him.

'Most maps are tools one uses as an aid in journeying. They do not usually give a destination.'

'And the other crystal?' asked Peter hesitantly. 'The amethyst crystal? Did it show a destination, Queynt?'

'A wrong one,' he sobbed. 'Yes. A wrong one.'

'Shhh,' I said, putting my arms around him, cradling him to me as though he were a child. 'Shhh, Queynt. Tell us. What do you mean, a wrong one?'

'It summons to another place. Not on the map I was given at all. To some horrid cavern beneath the earth where monsters roar in the dark and all dreams are murdered.'

'Summons you, Queynt? Against your will?'

'Not against my will, child. Making it my will to go! That's the horror of it! But bless you, child, the blue one is there as well, saying, No, not the right place, not the right thing to do.' He could not say any more. Perhaps he would not say. I sat there cradling him well into the night, he still crying without a sound and Peter sitting by, the fire making mirrors of his eyes, glowing disks turned in my direction. At last Queynt slept.

'Well, Wize-ard?' said Peter.

'I won't let it happen,' I said. 'I will prevent it.'

'What will you do to save him?'

'I don't know, Peter. I don't know. Whatever it is is inside him. Perhaps by morning it will have worn off. Perhaps it's addictive, as the yellow ones were. We must watch him, protect him. But I don't know what I'll do if he isn't well by morning. I haven't any idea at all.'

It was some time before we slept.

I woke Chance early, while it was still dark, whispering to him, 'I need to know what was said about that amethyst crystal, the one Queynt tasted.'

'What was said? Little enough, girl. Let's see, there was five of us gaming. Man named Chortle, two brothers from a place somewhere north of Bloome, man named Byswitch, and me. Byswitch had most of the coins and the big crystal. Said it was new, no one had anything like it, very unusual. Said I ought to try it. Share it with my friends. Just came, he said, from That Place.'

'That place?'

'I don't know. That's what he said. "That Place north of Fangel where the Dream Miner is."'

'Would you say – Chance, would you say the fellow lost it easily?'

'Didn't put up much of a fight, that's true. We gave him a chanst to get even, but he wasn't up to much. Said he had a woman waiting for him.'

'Who lost, besides him?'

'Nobody much. All the rest of us was more or less even.'

'So he lost, you won, and nothing else much changed hands?'

'You're thinkin' it was a plot? Thinkin' I was supposed to bring that thing where Queynt could get it?'

'Queynt, maybe. Or Peter. Or me. Or all of us.'

'More likely Queynt, I think. He's been around long enough to attract attention. You, girl, you're practically brand new.'

I didn't talk with Chance further about the Dream Miner. So far as we all were concerned, it made little difference which of us was the intended victim. Perhaps any of us would have served. If Queynt had not been to some extent immune, perhaps all of us would have been.

I lay down, only for a moment, to wake much later with the sun a handsbreadth above the eastern mountains. Queynt was sitting up, staring at his hand from which the two remaining blue crystals winked and gleamed like eyes.

'Two,' he said, noticing that I was awake. 'I have two left.'

'And the other?'

He shook his head. 'Like being drunk. I can see the map I have carried for this thousand years: forests and roads. Sparkling. Whizz. Dart. All speed and sureness. Mmmm. Cities, full of. Full of people. Not quite. There's a white road leading to a good place . . . an inn. A place to rest. And over that is another, dark and hideous, and yet seductive. Leading to that terrible place. Buried down. Oh, too deep. Too deep.'

'Are you going to take another of the blue ones now?'

'I'm going to wait to see if the other wears off,' he replied with great dignity. 'It is less demanding already than it was last night. Foolish of me to have done that. I was so sure I was immune. Why should I not be?'

'Because the crystal you tasted had been sent particularly for you,' I said. 'I think. Designed for you. Designed to get through whatever immunity you might have. Hell, Queynt, you've been wandering the world a thousand years. You think nobody knows about you? You think nobody knows about the blue crystal? We can't be the only ones you've told. You must have had wives. Lovers. Friends, at least. You must have got drunk sometimes and talked about things.'

He flushed. 'Perhaps I have. Long ago. The Eesties knew I had it, of course. And perhaps there are Seers and snoops in various guises all around us. Why me?'

'Why any of us?' I asked. 'Perhaps it was designed for any of us or all of us. Why? Why did Porvius Bloster get an order to do away with me from Dream Miner and Storm Grower – it's no fiction, I saw the parchment myself, read the writing on it. I didn't even know such a thing as a Storm Grower or a Dream Miner existed. So, if it is nothing in my past, our pasts, then it is something in our future. Perhaps some Seer has told these two, whatever they are, that in the future something will happen which involves one of us, or all of us.'

'I thought your search for these creatures might be a foolish one,' he said. 'I did not even think they existed. Now we are sure they exist, perhaps it would be wiser not to seek them!' He sighed. 'Though perhaps we will learn more in Fangel.'

Queynt shut himself in the wagon that morning. I did not ask him what he was doing. The art is a secret art. Each Wize-ard had his own solitary ways. I know he worked to do what I could not do for him, protect himself. He did not ask about the amethyst crystal, and I did not tell him it was hidden away in a pouch beneath my skirts. Besides the crystal, it held the locket with my Wize-ard's fragment in it and a lock of Peter's hair. Since Shifters could grow hair as they pleased, of any kind and color, I had never been sure why this sentimental gesture had occurred to me. Nonetheless, I carried it just as I carried the star-eye around my neck, as a symbol of what I was and what I intended.

It was a steady climb from the campsite to the city of Fangel. We passed the trail to Woeful at midmorning and stopped only briefly at noon. We walked a good part of it to save the krylobos and by late afternoon could see the walls of the city on the heights above us. We were no longer alone on the road. Other wagons and riders had filtered in from the east so that we were hard put to it to find a space for ourselves and the fire. We camped on a rocky shelf separated from the height by a tangle of steep roads and paths with no wood nearer than the jungle far below. A charcoal vendor moved among the wagons, doing brisk business, and we bought a sack to warm our supper over.

'When are the Merchants' men due in the city?' I asked Queynt.

'Tomorrow, I think. About noon. The Dream Merchant will meet the various Merchants' men in the residence, according to Brom, to be given their instructions. Merchants' men change frequently, he said. No one will wonder that I have a face new to them.'

'If it is new to them,' grumbled Peter. 'Let us hope none of them have seen you before.'

'Well, I must take the chance of that. However, the rest of you may do better. Remember those half veils the people in Zinter wore? I bought some when we came through there, along with several sets of their black dress. It occurred to me then we might need a disguise somewhere along the road. All three of you can be travelers from Zinter. They're known to be belligerent when bothered, like those from Zib and Zog, so the likelihood is you'll go untroubled.'

'And when does the delegation from the south arrive? The Duke and his unlikely allies?'

'Also tomorrow, I think. It gives us little time to look around.'

I had been somewhat distracted by my own thoughts, but this mention of the Duke reminded me of something, and I asked if Brom had said anything about the location of the crystal mines near Fangel. 'Where are they? How can we get there?'

Peter stood thinking for a moment, turning to look up at the town above us. 'Near here, I think. Chance? Brom said the mines were just below Fangel, didn't he?'

Chance went on stirring the pot as he tried to remember. 'I didn't pay that much attention, to tell the truth. No. Wait. He said there was an old fella lived there, remember? While we were dressin' him up. He talked about it.'

'Buttufor,' said Queynt. 'Gerabald Buttufor and his wife, Jermiole. Guardian of the mines. Right?'

'Where?' I was cross with myself for being impatient with them, but I was impatient with them, though there seemed to be no reason for it. 'Come on, where?'

'Well, while the pot boils, we'll see if we can find out.' Peter stalked away among the wagons, asking questions, smiling, chatting, playing the good fellow, Queynt off in the opposite direction doing the same. They returned almost simultaneously with the same story.

'Down that southernmost path. Not far. We can go now, if you like. Food will stay warm on the fire.

I did like, leading off in the direction they'd indicated with a haste almost frantic. Curiosity, yes, but not only that. Something more than that. Since Queynt's disastrous accident, it had become very important to me to learn everything I could about the dream crystals.

We came to a small house at the edge of a pit, two old folk sitting on the stoop, he with a pipe of some sweet-smelling stuff, she with a mug of some kind of happiness, chirruping like a tree frog in the evening. 'Well, and well, visitors, travelers, folks bound for Fangel. Come to see the mine? Not much going on here anymore, not since the crystals started comin' up spoiled, but you're welcome. You're welcome.' Nodding like a little doll, smiling at the shadows: I realized with a start she was blind.

'You folks like a tour?' Gerabald Buttufor heaved himself to his feet, leaning heavily on his cane. 'Noticed two or three nodules this mornin', 'bout ready to bust. Interestin' to see. Can't use the crystals. Like Jermiole says, all spoiled now. Can't say why. Don't know why. Are, though. All spoiled.'

Queynt passed coins into the old man's palm. 'We'd like to see it. Lucky we got here before dark.'

'Oh, you could'a seen it after, as well. Nodules get all hot and feverish, shine like little moons, they do. Get along down here.' He led us, stumping along with the cane, down a twisting path into the declivity. The sides and bottom of it were pitted with rounded scars, as though from a shower of great stony hail or meteors. He went along a path, stopping abruptly beside a fist-sized dome of stone.

'Here.' He tapped it with his cane. It rang, twangingly, a harsh, ugly sound. 'Good crystals don't even sound like that. Used to like the sound of the good ones. Now you watch.' He struck the stone again, sharply, several times in one place. The cane was shod with iron. The ugly sound repeated, but on the last blow the rock broke.

Fragments flew, disclosing the center. Like an egg, it held a yolk, a yellow crystal swimming in silvery liquid that oozed over the broken edge of the stone and into the ground. Peter leaned forward.

'Don't touch it!' I cried, seeing what it was.

'That's right, lassy. Not many know that unless they've worked the mines. Can't touch the crystal milk, boy. That's what we call it, crystal milk. Burn you right through to the bone.'

I had last seen similar stuff in a great pool deep in the Citadel of the Sevens; I carried a fragment dipped in that pool as one of my most cherished things. It had been approached with great care and considerable reverence when I had seen it, enough so to make me wary of it. 'May I borrow your cane, friend Gerabald?' I dipped the iron tip in the liquid to hear the same high singing I had heard in the Citadel of the Sevens, far beneath the surface of the earth. I clutched the pouch containing the locket, disbelieving. So! That most marvelous and esoteric stuff was, in fact, well known elsewhere.

'How do you get the crystal out?' I asked.

'Why, that's no trouble.' He bashed away at the stone once more, breaking it so that all the liquid ran away, raking the crystal out onto the stone. 'Soon as it dries, you can pick it up. Don't taste it, though. It's one of the death ones.'

The others wandered off, but I waited while it dried, while the evening came on, bending at last to pick it up, piss-yellow and deadly as poison. I crouched over the empty shell, rising at last in some puzzlement.

'Peter,' I called, seeing him turn and move toward me with more eagerness than I needed. 'Lean down here,' I whispered. 'Shift your eyes. I can't tell, it's too dark, but isn't there a kind of channel or duct at the bottom of this hole?'

He stretched out on the stone, taking the opportunity to put one arm around me as he stared into the hemispherical hole. Shift eyes, Shift nerves behind eyes, peer deep. Even in the deepening darkness he could see it. 'Yes. A twisty little duct, leading down into the earth. You want me to look at some of the others?'

'Please. Do. See if they're all alike.'

He wandered away, keeping his face with its oddly Shifted eyes turned from the loquacious old man who was lecturing Queynt and Chance on the intricacies of dream mining.

'Sometimes there'd be a dozen little ones in one nodule, sometimes only one. Used to be pretty green ones in this mine, good ones, too. Happy stuff, no death dreams; forests and birds mostly. I 'member one was about flyin'. Oh, me'n Jermiole shared that one, flew all over. Mountains, valleys. One great chasm we saw all full of cities built on tree roots, if you could believe that. Great groles down in the bottom of it, too, and up on top the hugest beasts you've ever seen. Saw parts of the world never knew were there. Well, p'raps they aren't, if you take my meaning. In the crystal they were, sure as certain.'

'Were a lot of these yellow ones dug out of here and put into commerce?' I asked Gerabald.

'None from here. Fella used to work here dug up the first one, tasted it – well, we almost always did, you know. Didn't know what to ask for 'em until you tasted 'em – and we found him four, five days later where he'd wandered off to, deader'n a baked bunwit, half the crystal still in his hand. Well, if that wasn't enough, came some ijit through here a few days later, didn't ask, didn't tell anybody, and dug a bunch of 'em, gave 'em to his entire party, parents, children. They must've shared 'em around, cause we found 'em all gone. That was enough, let me tell you. We never sold another from this mine after that.'

'If we've seen a lot of these on the road, then, they must have come from somewhere else?' I asked.

The old man stumped over to me, looked up at me with rheumy eyes, whispered, 'Way I hear it, lassy, they're coming up ever'where. Used to be a mine over near Smeen, nothin' but pure greeny-blue crystals. Most greeny-blue ones are the best kind. Make you healthy, they do. Long-lived. Me'n Jermiole'r more than a hundred ten, you know that? We just go on, cheerful as tumble-bats from the ones we used to get fifty, sixty years ago. Well, that mine's nothin' but these yallery things now. So I hear. Sad, too. I've got a few of those old ones left, but sad to think there'll be no more.' He stumped away again.

That was more than merely troublesome. It was scary. Peter came up behind me, began stroking my back. All I wanted to do was turn around, but I gritted my teeth and told my belly to stop melting in that ridiculous way. 'All of them,' he said, continuing the stroking. 'All of them have that little tube coming up from deep in the earth somewhere.'

Gerabald Buttufor looked back at me, calling loudly, 'Better throw that yallery thing away, lassy, pound it up to powder. Dangerous, those are.'

'I know.' Who knew better than I? No one else had buried more of the victims than I had. Still, the thing went in my pouch. Sometimes one had need for dangerous things. This crystal was one. The idea I had just had was another.

CHAPTER SIX

As soon as it was light, Queynt arrayed himself quasi-fantastically as suited a Merchant's man from Bloome. He wore the seal of office, the plaque of jet with the letters 'DM' picked out in brilliants in a circle of multicolored gems. We three others put on the black garb from Zinter that Queynt had provided from his costume store. I considered it inauspicious clothing while accepting that nothing could be more anonymous. A stretchy black garment covered the body and head with a half veil over nose and mouth. Over all this went a voluminous cloak, dark as midnight, with one stripe, the color of dried blood, running from throat to hem. The cloak had a larger, metal-lined hood hanging at the back to be used in case of hail. The people of this region were preoccupied with the possibility of storm, and we were beginning to understand why.

There were no boots among Queynt's provisions, so we wore our own, decorated with new ornaments to make them look foreign and strange. I chose a pair of gilt snakes for the outside of each boot: Peter chose salamanders and Chance a pair of Basilisks. At the sight of these last, I couldn't help shuddering.

'What's wrong?' Peter came to my side with a concerned expression.

'Nothing much. It's those Basilisks on Chance's boots. Made me think of Dedrina Dreadeye. Dedrina-Lucir's mama.'

'Lucir? That was the one who tried to kill you?'

'Yes, she tried, but I succeeded. I killed her, and I've walked in fear of the Basilisks' vengeance since. Dedrina Dreadeye is still alive; sometimes I remember that and it makes me go all over cold. Porvius Bloster came northward, I remember. Likely his sister Dreadeye did, too. I keep expecting to encounter her, or him, or both.' I wandered toward the rocky edge of the shelf we had camped upon, stood looking toward the eastern horizon.

'We've seen no sign of her, or him.' He stood beside me, giving me lecherous looks. No. I thought of them as lecherous. Perhaps he intended them only to be admiring.

'True. I'd feel happier if we had – if we knew, for instance, she was headed off in some specific direction, preferably away from us. Ah, well. Not important now. What is important is Queynt. How's he feeling?'

'Seems in good spirits. Asked me what we'd done with the amethyst crystal.' He turned to look back at the wagon, where Queynt and Chance seemed engaged upon wheel repair.

'What did you say?'

'Told him I hadn't seen it since the event.' He moved toward me with a purposeful leer.

'Peter,' I begged weakly. 'Don't.'

'Peter, don't!' he mimicked savagely. 'Gods, Jinian. I've had enough of "Peter, don't." '

'You know why. It isn't that I want to say it! It's that you'll never listen.'

'I've listened long enough. You're not studying the art now. The seven aren't here. But you're here, and I'm here, and all this going on about your oaths is meaningless. I know you love me – want me. Unless you've changed completely since the Wastes of Bleer. I remember a certain night there. If we'd had a little more time, the oath wouldn't have mattered then!'

'You know I haven't changed. But we thought we were going to die then.'

'I know. And we could die tomorrow. Which makes this oath business even more stupid. Well, Jinian, love, I'm not going to go on like this . . . ' He had the look of a man who had spent a restless night

80

of frustrated desire and was determined it should be the last.

What I might have said was stopped by Queynt's voice.

'Time to move,' accompanied by a bugling cry from the krylobos.

'I'm not going to go on, Jinian,' Peter repeated in a thick, passionate voice, pulling the veil up over his mouth so all I could see was the determination in his eyes. 'If we're to travel together, we're going to have to be together. I can't take much more of this.'

He strode off, not waiting for me. Chance was already on the wagon seat. Queynt was mounted. 'So far as Fangel is concerned,' Queynt said, 'I am a mere Merchant's man. You three black-cloaked Zinterites are the owners of this strange equipage. We travel in proximity, but not together. Isn't that so?'

We started off, Peter riding close beside the wagon, Queynt slightly after. Others from the campsite creaked into motion as well, a fragmentary snake crawling toward Fangel.

The city lifted its roofs before us. Its towers bore long black pennants, like great tattery bats flitting silently above the hill. There was no sound from Fangel, not the creak of wagons nor the sounds of commerce, no vendors' shouts, no children's laughter. A silent city, it poised above with expectant gates like open mouths.

It had no smell, Fangel, no woodsmoke, cookery, market goods, people-cum-animal smell. If there had ever been a kindly stench of people there, the jungle wind had blown it away. Now was only the graveyard odor of stone and dust.

Outside the open gates a troop of guardsmen stood, each arrayed with the Dream Merchant's insignia, looking us over with long, calculating stares.

'Business?' asked one, leaning on the wagon step.

'On our way to Luxuri,' said Chance. 'No real business in Fangel.'

'Turn aside to Dungcart Road, to your left outside the walls.'

'We heard there was a procession. Thought we'd go in to see that.'

'Procession this afternoon. In that case you can park the wagon off the avenue in the park. Leave before dark. No fires in Fangel. No rooms, either, and no food served after dusk, so don't think of staying. We've plenty of room in the prison for vagrants who remain after dark.'

Chance clicked to the birds and they moved through the gate. 'Friendly,' he remarked. 'A real friendly place.'

Behind us we heard the guard saying to Queynt, 'Business?' and Queynt's reply. 'Merchant's man from Bloome, summoned for the reception.'

We dawdled, letting Queynt pass us. High walls enclosed the street, blank walls marked again and again with the linked letters of the Dream Merchants. Above the featureless walls jutted ornamented façades of great houses or blank sides of long unwindowed buildings.

'Factories?' I wondered. 'Warehouses? Is this a manufacturing town, then? At this height?'

The streets were empty. No person walked there; no curious head protruded from a convenient window. Our scanty caravan wove through the city to a central park, a place of mown grass, trees, and wide basins of polished stone in which water lay quiet. Even here there was no smell, as though the trees had been made of some inorganic material, the water poured from some sterile vat. Across a wide avenue a twisted metal fence made a barrier between the park and the much embellished walls of the residence. As we watched, the doors of this ornate building swung wide to emit a voluminous, almost architectural robe. A square head protruded from the neck of it, close-clipped no-color hair, a promontory of nose overhanging a clifflike upper lip beneath which the mouth writhed wave-like around fallen stones of teeth. 'Thtrike,' said the mouth in a sibilant shout as the robe gestured with practiced drama.

'Gods,' mumbled Chance, looking at the gong they were about to strike. 'Look't the size of that thing. Hold your ears!'

The warning came barely in time. An earth-shaking '*Bong!*' set up a trembling reverberation throughout the city, the very ground shivering beneath us, the sound seeming to gain strength as it continued, permeating the buildings with an inexorable message. '*Bong!*' again, and yet again. Then a slow falling into momentary silence, broken at once by other sounds. Doors opening, people speaking, carts moving out of warehouses and onto the streets, a child screaming laughter, fountains suddenly splashing. Somewhere a band started to play.

It had been like a stage set on which the curtain had suddenly gone up. It was unreal. I did not believe it.

Queynt sat on his horse only a little way from us. 'The man in the robe was the Dream Merchant,' he remarked. 'Brom described him to me. The gong could be a kind of curfew, to keep everyone off the streets at night.' He did not sound convinced of this.

Across the avenue the guardsmen opened the iron gates and propped them wide as the Dream Merchant retreated into the residence. Waiting beside the convoluted fence was a bulbous, beak-nosed man displaying a seal of office much like the one Queynt wore. He raised his hand to Queynt, beckoning. 'Merchant's man? New at it? From Bloome? Ah. I'm here from Woeful. We can check in with the Dream Merchant now if you like. I'll show you the way.'

Queynt dismounted, tied the horse to a convenient tree, and walked through the gates with the other Merchant's man, leaving the three of us to ourselves.

'I smell food,' said Chance. 'No inns, but lots of food carts. Suppose I get us some breakfast.'

'Do that,' said Peter. 'Meantime I'll take a short prowl around and see what's to be seen. Jinian?' He invited me with a gesture.

I didn't want to go anywhere. If truth were told, I wanted to get out of Fangel, the sooner the better. The silence before the gong went; the lack of smell to it; the way the people moved; everything about it gave me the shakes. 'No. It'll be easier for you to go here and there without me. I'll keep an eye on the wagon while you two roam about.'

He turned away with rejected sulkiness, moving into the gathering crowd that was assembling to stare at the krylobos.

'Aren't they pretty things,' gushed a lady of Fangel, got up herself as a pretty thing, all ruffles and bows. 'Great beauties. What do you feed them?'

Not of a mood to be tactful, I said, 'About a twenty weight of raw meat a day, including the guts.'

The lady made a moue, tossed her head. 'So savage! And where are you from? I have not seen garb like that before.'

'From Zinter. It is the usual dress there. Our people have a dislike of displaying their faces.' I tried to look the woman in the face, tried to make eye contact. Each time I came close, her glance slid away as though greased. Her expression was not unkind, and yet there was something about her that set my skin aprickle.

'Is it a Games dress of some kind?' She evidenced no particular interest in my answer, but I didn't like the question.

'No, madam. It is the ordinary dress of our people.'

She posed, simpered, displaying her own face in several well-practiced expressions. On her bodice she wore a jet plaque with the letters 'DM' picked out in brilliants.

'How exotic. Do you allow others to know your names?'

So here it was. 'Jambal,' I replied. There are many

spells, seizings and sendings that can be done against those whose names were known. Silly to suspect this stupid-looking woman of any villainy. Silly. Why then did I suspect it? 'My name is Jambal.'

'I am happy to meet you, Jambal. My name is Sweetning Horb. I live over there' – she pointed at one of the high-walled mansions along the avenue – 'in Horb House. Perhaps you will come to dine with us?'

'Alas, lady, no. We are expected in Luxuri and will leave before long.' Thank all the gods.

'All honor to the Duke of Betand. Hail Huldra. Hail Valearn. Hoorah for Dedrina Dreadeye. What a pity you must leave so soon.'

I heard the name but did not. Dedrina Dreadeye. Frozen with shock, I was still alert enough to see that Sweetning Horb wore a dream crystal about her neck. It was a pinkish stone set in a gold bezel. Nausea struck at me; it was hard to raise my hand to stop her, but I managed to put a hand on the woman's arm. 'Please, who are these people you exclaim honor upon?'

'Honor? Upon whom, Jambal?'

'You said, "Honor upon the Duke of Betand." '

'I did? Well, undoubtedly he is an official visitor worthy of honor.'

'But who is he?'

'But my dear, I haven't the least idea. I must run. Lovely to have met you, and your huge savage birds.'

I was given no time to recover. An oldster with a raffish beard stood importunately before me demanding to know the names of the birds.

'Yarnoff and Barnoff,' I said at once, trying to keep from shaking. 'Yarnoff is the female.'

'And where were they captured, madam? I am zoo keeper for the city of Fangel and would be glad to know where a specimen could be acquired. Honor to the Duke.' He wore the jet badge, the pinkish crystal.

'It is my understanding they were taken as chicks from the mountains above the Southern Sea. However, since they came into my care as adults, I cannot vouch for the truth of this.' All lies, good safe lies.

'All honor to the Duke of Betand. Hail Huldra. Did I understand you to say they are fed raw meat?' When I nodded, he went on, 'From my own experience, I would counsel the addition of cooked grain. I have been told that krylobos in the wild do eat grain, and it might be their health would suffer from a diet of meat alone . . . ' He took his crystal in one hand and licked it reflectively.

'*Idiot*,' commented Yittleby to Yattleby. '*I'd feed him stewed grain. Actually, Jinian, a few ripe thrilps wouldn't be amiss . . .*'

'Hail Valearn,' said the man, looking at me earnestly. 'Hoorah for Dedrina Dreadeye.'

'I'm sorry,' I replied. 'I didn't hear. What was that you just said?'

'That their health might suffer from a diet of meat alone.' He licked the crystal again.

I shivered deep inside, trying to keep it from showing. 'Whether it would or not, sir, they must be fed now. Will you excuse me?' Then, almost silently, '*Yittleby, couldn't you two clear the area somewhat?*'

Yittleby charged the onlookers with a hungry caterwaul. Yattleby began to kick, missing his targets but only slightly. The oglers drew back in dismay, some reaching for the pinkish crystals that all of them wore. Some sucked upon them, seeming not to notice that they did so.

'The krylobos don't like crowds,' I called, voice cracking. 'Stand well back.'

Now, I said to myself, it will be only a matter of moments before someone appears at my side with a pink crystal and insists I have a taste of it.

It was Chance who appeared, however, bearing

fragrant meat pies and pastries. 'All honor to the Duke of Betand,' he remarked. 'This place is enough to give you the grues. I've decided my name is Biddle, by the way.'

'Thank the gods you were cautious. I'm Jambal. I hope to hell Peter had sense enough to – '

'Don't worry about him. He's all right. Tell you something interesting, though Jin . . . Jambal. There was a fella over there on the street in Tragamor dress. First Gamesman I've seen since we left Zinter. Came in on a wagon just behind us. Well, he was picked up by some woman dressed up like a Festival Horse, all ruffles, and before he could get two steps away from her, she'd given him a dream crystal right off her neck.' Chance wiped his brow as he set the food out on the wagon seat and cocked his head to the bird's uproar. 'Lemme get those birds some food and I'll tell you the rest.' He went to the rear of the wagon where the meat stores were kept.

I sniffed at the food ravenously. Seemed all right, but just to be sure I murmured a renewal of the Fire Is Sparkening spell, which would warn if anything unhealthful were encountered. I was halfway through a savory meat pie when Chance returned.

'So, like I was sayin', this flouncy high-nosed dame gave him this crystal, right off her neck. Then she teased him into tasting it. Well, that's all right, just a taste doesn't usually – you know. But it was like those yellow ones, Jin . . . Jambal. He tasted, then he took off his helm and left it lying, and as he went off with her over there, he was sayin', "All honor to the Duke of Betand." Now, I ask you!'

So this was why they had seen no Gamesmen. Gamesmen were particularly targeted to be supplied with crystals. And once given them, it seemed they were not only full of praise for the coming visitors, but also forgetful of their own status. Praise for the visitors did not so much distress me. The mention of

Dedrina Dreadeye did, however, coming as it did out of the blue. Down the avenue we could see a tall black form returning. Peter.

He arrived somewhat breathlessly. 'Hail Dedrina,' he whispered. 'Have you heard?'

'Could anyone not hear? You didn't tell anyone your name, did you, Peter?'

'Nobody asked. I was moving too fast to get into conversation. Good idea not to, though. I'll be Chorm.'

'Jambal,' I announced. 'And he's Biddle. I wonder if Queynt – '

'Queynt will take care of Queynt. He got along for some thousand years before you came into his life. Sometimes you sound like his mother. And mine.'

He sounded grumpy again, still, very much like someone working himself up to some irrevocable pronouncement. Sensibly, I said nothing. Across the way the doors of the residence opened and Queynt emerged, along with his beak-nosed new acquaintance. They came across the avenue. 'Ah, the travelers from Zinter. May I introduce you to the Merchant's man from Woeful. Ballycrack Willome. My fellow travelers from Zinter. I'm sorry, I've forgotten your names?' His eyebrows waggled caution at us.

'Jambal,' I said, bowing. 'Biddle, there with the birds. And this is Chorm.'

'I am gratified to know you,' said Willome. 'All honor to the Duke of Betand.'

I looked at his chest. Yes, he wore one of the pinkish crystals. And so did Queynt.

'Hoorah for Dedrina Dreadeye,' Queynt said softly, shaking his head at me. 'We are so looking forward to the procession and reception.'

'The procession will enter Fangel shortly after noon,' announced Willome. 'We Merchants' men and you other visitors will cheer and exclaim with delight from the park here. Residents of Fangel will cheer from their windows or the streets. The Duke of

Betand with a great retinue will arrive. Also the Witch, Huldra. The Ogress, Valearn. Both with their followers. And the Basilisk, Dedrina Dreadeye, recently allied with them.'

'How exciting,' commented Peter, one hand on my shoulder to stop my shaking.

Queynt went on, 'When the honored guests have arrived, the Merchants' men are invited into the residence grounds for the reception. After which we must take our latest shipment of crystals and get back to our own towns, eh, Willome? Hail Huldra. Hail Valearn.'

'All honor to the Duke of Betand,' intoned Willome. 'Will you all excuse me while I get some breakfast?' Belching gently, he moved away through the crowd, somewhat lessened since the birds' threat upon the spectators.

'I keep expecting someone to show up and force those things on the rest of us,' I said. 'Queynt, you didn't –'

'Calm down, girl. No, I didn't. Though it was chancy there for a moment. A little sleight of hand and enough sense to mimic what was going on around me seemed to do the trick. I'm using the name Abstimus Baffle, by the way. One of my oldest noms de guerre.' Seeing our puzzlement, 'Never mind. A phrase from a former life.

'Now, I think they will not force anything on you as long as you attract no more attention than our krylobos friends have already done. The pink crystals are only temporary, only for this event. They will be used, I suppose, so long as the Duke and his entourage are in Fangel. Since you are to be gone before dark, it is not necessary to "crystallize" you, so to speak. I, on the other hand, will be attending the reception and must be relied upon to act correctly. So.'

Peter was astonished. 'Do you mean to tell me that they have given those foul things to an entire population in order to assure the Duke gets welcomed appropriately? What do they do between visits? The people, I mean? And where do they get the crystals? Do they really come from mines?'

'Why should there be a town here at all on this sterile height?' I asked. 'There's no water. There's no agriculture to support the population. No reasonable explanation why commerce should center here. But it is a fortress easy to control. The population has to be engaged in the crystal commerce somehow. Or in something we can't even imagine. I'll tell you, this place makes me crawl.' I stared out at the street where the populace moved, buying meat pies and fruit, hot sweet breads and sugary candies, confetti and flags, moving and talking as real people move and talk, and yet every other breath stopping to put the pinkish crystals to their mouths, moving then again, to spew, 'All honor to the Duke of Betand,' without knowing or caring what it meant.

'Still, we're here,' murmured Queynt. 'Let not the time pass us by. Peter, learn what you can, will you, my boy? And you, Chance. Meantime avoiding those crystals as though they were Ghoul Plague! We should all be back here shortly after noon when the procession arrives.'

Obediently we scattered, Queynt and I staying together as we walked the streets of Fangel. All the large, blank-faced buildings opened off secluded courtyards, and these courtyards had guards posted outside them. 'By noon,' murmured Queynt, 'Peter will have investigated a dozen places in as many shapes, I doubt not. You may be right about their crystal factories, though the probable methodology escapes me.'

'I envision it having something to do with that silvery stuff the crystals grow in. Crystal milk, Buttufor called it.'

'Is it the wize-art tells you this, Jinian Footseer?' He sounded amused.

'It is my troubled heart tells me this, Queynt. That

90

and what I saw at that little mine outside town.' Before I could go on, we were accosted.

'Jambal! Are you enjoying Fangel? Sweetning Horb, remember? We met this morning! Oh, my, have you left those great brutal sweet birds alone? Oh, tisk, they'll eat half the populace by the time you get back. I hope you tied them tightly!'

'I did, yes. May I present Abstimus Baffle, Merchant's man from Bloome. We traveled more or less adjacent from Bloome. Abstimus Baffle, Sweetning Horb.' I stepped back to let Queynt take over, which he did, bearing the woman off on a flood of words that put the quantity of her own to shame. I didn't follow them. All day my discomfort had grown, my skin crawling in a spontaneous writhe of escape, convinced that someone was watching me. It was impossible to go on moving and acting as though nothing were wrong. I turned back to the wagon.

'*Was a twit here, Jinian,*' said Yattleby. '*I stomped him, only a little. Tried to poison us each with some pink thing.*'

'*The whole town's a trap,*' I mumbled. '*Keep watch, will you. I'm going to sleep in the wagon. I'm exhausted.*' Peter had not been the only one to spend a troubled night.

I fell into sleep as into a pit, disturbed by pertinent dreams of crystals and mines and dead bodies along the road, wakening when the others returned along about noon.

'The lady wanted to be sure I shared the town's need to honor the Duke,' Queynt confessed. 'I came very close to tasting this pretty pink crystal, friends, though I managed to avoid it with a minor Wizeardry. They are persistent here.'

Peter was very white-faced and not in a mood for this jocularity. 'Jinian was wrong,' he said. 'The buildings I could get into are all full of people. Laid out on the shelves like so many sacks of grain. Children. Men. Women. And creatures, lizardy things. Furry things. Asleep, I think. When the gong goes, some of them must get up, but the others just stay there. There's nothing in those houses but storage. And all of them have crystals in their mouths.'

'Gods!' I had not even imagined this. 'What do they have the look of, Peter? An army, perhaps?'

'Could be.' He pursed his lips, thinking, making quirky wrinkles around his eyes. 'Come to think of it, most of those on the shelves are fighting size – big. Men or other things, both big. Some smaller ones, but I'd say nine out of ten could be warriors.'

'Gamesmen?'

'It would explain where they'd all gone.'

That was a disquieting thought. We didn't have time to worry over it, however, for there was a trumpet blast that spun us around facing the avenue. Heralds rode toward us, horns in hand, tabards gleaming. 'All those within sound of my voice give ear! All those give ear! His Grace, the Glorious Duke of Betand. Her Highness, Valearn, Queen of the High Demesne. Her Worship, Huldra, Heiress of Pfarb Durim. Her Eminence, Dedrina, Protector of Chimmerdong!'

'Heiress of Pfarb Durim,' stuttered Peter. 'Still claiming the city, is she? Not damn likely.'

'Protector of Chimmerdong,' I snarled obstinately, even while my body melted in a sweat of terror. 'Over my dead body.'

There was no time to say more. The first of the procession was passing, a sonority of trumpets, a frenzy of drums, so loudly bellicose as to drown all other sound and all thought. Then striding banner bearers, then muzzled pombis shambling in formation with small, frightened shapes tied to their backs.

'Shadowpeople!' hissed Peter. 'And not here of their own will.'

A huge cage on wheels with a gnarlibar inside, asleep: twelve chained krylobos who screamed such a cry as could have been heard in Schooltown far to the south when they saw Yattleby.

'*Rescue! Rescue!*' they cried.

'*Wait! Wait!*' cried Yattleby in return, a vengeful shriek. '*We will!*'

Several of the guards along the route turned at this, scowling. '*Hush,*' I hissed at them in their own language. '*You will betray your purpose.*' The great bird subsided, his anger shown only by the huge toenail tracks he was scratching in the earth. '*Shhh,*' I said again.

'All honor to the Duke of Betand,' piped Queynt, giving us cautionary looks out of the sides of his eyes. 'All honor to the Duke of Betand!' He waved his fists, smiling as the cart came toward us on which the corpulent hulk of the Duke rode, canopied with silken draperies and jeweled like a Tragamor's helm. He bowed from side to side, waving a puffy, negligent hand. Behind him marched his retinue, and behind them a line of captives in chains, both men and women. Most carried treasure on display. One stalwart couple carried a huge woven basket between them.

Just behind them was a young woman in rags, carrying a child. She was a pretty thing, little more than a child herself, and I was about to say something to Peter about her when he made a strangled cry.

'Sylbie!' he shouted, so loudly that the chained young woman heard him and turned searching the crowd. Her face was very lovely, though tracked by tears. The child she carried had a wave of ruddy hair across its forehead. 'Sylbie,' Peter said again, a guttural snarl. 'That bastard broke his bond.'

The marching woman was not the only one who had heard. So had the Duke. He heaved his bulk upon the cart, trying to see who had called out, spoke sharply to one of his guards, who spurred away from the procession and into the park.

'Happy *he'll be*,' Queynt caroled in frantic rhyme with Peter's exclamation. 'Happy *he'll be*. All honor to the Duke of Betand.' He had made his voice sound almost like Peter's.

The guard stopped, came forward more slowly. 'What's that you're yellin', Merchant's man? Somebody's name?'

'No one's name. No, only a fervent wish for the Duke's happy future, Guardsman. All honor to the Duke of Betand!' This was echoed by the others in our group, and the guardsman galloped back to his place beside the Duke's cart. We saw him speak, saw the Duke heave himself up to cast a smiling wave in our direction as the cart turned the corner to circle the park. 'Gods,' murmured Queynt.

'Don't scare me like that again, Peter. Thank all the gods you've got that veil over your face. Who in the name of all that's holy is the girl?'

Peter didn't answer. Only his eyes showed above the veil, the skin around them very red, then very white. I watched him with a sick, sinking feeling. 'Someone you knew?' I prompted him.

He nodded. 'Someone ... ah, someone I met in Betand. When I went through there some – oh, it would be almost three years ago.'

I had judged the baby the woman was carrying to be about two. So.

'You said the bastard broke his bond. You meant the Duke?'

'He was set on having Sylbie for himself – set on having her dowry, at any rate. I did the town a considerable service while I was there. In payment, he was to let Sylbie choose her own husband. I don't know what he's done to her, but she was a wealthy girl when I left Betand.'

Wealthy and pregnant, I said to myself. Queynt threw me a sidelong glance as though he read my mind.

Peter was still worrying at it. 'If she's a captive in the Duke's train, he's done some foul thing. He was a mean-spirited bastard in Betand. It's unlikely he's changed.'

'If she is a friend of yours,' I said in a voice as calm

as a glacier, 'then we must rescue her. Her, and some Shadowpeople, and several krylobos. It seems we have our night's work cut out for us.'

'Where'll all that mess be stayin'?' asked Chance. 'Inside the residence grounds?'

'There's a large guest compound there,' said Queynt. 'Together with barns and dormitories. I saw it this morning. I'll try to get a better look during the reception. Gods, Jinian, you mean to try getting the krylobos out, and the Shadowpeople, and the girl and her baby?' He popped his eyes at me in pretended astonishment.

'Well, Queynt, I don't think Yittleby and Yattleby will give you a choice about the krylobos. Either we do it or they will. In case you hadn't noticed, Yattleby is about to take on the Duke of Betand and all his retinue, all by himself. He won't restrain, so I wouldn't try it. As for the Shadowpeople, I've wanted to meet them ever since Mavin told me about them. And the girl? Well, I think that's Peter's baby she's carrying, so we have no choice there, either. Wave, now. Smile. Here comes Huldra!' Amazed at my own chilly calm, I waved.

And there was a cavalcade of mounted drummers, beating an erratic thunder on great copper tubs, followed by a high, black cart with the still-faced Witch upon it, long dark hair curling around a white, red-lipped face with eyes that burned. The dangerous, watching feeling I had been having all day suddenly intensified like fire. It burned. There was a seeking feeling in the air, as though a creeping tentacle reached toward us. Peter turned to one side, hiding even his eyes. The invisibly flaming hunter passed with the creaking cart, turning the corner to continue the procession. Some kind of seeking spell. I shivered.

Next a row of fan-horns, shattering the air with dissonant blasts to announce Valearn, gray hair standing in great spikes around her ravaged face, eyes like dead coals, black and lightless, and the skeletons of children rattling on the wheels of her wagon. It should have sickened me. Instead, I felt anger, hot and horrid. Queynt put a hand on my arm, hissed at me.

Then came a row of men bearing huge wooden spirals that emitted a blood-chilling hiss when stroked, endless and chilling. Dedrina Dreadeye, mounted upon some great lizardish form that none of us had seen before, its monstrous tail heaving back and forth as it waddled down the avenue, head swinging left and right, as did its rider's, left and right. At her side on a blindfolded horse rode Porvius Bloster, looking old and ill. This time it was I who turned my face aside. I felt the Basilisk's attention on the crowd. She looked exactly like Dedrina-Lucir except for age, and seeing her was like peering back into time. I had already killed three who looked like this. Daughter and two sisters of this one. I had killed them with the Dagger of Daggerhawk Demesne. On my leg, that same Dagger burned and throbbed.

The head of the procession had come around full circle and moved into the grounds of the residence, musicians, guards, and animals moving off to the left, honored guests to the right. The girl and her child went to the left. I asked Queynt, 'Do we have a better chance during the reception, Queynt? Or after it, when all visitors are presumed to have left Fangel?'

'After, Jinian. After,' he whispered. 'My suggestion is that you depart northward now. I am expected to leave by the south gate when this affair is over. Is there a path from north to south outside the walls of this place?'

'Dungcart Road,' answered Chance. 'Along the western wall. Shall we wait for you then, Queynt? Outside the north gates?'

'Wait for me there. Except you, Peter. You might slip along Dungcart Road and offer me help, if needed.

Hard to say how many there'll be in company when we leave. I'll have to get away from them somehow.'

Thus quickly were we determined. Two of us three putative Zinterites began hitching the birds while one talked with highly irritated krylobos. *'We'll come back, Yattleby,'* I kept saying. *'If we stay now, it will attract attention, and some of your kin may end up getting killed. If we leave, they'll all go to sleep thinking there's no danger. Wait until dark. Come on, now. Take the harness and quit kicking. We won't leave your kinsmen – ah, kinsbirds behind.'*

Eventually the giant bird agreed, though I knew very well he wouldn't go far from the walls. His eyes were red and furious. I had never seen them like this before. He was too angry even to talk to me.

Queynt went to the residence, nimbly bowing and smiling, full of quirky gestures and fulsome words, echoing the universal greeting. 'All honor to the Duke of Betand.' I know from him what he learned there and will tell it here.

Inside the gate he encountered Willome once more, and they made their way to the tables where liquid refreshments were provided. 'Will we be introduced to the guests of honor?' Queynt asked offhandedly, seeming to pay attention only to the spitted chime birds he had been offered.

Willome shook his head. 'I think not. Hoorah for Valearn. They have not done so on any occasion heretofore. We are here to fill the grounds, I think. As is proper.' He bit a crisply toasted bird in half, spluttering bone fragments in all directions. 'Hail Huldra.'

'Hail Valearn,' said Queynt. 'I must find a place to relieve myself.'

' 'Round back,' said Willome. 'Near the stables.'

But it was to the residence itself that Queynt repaired, carrying with him, so he said, the worried look of a man seeking a necessary with a view to immediate utilization. He carried the expression only so far as the deeply carpeted corridor leading to an ornate audience chamber he had located from outside. Here, sheltered from the glow of midday but visible to the mob on the terraces, the guests of honor and their more highly placed attendants eddied to and fro in a swirling slosh of sidling waiters. Here, hidden from observation behind heavy portieres of gold-crusted velour, Queynt came to rest, poised on one foot to flee if necessary, ears pricked and one eye applied to a judiciously located crack between the hangings.

The Dream Merchant, seen only at a distance that morning, was less than a manheight away, his long face still as a carving, the looming upper lip immobile as stone, undisturbed by the words that sprayed from its foot.

'Well, Betand! Tho you have come to Fangel at latht.'

'Well, Merchant! So I was invited at last. Little wonder I came.'

'Invited for what, I wonder. Has the Backleth Throne determined upon thome action? Ah?' The Merchant regarded his guest with suspicion. 'Thtorm Grower and Dream Miner, my lovely parenth? Have they told you why you are thummoned?'

The Duke belched lovingly, threw bones over his shoulder which struck the hangings before Queynt's nose, almost startling him into betraying movement. 'Have they told me? Come now, Merchant. Do they write me letters? I got this!' And he waved a bezel-mounted crystal in the Merchant's face. 'This. As did those three crones with me. Give it a lick and you'll know everything I do. We're off to *That Place*, higgy-piggy, as may be, and Devils take him who lingers. I am much bewitched in this endeavor, may I tell you, Merchant, with three such ugly dams as you have yet to dream ill of. I will tell you that Valearn is enough to give a child nightmares for all his life, whether she threaten to eat him or no, and the lovely Dedrina does the same for me.'

'And yet, even in thuch company, you go?'

'Do you hear me preaching rebellion? There is profit in following the Backless Throne. They suggest this alliance, and so we ally. I do well by the Throne and they by me. I have always felt well paid.'

'And you are taking all thith entourage with uth?'

'Unlikely, Merchant. That lizard of Dedrina's is only something Huldra called up and will as easily let go. The others . . . well, when I go hence tomorrow night, I will leave most of the traps and booty here in your charge until I return.'

'Not in my charge, Betand. I am to go with you. I am thummoned ath well.'

'We will be six, then. Valearn will go, and that Witch, and the serpent queen, Dedrina Dreadeye, with her lackadaisical brother, Bloster. He wants only a minor catastrophe to kill himself over, so depressed he is. Well. We will go and find out what's wanted and then return.'

'I take it you have not been there before,' said the Merchant, sulky and offended at the Duke's offhand tone.

'If you knew what you will find there, you would thound leth casthual. I have not been there for a very long time, but I do not ekthactly look forward to the vithit.'

'So much the better for us, to have your company. Though I am told some visitors don't come out as well, I suppose we need not fear that. So long as they need us to distribute the crystals they send.'

'They require enough of that,' he replied sulkily. 'More and more crythtalth, more and more every theathon.'

The Duke turned at this, piggy eyes burning into the Merchant's face. 'And what do the new ones require, Dream Merchant? More of the same? A little perversion there? A little treachery here? Self-interest in odd quarters? Subversion and deceit? Or is there something new?'

'They will tell uth when they are ready for thome-thing new. They thay they are not ready for the latht thingth, not yet. And I mutht thit here until they are.'

They were interrupted by the close approach of another guest, that woman who had been so curious upon the streets of Fangel. She simpered toward the two men, curtsying and nodding like some doll on springs, face creased like a nut in a hundred sycophantic puckers.

'Sweetning Horb, Your Grace. I've been busy among the visitors to Bloome, as I was bid. I thought you might want word of them – though there's little enough to tell.' The three drifted away from the portieres, leaving Queynt straining his ears. He could hear only fragments. 'Say they're Zinterites . . . got their names in case you want them . . .'

Queynt watched as they turned away, then drifted out onto the lawn once more, thoughtful, breaking his concentration from time to time only to utter the obligatory 'Hail to Valearn.'

Meantime, we three had departed through the northern gate, where the guardsman referred to a list, checking us off as we went. They were careful to be sure all visitors who came in also went out. It made me nervous, this great care. What had there been in Fangel we had not seen? 'Pleasant journey,' the guard wished us. 'Hail to Huldra.'

'Hail to Huldra,' snarled Peter, no happier than were the krylobos.

Poor thing. Wasn't he caught in a dilemma? It was Sylbie, and he had no doubt of it. It was his baby, and he'd no doubt of that, either. Perhaps he had even known that she was pregnant when he'd left Betand. Evidently he had taken some steps to provide for her, yet here she was, unprovided for.

And here was Jinian. Not saying anything. He

watched me from the corner of his eye. I didn't help him, though it would have been kind to do so. He knew I had not missed any of it and knew well what he was thinking.

'Oh, shit,' said Peter, muttering. 'Pombi piss. Hell and damn and may the Hundred Devils dine on my gizzard.' He did not need to have invoked them. Seemingly he was feeling as though they already were.

The road continued upward for a short distance before entering the jungle which had climbed to meet it. Out of sight of the walls of Fangel it began its twisting descent toward Luxuri. Here we left the wagon, unhitching the birds.

'I think reconnaissance,' I said to Peter, keeping things quiet and emotionless. 'They took the captives off to the left after they were inside the gates. Also, we will need something to cut chains if we're to free the birds.'

'That's my metal saws,' said Chance. 'All neat and nice in the tool box, sharp as a file can make 'em. You goin' to have a look around?'

'Yes,' said Peter in a surly voice. 'Jinian. Jinian?'

'You'd best go,' I said. Now wasn't the time to talk about it. Or perhaps it was, but I wasn't willing to do so.

He went. Under cover of the jungle he laid the Zinter clothing aside and changed it for a fustigar's hide. Once at the walls, he would change again. For now, however, he gave his soul some peace by growling hugely, setting up echoes that ran along the distant valley.

'He's upset some,' said Chance.

'That was his baby with the girl,' I said calmly.

'Well, happen I know a bit about that. It wasn't any love affair, if that's what you're thinkin'. He did it to remove a curse from the city of Betand, and that's the truth.'

'Unlikely.' In a fatalistic mood, I was not allowing myself to accept logical explanations.

101

'I don't care how unlikely, it's true. Some Necromancer or other had raised up the spirit of someone yet unborn and set it to haunt the city. So, all the travelers had to beget when they went through. Tryin' to get the unborn born as fast as possible, that's what they were doin'.'

'He remembered her name.'

'Well, it wasn't that long ago and likely it was his first time, lassy. That kind of thing sticks with you. Mine's name was Barbra. Barbra Queet. She ran an alehouse in Sabistown, beside the Southern Sea. She took pity on a lustful young squinch with two left feet and 'nitiated me. Ever' now and then I say a prayer-like thank-you for Barbra Queet.'

I did not reply. It was not from lack of sympathy, but from seeing likely what was going to happen. It could hardly fail to happen. Not given Peter, as Peter was, and me as I was, and Sylbie – heretofore unknown but now known all too well. 'Never mind, Chance. I'm not blaming him for anything. I've got to go settle the birds down.'

'Why don't you just say "talk to 'em," ' said Chance, miffed. 'We all know you can.'

I know that I flushed. There were no secrets. Silly to imagine there could be.

Dusk was falling when we saddled the birds. *'Slowly,'* I counseled both Chance and Yattleby. *'We want to arrive outside the northern walls under cover of darkness, not fly over it while it is yet daylight.'*

We got there shortly after dark, well enough, only to wait about in increasing impatience and worry, waiting for Peter and Queynt. By the time they arrived, it was almost midnight.

'Gamelords, what a mess,' moaned Queynt. 'There were a full dozen of us left the southern gates all at once, and nothing would do but that we travel together. Willome had a grip on me like a vice. I tried everything I could think of to break up the group. Finally, Peter had to Shift to gnarlibar shape and

102

stampede the horses. Mine went with them, but I fell off. Luckily. I don't think they'll be back to look for me.'

'Had to take on bulk to make the gnarlibar,' said Peter, 'and it took me a while. Before that, I did find out where the captives are, though. Sylbie's in a kind of dormitory right against the residence walls, along with some other captives. The krylobos are in a barn alongside that. The Shadowpeople are in the barn, too, in a cage. The krylobos are the only ones chained up, but it's the kind of chain that runs through a metal loop on a metal cuff, so we'll only need to cut one link. That'll leave them with the cuffs on, of course, but we can deal with that later.'

'Did you get a chance to speak to her?'

'Sylbie? No. I was in the shape of a snakey thing, and I didn't want to scare her to death. She has no idea I'm a Shifter. When I knew her, I barely knew it myself.'

We stood there, looking at the walls, no one moving, as though we were all equally reluctant to go over. 'Queynt and me can take care of the north gate,' said Chance at last. 'You do the rest, and we'll have it open by the time you get back.'

We agreed. It seemed the best plan.

Yittleby and Yattleby bounded over the wall. Peter Shifted into a huge, spidery shape with long, taloned feet and lifted the rest of us over. Queynt and Chance sneaked away into the darkness toward the north gate as we crept through the silent streets to the residence. Something about those streets set my teeth on edge, no less in the dark than it had in daylight, a kind of watching terror, as though some-thing hugely ominous were held on a fragile leash which might break at any moment. Do you know that dreadful dream feeling? Walking up by the lair where the dragon is *probably* asleep. Stepping through the swamp while the Basilisks are *probably* away. In Fangel I always had the feeling that *probably* some-thing awful was about to get loose.

When we reached the residence it was dark in most of its windows; only a fugitive glow betokening some servant up late on the business of fires or breakfast. I needed no help to get over this wall. It was mere decoration. Evidently the city of Fangel relied upon its crystals and its curfew. Otherwise, except at the gates, it did not post guards at night. Otherwise, I amended to myself, it does not seem to post guards at night.

There was one, however, lounging sleepily against a doorpost. Yittleby stepped forward without a sound and brought her beak down on top of his head. He slumped silently onto the stones. Peter leaping to catch his sword before it made a clatter. Inside was a babble of bird talk.

'Krerk,' said Yattleby to his kin. *'Be quiet.'*

We pushed open the heavy door, hearing the rustle of feathers, the harsh scratching of talons upon the boards of the floor.

'Please tell them who we are,' I asked Yattleby. *'And what our needs are in this venture.'*

'Krerk, gargle, quiss,' said a voice from the dark. *'Why don't you speak for yourself, girly-person?'*

'You might as well,' krerked Yattleby. *'They can hear you anyhow.'*

'We are releasing some prisoners, yourselves among them,' I said. *'You can help us if you will by remaining together and quiet and assuring that we all get out safely.'*

'Whirfle krerk. *Will you release the little people?'*

'The Shadowpeople? Yes. Of course.' I had already heard a line of plaintive melody which located the cage of the Shadowpeople for me. The latch was tied down outside the reach of the captives, but Yattleby reached over my shoulder to make short work of it. The tiny forms went past us in a scurrying cloud, calling songfully as they fled into the night. 'Lolly duro balta lus lom. *Walk well upon the lovely land.'*

Peter was busy with the chain. 'Krerk quiss?' the birds demanded urgently.

'I'm sorry?' I turned to Yattleby. *'I didn't understand that.'*

'Whistle whistle krerk quiss. Rrrr.' What was this they were telling me? I turned to Peter in astonishment. 'Did the Shadowpeople make a song for your mother?'

'They did, yes. When she was very young. It was at the time of the plague in Pfarb Durim.'

I turned back to the birds. 'Krerk, *Mavin Manyshaped,* quiss rrr quiss.' This went on for some time.

'They say,' I told Peter, 'that there are two human people among the captives who came looking for Mavin Manyshaped. The Shadowpeople heard them say her name. We saw the people in procession. Carrying a huge basket.'

'Friends?' asked Peter doubtfully.

'Someone Mavin knows. Or someone who knows her. I don't think we dare leave them, just on the off chance—'

'All right, all right. Will the krylobos help us?'

'Yes. They'll help us. Out of curiosity, if nothing else.'

'Quiss rrr,' said Yittleby. *'Out of wonder at a person who can talk their language.'*

Peter was halfway through the heavy link, watched with intense interest by fourteen pairs of krylobos eyes, fourteen great beaks hung above his head like a threatening crown. He cut through with a muffled exclamation, and the krylobos began to pull the chain through the links of their leg irons, freeing themselves in moments. They stalked out into the paved court.

'Next door,' Peter whispered. Here there were no guards at all, but the door was securely locked. Peter remedied this with one tentacular finger. We pulled it open, the birds standing about outside like so many great sentinels.

'Sylbie?' Quiet into the darkness.

'Who is it?' Plaintive.

'Peter,' he said. 'Ah – Nobody. Do you remember Nobody from Betand? When we broke the curse?'

'Peter?' Wonderingly.

'Are you tied or chained?'

'No. No, I'm coming.' A glad bleat of words.

'Is someone here looking for Mavin Manyshaped?' I called softly into the dark.

'Here.' A woman's voice, deep and humorous.

'The person with me is Mavin's son.'

'Ah.' The woman laughed, 'Come, Roges. It seems we have once again encountered a doer-good and are being rescued.'

They came into the half-light of the courtyard, Sylbie staggering under the weight of the child, one shoe half-off, flinging herself into Peter's arms with glad tears and he patting her there, soothing her, while I tried not to see him do it. The woman and her companion still carried the great basket between them.

'What's in it?' I asked. 'Treasure?'

'In a manner of speaking,' said the woman. 'At least, it is something we should not leave behind.' She took a deep breath. 'My name is Beedie. Who-ever you are, I thank you. Now, how do we get out of here?'

The Shadowpeople had already fled. However, with five people, six counting the baby, and fourteen birds we were still a mob. Burdened by the basket, the two strangers could not be expected to move very fast. The dilemma was solved almost before I thought of it. Yittleby and Yattleby stepped to the basket, each bending to take one handle, then moved into the night in their usual unvarying stride. The other krylobos spread at either side like skirmishers, and we went over the wall into the silent street.

I reached out to take the baby. 'Let me have him,' I

said. 'You fix your shoe, or you'll trip before we're halfway there.' The child snuggled into my arms, reaching to pat my face. Tears burned in my throat. I had had dreams, betimes, of carrying Peter's child. Needless to say, I had not dreamed it like this. Peter went ahead, half carrying Sylbie by one arm.

The streets echoed, footfalls magnified into approaching hordes that dissolved at each intersection into silence. Despite this, every building seemed to watch, to be intent upon us. The jeweled insignia of the Dream Merchants peered down from every wall. I squeezed eyes half-shut, concentrating. Something in those buildings was watching, not yet moved to intervention – but soon. I could not make an effective protection for us unless I knew what to protect against, but nothing betrayed itself. No creature could be seen. We were almost at the north gate when the alarm bell rang, breaking the silence with a hideous insistence.

'Run,' cried Peter, setting his own command in action, swooping Sylbie into his arms and lengthening his legs all in one movement. I felt myself seized from behind by my belt: I squeezed the baby tightly with one arm and grabbed the bird's neck with the other as one of the freed krylobos deposited me on its back and began to run. I gritted my teeth, thrust my legs in front of the stubby wings, gripped the baby as in a flitchhawk's talons, and prayed we would not slide off. Beside me, Beedie and Roges had been unceremoniously mounted in the same fashion. We dashed down the street, the gate appearing impenetrably shut. Just as we came close we saw one of the mighty halves standing sufficiently ajar to let us through.

'Krerk quiss rrrr, quiss!' I screamed. *'Someone pick up those two men!'* Then we were racing away up the long road toward the jungle as a flight of arrows struck the gate at our back. Something had wakened at last. Another flight whistled through the opening, shrilling above our heads to rattle upon the stone. I could hear Chance cursing and knew he had been wounded. I didn't hear Queynt's voice at all.

We came to the wagon. 'I think we may expect pursuit,' said Peter breathlessly. 'You, Jinian, take Sylbie and the baby and these people in the wagon. Take Queynt, too. He's been knocked silly. Chance, get the horse and go with them. If Yittleby and Yattleby will pull and one or two of their friends will go along as guard, perhaps the others will stay and help me?'

I croaked this request in bird talk, voice breaking. The stalwart man and woman seemed accustomed to this speed of activity; at least, they were holding up the harnesses for the krylobos as though they had done it a thousand times. There was much krerking among the freed krylobos, then the matter sorted itself out. The wagon was moving speedily down the western road, past the fork that would have taken us to Boughbound Forest. Chance rode before us, dabbing at his shoulder with an already blood-drenched rag. Just behind us were two additional krylobos, one of them a giant of his kind, larger even than Yattleby, and behind us on the road something huge and furry was beginning to form itself.

'What's happening?' begged Sylbie in a small voice, looking back. 'What's he doing?'

'He's a Shifter,' I said flatly. 'He's Shifting himself into something very huge and horrible to turn back any pursuit that comes after us.'

'A Shifter?' The offended tone made me quite angry.

'A Shifter, yes. And you'd better pray, little girl, that he Shifts monstrously, or you may be back in the Duke's clutches by morning.'

'I didn't mean it like that,' Sylbie whispered. 'I was just so surprised. I wouldn't ever say anything bad about Peter.'

'Never mind. There'll be time to sort it out tomorrow, if we're still able to sort anything out. You go back there and sit down. All of you. Keep quiet. Keep out of my way. Right now, I've got to concentrate on driving.'

Liar. Liar. No one needed to drive Yittleby and Yattleby, who would find any road needful, any hiding place needful by themselves. Liar.

I didn't care. At the moment all I wanted to do was forget that Peter or Sylbie or Sylbie's child had ever existed.

CHAPTER SEVEN

The first of the sendings came on us just before dawn.

I was nodding on the wagon seat next to Chance. He had tied the horse to the wagon and taken time to bandage himself with much cursing and help from the strangers, Beedie and Roges, friends of Mavin Manyshaped from far over the Western Sea, so they said. They had been useful in bandaging, useful in watching, and had offered to drive if I needed help, which I had refused, preferring to keep busy or at least appear so.

Yittleby and Yattleby had passed the time in conversation with their kin, a bird tribe now mightily angered at the Duke of Betand. 'Yerk quiss krerk,' conveyed fury and the details of their capture.

'How did you folks get picked up?' asked Chance of Beedie and Roges.

'We came into Hawsport on a ship,' said the woman, 'asking in the port where we might find Mavin Manyshaped. We had gems to pay our way and buy information. A black-haired eel of a man attached himself to us, saying he knew where to find Mavin. The next thing we knew, we had been dragged off to Betand, where we were questioned at length about the source of the gems. The Duke's people didn't seem to be interested in anything but that. When we told the sleek one he could find the mines three years' journey west and oversea, he cooled somewhat, but made no offer to release us.'

'You don't think it was using the name of Mavin that got you into trouble?' I'd been worrying over this.

110

'Not then. Though when we spoke of her later, in our captivity, it seemed to stir the little furry folk.'

They fell silent. Sylbie and the baby were asleep. Far off on the eastern sky lay a thin greenish line heralding light.

It was then the sending came.

It came shrieking down the trail far behind us, clearly visible over the trees at the top of the slope as it cast back and forth like a scenting fustigar, a blue, skull-jawed haze with a voice that shattered the dawn. The voice cried, 'Jambal!' and then again: 'Jambal.' Birds fled from dark foliage, screaming terror. In the underbrush small movements ceased. Yittleby and Yattleby stopped, frozen, turning their long necks to see what came.

'Gods,' I hissed. 'I should have been prepared for this. Quick, Chance, get out of those Zinterite clothes.' I was ripping the black clothes off, shouting hissing directions to Beedie meantime. 'There's a sack of straw back in the wagon somewhere. Find it. No, it's bigger than that. That's it. Here, stuff this garment with enough straw to make it shapelike. Tie the hood on top. Here's the veil. Pin it. Cloak over the whole thing. Paper. Paper. Gods, Queynt, where did you put the paper? . . .' Stumbling over Queynt's unconscious form, I fumbled on the shelves. 'Here. Now – hell, give me a piece of that charcoal.'

I muttered a likeness spell, half stuttering in my haste, then leapt half-naked from the wagon to fasten the dummy high upon a branch. I labeled it with the torn paper, hastily scrawled in charcoal with the name 'Jambal,' and left it dangling in the dawn wind as the blue haze circled down toward it, shrieking triumphantly, 'Jambal.'

We fled, leaving the haze to eat the straw manikin with great munching, masticating noises and cackling screams.

'By the Lost City,' murmured Roges, 'what was that?'

111

'A sending,' I panted. 'Sent by that Witch, Huldra, I've no doubt. It seeks an entity named Jambal. The entity named Jambal is hanging on that tree. That's all Jambal was, thank all the old gods, a costume, a bit of playacting. Luckily. If it had my real name, I'd be Witch's meat by now.' I flushed, began to look for shirt and trousers, only then conscious that I was shivering in my smalls. 'Hurry up, Chance. They'll be hunting Biddle next.' And to Beedie and Roges, 'Get Queynt's clothes off him, too. They may not connect him to us, but best we be ready if they do.'

The dummy labeled 'Biddle' was mounted high on a branch before the next sending announced itself, a purple haze with Demon's face and banshee voice, howling the jungle silent in its wake. I didn't remember the birds until this sending fastened itself with hideous voracity on the strawman; then I remembered my own voice saying, 'Yarnoff and Barnoff,' or some such fool thing. They, too, had been named to a resident of Fangel. I chattered in krylobos, yelling at them when they refused to understand. It was the huge stranger krylobos, stepping forward to krerk at Yattleby in tones of unmistakable mastery, who prevailed. Sulkily, they tugged plumes from each other's topknots, a few feathers from wings, legs and breast. Soon there were feather tufts mounted high, labeled 'Yarnoff' and 'Barnoff,' while I was frantically wondering if it mattered whether I had put the right feathers with the right names.

It was not done too soon. Wraiths red as hot iron came screaming from the sky to settle upon the hasty bundles. If we had delayed a moment, we would have delayed too long.

'Now what?' begged Beedie, pale as milk. 'We have no such things as these in the chasm.'

'What chasm is that, lady?' asked Chance, breathing heavily. He had not liked the look of those wraiths and was eager to talk of something else.

'In the chasm where we live, on the great root cities.'

'Great root cities,' I said distractedly. 'Are there things like groles there? Great things like huge worms?' And on being told there were, I was confirmed in an earlier supposition and saddened thereby.

'I ask again,' said Beedie, amazed at this easy change of focus. 'What now?'

I rubbed my head wearily, trying to remember. 'Well, now the Witch will be told by her wraiths that they have found and eaten the ones she sent them after. If she is not too clever, that will be enough. If she is very clever and does not mind the time it takes, she will examine the wraiths for blood scent and, finding none, know she has been tricked.'

'At which,' came Queynt's heavy, pained voice from the wagon, 'she will be very annoyed. You should have put some fresh meat in the dummies, Jinian.'

I was ashamed to have forgotten it. There was no excuse for it except funk, fear and funk from a growing supposition that something was terribly wrong. 'I forgot.'

'Well, you had little time to do anything. Sorry I was of so little help.'

'Any meat? Why not blood of your own?' Roges asked.

'Because that would feed the wraith and lead it directly to the source,' said Queynt. 'No, any non-human meat would do. It is a clever Witch indeed who can tell the difference between man blood and zeller blood by smell. Of course, Huldra may be that clever. We know almost nothing about her, including the source of her animosity.'

'Let us take her animosity as proven, Queynt, without worrying about its source.'

'Not only hers,' he said. 'The Dream Merchant spoke to the Duke concerning Storm Grower. They travel to meet with Storm Grower and the Dream Miner, who also have animosity toward you. I wonder why.'

'Before traveling to the north with you, Queynt, I had heard the name twice. Once in Chimmerdong Forest, when Porvius Bloster said the order to kill me had come from "them, the Dream Miner and Storm Grower". Then again on the Wastes of Bleer, Sorah the Seer said something to Peter about a Storm Grower. It made little enough sense, then or now. *"Shadowmaster. Holder of the key. Storm Grower. The Wizard holds the book, the light, the bell."* Make what you will of that, Queynt. It meant nothing to me.'

'I make nothing of it yet. Nonetheless, there is a Storm Grower, and a Dream Miner, both somewhere together. And tomorrow the Duke goes there with his ghastly maidens.'

I tried to make sense of this. 'Oh, Queynt, I am too tired to think! I wish Peter and the other krylobos would come tell us pursuit has been sent aside.'

Privately I was thinking it was not a long leap of suspicion from Jambal to Jinian, if the Witch knew Jinian existed. If the Witch cared. If the Witch were a creature of the Dream Miner. If. If. If. Perhaps another sending would come before long.

As though summoned by my thoughts, a cry from the forest brought an answer from Yattleby. *'Pursuit ended. Peter comes.'*

'We can stop,' I said thankfully, reaching for the reins. *'We can stop,'* I krerked to the birds.

We did stop, gratefully, waking Sylbie and the baby in the process but otherwise much gratified to be able to stretch, walk about, go into the woods to relieve ourselves.

'Doe see birs!' demanded the baby.

'What's his name?' I asked, in a fatalistic mood.

'Bryan,' said his mother, surprisingly. 'It was my older brother's name. He had hair just this color. My mother always said I should name my first child after my brother, if it was a boy. This is Jinian, Bryan. Can you say Jinian?'

So much for Peter's inherited red pate! I stood by as the baby did go see the birds, seeming totally unafraid of the great creatures. 'This one is Yittleby,' I instructed. 'That one is Yattleby.'

'Yilby,' crowed the baby. 'Yalby.' He had a fine grasp of infinitesimal distinctions, this one. 'Jinny,' he went on, giving me an effulgent smile.

'He's very friendly,' murmured Sylbie apologetically. 'My mother always said I was, too, as a baby.'

'A charming child.' I was cool, not very amused at myself for being so.

A disruption in the underbrush announced Peter. He came out dressed in his own Shifter fur and carrying the Zinterite garments. 'Damn,' he said when told of the wraiths. 'I liked those clothes. Besides' – hopefully – 'I didn't tell my name to anyone.'

'I did,' I apologized. 'Unfortunately. Sorry, Peter, but it'll be safest if you hang them.'

'What was the name we used for me?' he wondered aloud. 'I've forgotten.'

'Chorm,' howled a hungry wraith voice, far back up the trail. 'Choooorm . . .'

'Oh, yes,' he said, scrambling for the straw sack and the upward trail all at once, while I mumbled the likeness spell for the fifth time. When he returned he was paler. 'Nasty thing, that was. All greenish and flapping. Gamelords, but I'm glad I hadn't met a Witch before.'

'You did,' corrected Chance. 'We met one together on the road to Xammer. Before we met this Wizard,' indicating me, Jinian, with his elbow.

'Well, that one was nothing much. All Beguilement, as I recall. Nothing compared to this Huldra!'

'Huldra may have a Witch's Talent,' said Queynt, 'but mere Talent would not enable her to send these wraiths. No, she's studied the arts. Not wisely, but deeply in a narrow way. Found some corruptible Wizard, most likely, and bought the secrets from him.'

115

'Did I hear Chance say you're a Wizard?' asked Beedie curiously, eyes turned weighingly on me.

'Yes. Of a sort. A very young one,' I admitted.

'Can you do . . . things like that? Like those blue things?'

'I could, yes. Likely I wouldn't. There's a blood price for doing things like that. One I wouldn't want to pay, but that someone like Huldra wouldn't mind paying. For each wraith she sends, someone dies. It is lifeblood which empowers the creatures. To Huldra, the life of a pawn or follower would be nothing. Her whole family was like that, starting with Blourbast, so I understand.'

'Bloody intentioned,' agreed Peter. 'Though sometimes they hid it for a time, to further their own aims.' He was remembering the time at Bannerwell when he had been almost convinced – for a very short time – of Huld's honor.

Sylbie and Bryan returned from their bird watching. Bryan staggered to Peter and climbed onto his knees. Peter patted the child awkwardly as he blushed deeply. 'Tows!' the baby demanded vehemently. 'Tows!'

'Baby wants his trousers,' said Sylbie. 'I had to take them off him. They were wet and he was getting peevish. We were so long in the wagon, and I had no others to bring.'

'Well, now,' said Roges heartily, 'that's easy to remedy. Let's see if the wagon master keeps needle and thread and whether there is such a thing as a raggedy shirt no one needs any longer . . .' He picked Bryan up, jogging him expertly, and went to query Queynt where he lay beneath a tree.

'Roges misses ours,' said Beedie. 'Though none of them are babies anymore. The youngest is eight by now, five when we left.'

'Where is he? she?' I wanted to know.

'She. Our first girl. We named her after Mavin. She's home in Bridgers' House, being spoiled rotten

116

by my Aunt Six. We talked of bringing her, but the journey was so chancy.'

'How did you meet Mavin?'

'Oh, Jinian, that's a story for a week in the telling. She came flying from far over the sea, down into our chasm in the shape of a great, white bird. Just take it she saved my life, more than once, and did a great good to our part of the world, too. When this came up, well, we couldn't know what to do about it, could we, down in that great chasm with no contact with the outside? There seemed only one thing to do: bring it to the only outsider we knew well and trusted.'

'This thing?'

Beedie looked at Roges, and he at her. 'That man is Mavin's son,' said Roges, indicating Peter. 'And these others are his friends. Some others ought to know, Beed.'

'True. Others ought to know.'

She went to the basket, then, taking the cover off and removing some leafy wrappings from within. 'It may be,' she said, pointing to the basket, 'that this was the reason we were kept captives by the Duke. He may have intended our friend here for his zoo.'

'I aaam huuungry,' puffed a small voice from within. 'Pleeeez fooood.'

'Do you have any meat?' asked Beedie, her voice concerned. 'He hasn't been fed for several days.'

We gathered around the basket to peer within, seeing only a formlessness there, a roiling shininess. 'How much do you want?' asked Chance.

'A chunk, about head-sized.' She spoke into the basket. 'Meat coming, Mercald-Mirthylon.' When Chance brought it to her, she lowered it into the basket and put the lid back on. 'It will only be a minute.'

Roges was busy with needle and thread and an old shirt of Peter's, jouncing Bryan on one knee the while. 'Not a pretty sight, watching them eat, so we

117

don't. I suppose, from their point of view, watching us eat could be mighty unaesthetic, too. I'd better warn you, don't touch what's in the basket. It will eat you as quickly as it will that meat, not intentionally but uncontrollably. That's how it got the name of Mercald. Mercald was a friend of ours, a priest, and he thoughtlessly laid hands upon it.'

Beedie nodded. 'We call the race "the Stickies". They are sticky on top and dissolve anything that touches them. In their native chasm land, they live on insects and plants and small fish which brush against them. Or larger things, if such are unwary. And if a Sticky eats something with a mind, then the mind becomes part of it, too. So, we have a creature here in this basket who has eaten two living men – one named Mirtylon many hundreds of years ago. One only twenty years ago or so, named Mercald.' She looked around at the circle of disbelieving faces. 'Well, you shall hear for yourself.'

She removed the lid from the basket and turned it on its side. The moist shininess within rolled out onto the earth, settling itself into a thick disk, rounded upward at the centre, from which an ear and a small trumpet gradually extruded themselves. 'How do you do.' It puffed. 'I am gratified to meet you, Peter, Mavin's son. (Puff.) I knew Mavin. She was very wise. Wiser (puff) than I.' There was then a strange, strangled sound, and after a time we realized the thing was laughing.

'Jinian, you are very brave. (Puff.) I heard the sending screaming. Most frightening. (Puff.) Sylbie and the baby we knew already from the procession. (Puff.)' The trumpet collapsed into the general shininess, which quivered for a time before the vocal apparatus extruded itself once more.

'I feel much stronger, thank you. (Puff.) I am happy to meet Chance and Queynt. (Puff.) Also the birds. I was a birder priest. Birds are (puff) messengers of the Boundless. (Puff, puff.)'

118

Though I didn't understand this at all, I translated it for the benefit of the krylobos and was rewarded by an incredulous hoot.

'Well, perhaps they have not (puff) been taught of (puff) the Boundless.' The windy voice sounded sad.

'Tell them about the discovery, Mer-Mir,' said Beedie. 'You can talk about religion later.'

'Yes. Ummm. While wandering deep in chasm (puff) found tunnel leading deep. (Puff.) Took others and formed expedition. (Puff.) Tunnel went very deep. Fires there. Pools of strange stuff. Silver. Thick. Very poisonous. One of us was dissolved (puff) in it. Near the pool were scattered blue crystals. Many.'

'They brought a lot of them out to us,' said Roges, trying his handiwork on Bryan, who crowed delightedly. 'How they got in and out of there, I'll never know.'

'Very difficult. Took much time. Effort. (Puff.) But we had touched the blue crystal. (Puff.) Once we had touched it, we had to bring it out. (Puff.) Touched it. Knew we had to. (Puff.)'

'They touched it with themselves, absorbed some of it, and it turned out to be message crystal.' Beedie, striding about the clearing, swinging her arms, stretching.

'Message crystal?' These words were like the ringing of an alarm bell. Everything inside me sat up to take notice of the world. 'Message crystal?'

'The things you call dream crystals, we call message crystals. In our land we have a necessary tool, the root saw. The teeth of the saw are made from jewel gravel, hard jewel gravel from the bottom lands, glued to a flexible band. The saw makers buy the gravel from traders, so much a weight, and among the real gems are often tiny pieces of message crystal. When we were brats, we would "borrow" the gravel from the saw makers so we could suck through it for message crystals. Unsanitary, as my Aunt Six would say, but you know how disgusting children are.'

119

'What kind of messages?' I begged, sure that I already knew. 'What did they say?'

'Oh, pictures, mostly. Dim, dreamy things. The messages weren't intended for us, you know. Now that I've been to the bottom lands, I can guess some of them were messages to the great bottom worms. Locations of vines to eat. New hot springs with special minerals to cure skin troubles. I found one crystal once that must have been intended for a bird, full of flying, strangeness, lands and valleys below, and a queer town with funny doors, wider at the top, and a lovely tall tower. It was a tiny crystal. It dissolved in a minute, but I've remembered it for years.'

'The city you saw might have been Pfarb Durim,' I told them. 'It has odd doors like that. Lots of places used to have doors like that. Gerabald Buttufor once found a flying crystal, too. He said it was full of great cities built on roots.'

'Our cities are built on roots,' said Roges, amazed. 'Think of that! Messages concerning your cities on our side of the world, and messages concerning our cities on yours. Well, it's all one world, after all.'

'Excuse me,' puffed the thing from the basket. 'But we have to tell Mavin (puff) about it.'

I said, 'I don't understand this necessity. Is there some astonishing message in the crystals?'

'Astonishing?' Beedie thought about this. 'No, Jinian. Not astonishing. The only astonishing thing is that we haven't had this message before. You must see for yourself.' She burrowed deep into the small pack she carried, came up with what appeared to be a small, rough block of wood. 'We couldn't bring very many because of the weight. We got out of the chasm in a balloon made of flattree leaves, and weight was crucial. If we carried them openly, we were afraid they might be stolen. So, Roges made this.' She pressed the wood along one of its sides, sliding a thin slice away to reveal a cubby hidden inside, tipping it to drop something into my hands. A small, bright blue crystal. 'Taste it.'

I recoiled. I'm sure my face was flaming. 'I . . . I can't.'

'Let me,' said Queynt. 'I'm already overdosed on the damn things it can't hurt me worse than I already am.'

'It won't hurt you,' said Roges, shocked. 'I've tasted it, and Beedie. All of our children. Almost everyone in the chasm by now, I imagine.'

I didn't object. He took the thing from my hands. I couldn't watch him. In a moment, however, he gave it back to me and spoke in a puzzled voice.

'I can't taste anything, Jinian. It must be identical to the one the Shadowpeople gave me all those years ago. Why are you so nervous about it?'

I tried to laugh. 'Probably nothing. Nerves. The wraiths have put my skin on backward. Put it down to some personal quirk, Queynt.' I held the thing but did not taste it. 'If you are agreed that it should be taken to Mavin, then take it. And if you believe it should be taken quickly, then take it quickly. If it will undo some of the evil those yellow crystals are causing, then do it, soon as may be.' I turned the blue crystal in my fingers, passed it from one hand to the other. I thought I knew without tasting it what the intent of it was.

Queynt gave me one of his odd, concentrated looks. I stared him down, not letting him see how troubled I was. I could have been wrong. I wanted to think about it more. This time I couldn't be breezy and quick. This time I wanted to crawl in a hole and think, and sleep, and think some more. I put the crystal in my pouch. Beedie had others. I might have need for this one.

The baby, newly trousered, staggered toward Peter's lap and almost fell into the fire in transit. Under cover of this confusion, I leaned near the strange being – very careful not to touch it – and asked, 'Mercald-Mirtylon, in the cavern where the blue crystals were, was there any evidence of any living creature?'

'(Puff.) Nothing there at all. Stickies were the first (puff) and probably only. Very hot. (Puff.) Not good for living things.'

'Do you think the blue crystals had been there long?'

'Very long. They were (puff) far from the white stuff. At the edges of the (puff) cavern. Only yellow crystals near the white stuff. (Puff.) I think, very old.'

I thanked the creature, remembering at the last minute not to pat it, which would have been my instinctive gesture of thanks with most beasties.

The baby had been rescued, had gained Peter's lap and plumped himself down there, chattering in sleepy infant talk which even my language Talent could not follow. Sylbie came to curl beside Peter and the child, inserting herself neatly under Peter's arm so that he held her, perforce, without actually having reached for her. Still, he did not draw away. He looked up to catch my gaze, flushed in half guilt, then gave me an unrepentant stare as though to say, 'Well, you won't and she will, so gaze me no gazes, Jinian Footseer.'

'We must sleep,' I said carefully, keeping my voice expressionless. 'All of us need sleep.'

As I moved about the clearing, preparing for the night, I stopped beside Queynt. His eyes were still red, and there was a great lump on his forehead, but he looked otherwise his own indomitable self. 'These crystals the visitors believe are so important – perhaps you have known their contents so long you have not really thought about them, Queynt? Perhaps you have not considered the implications – if, for example, everyone had had one.'

He seemed surprised at this. 'Well, yes, Jinian. That's possible. In which case, someone new, someone like Mavin or Himaggery is needed to make a judgment. To consider, as you say, the implications.'

I stared at him, willing him to pay utmost attention. 'A bit farther down the hill, Queynt, there is a fork in the road. The southmost road leads down to Luxuri and thence to Bloome again. From there it is not far to the Great Road which comes north from Pfarb Durim. And on that road, the journey to the Bright Demesne should not take long – or no longer than any such journey will take. If you can get there, and if you can get Himaggery and Barish to quit calling meetings to discuss the hundred thousand, perhaps they would consider what the true meaning of the blue crystals may be. Perhaps Barish would do it for you?'

'I can ask him,' he said.

'It's important enough to go, and quickly.'

There was no point in further talk. No sense in worrying them with questions that could not yet be answered. We arranged ourselves for the night. To rest, if that were possible. Roges lay looking at the dark. Beedie close beside him. The creature was back in its basket. Peter had stretched himself out on a blanket by the fire, with the baby beside him, and Sylbie lay against Peter, half-curled around the baby. Peter slept, one arm across the child, the hand touching Sylbie's breast, and she not moving away from this touch. I, wandering late, saw this. Well, where else would Sylbie sleep except beside the one among them she knew as a friend?

I lay down away from the fire, able to see the flames as they undulated against the black of the forest yet unlit by them, lost in a pocket of darkness as in some secret closet, spying upon the outer world as through the keyhole of that closet, closed about with baffled jealousy coupled with the anxiety that my suspicions had aroused. If they were true, did it matter what Peter did?

None of them saw. All the myriad clues were there in front of them, and none of them saw. Not even Queynt. Queynt, who should have seen long ago on the Shadowmarches, when he was given a blue crystal by a Shadowman and interviewed by the Eesties. Oh, yes, Queynt should have seen then. But he did not. Only I believed I saw, from this cavern of quiet darkness.

And I could be wrong.

But if I were right, could I do anything useful if I stayed here? Where Sylbie was and Peter's child? I thought of the baby, opening each day with his bubble sounds, crowing like some cock-bird from his basket, pure joy unalloyed. Could I accept that, not grieve over it, and get on with what must be done? Even if I could accept it, what good could I do here? Could I think of staying only to stand between Peter and Sylbie and the child? Would Jinian take a parent's love away from a child? Jinian, who knew well enough what it meant to be the victim of an abductor of love, a robber of faith? Should I do to another what Eller of Stoneflight had done to me?

There was an easy way to do it. Jinian could go into these dark woods and gather the needful things: sixteen herbs and earths, and those easy to find, not scarce in any land, not difficult to locate even in the dark. A torch would be enough light. Her own senses would serve without any light at all. To make a love potion. To guarantee Peter loved Jinian, not Sylbie but Jinian, not the crowing child but Jinian. A simple thing, taking only from now until dawn. And then she could bring him his tea and sit by him looking into his face while he drank it . . .

There was a pig that had loved me in the Forest of Chimmerdong, loved me well, unable not to love me. So would Peter be unable not to love me. And if I were a monster, he would love me still. And if I were Valearn, Ogress of Tarnost, still he would love me. And I, knowing that, would feel – what would I feel?

If crystals could compel without blame, could not one small Wizard? And if what I feared was true, who would be alive to judge me for it? And if what I feared was true, what time would there be for any alternatives? And if what I feared was true, what point in refusing to taste the blue crystal and verify what I believed?

Except that if I knew, I might be too terrified to act. But as long as there was doubt, however small, then action could take place.

Exactly.

Even if I did it totally alone, I had to do something. This was the lesson of Chimmerdong.

So, not the sixteen herbs and earths. Not the liquor of love, the efficacious potion. Not love at all.

And not a patient traveling with them, either, coming between them, becoming less myself with every passing hour as I sought to become whatever it was he loved, forgetting my oath, changing myself to the needs of love rather than being true to myself and doing what must be done. Not jealousy.

And not the mere running off in a huff, to sulk in some distant place until the world was changed. Not anger. No. Not love, not jealousy, not anger. Duty instead. The lesson of Chimmerdong instead. I would need to depart, but depart to some purpose.

I sneaked from my pocket of darkness to gather the things any traveler would need. Quiet as shadow I drifted into the forest, up along the hill, back toward Fangel. Morning would take me far enough from this place that they could not find me, even if they looked, which they would not. The need for them to move southward was too imminent, too persuasive. Pray Queynt understood this. A man as perceptive as he must understand it. Pray they did not delay.

And I would do what I had to do. This was to find the Dream Miner and this companion, this Storm Grower, and see if they knew why the foul yellow crystals were being spread across the world. And, I reminded myself, learn why they wanted me dead.

Behind me, a log broke among the flames, showering sparks, shattering into coals. An omen. Even the hottest fire would break and cool in time. It was a better hope than nothing. I moved into the night, pacing leagues back toward Fangel between myself and the sleepers.

It was again near dawn the final sending came, high in the eastern sky, a pale gray blot white-fanged against the dark, the voice a howl of wind from between the stars. 'Jinian,' and again, 'Jinian.'

So, whoever it was in Fangel had found me out, put two and two together to come up with six; put Jambal and Biddle and Chorm in a pot to pour out Jinian. Was it Huldra behind this sending? Or Dedrina Dreadeye? Or Bloster? Whichever, this one would not be put off with strawmen.

There were defenses against sendings. Defense was a paltry game that waited upon others for its intentions. I was too tired and angry for defense. Therefore, let the forest beware!

I left the trail, moving into the forest. Then.

The amethyst crystal from my pouch. Set upon a stone. Then Music and Meadow to bring an innocent creature near, to wring its neck quickly so that it died without fear or pain. Unjust to use its blood so, and yet I could not use my own. Bright the Sun Burning set upon crystal and blood. Dream Chains to Bind It to hold an image there.

'Oh, here I am, Sending,' I sang in the false light of predawn, dancing widdershins about the crystal on the stone, blood on the stone, song on the stone, herbs and twigs on the stone. 'Here am I, Sending, deep in amethyst halls, deep in crystal silences, within, hidden within. "A twig of red rowan, a sprig of midnight tree, a leaf of web willow, shall summon you to me." Come, Sending, to find Jinian where her blood leads you. Come, Sending, and feast where your hunger waits.'

'Jinian,' the sending called, spiraling down from the empty sky. 'Jinian,' in a husky, hungering voice which raised bumps on the skin as a cold wind might. 'Blood,' it called, rejoicing. 'Blood.'

Down to hover above the stone. It did not see as others saw, did not perceive as others perceived. It was both sent and summoned, and the blood led into another place. Into which it went, all at once, like a wisp of smoke drawn into a chimney, and then Jinian gathered the last of her strength to do Dream Chains once more, quickly, holding the wraith where it was, within the crystal, where it could not get out.

And when it was done, she fell on the earth like a felled sapling, unconscious, limp, all strength gone and drained away, the place cold as a glacier around her. 'She,' not I, for I was far away already, lost in some inner maze without any way out. On the stone the amethyst crystal burned, trembling. Around her, me, the dark changed slowly to day.

CHAPTER EIGHT

I was awakened by something, then lay for a long time on the cold earth wondering if me and I and whoever had reassembled themselves to be a person again. Where that person might be was another question which took some time to settle. I was near the trail that led from Fangel, hidden from it by a slope and a line of trees, and there were voices coming from the trail. I had lain there for about a day. I felt fairly weak, without much will or ambition, but otherwise normal. Beside me on the stone the amethyst crystal rocked as though inhabited – which it was in a sense – and I put it in my pouch rather unwillingly before crawling into the trees to see who came forth from the city into the dusk.

It was the Duke of Betand, traveling from Fangel with far less panoply than when he had entered. His allies and the Dream Merchant traveled with him, escorted only by Porvius Bloster and a few Armigers and Tragamors, men evidently not corrupted by the crystals, for they went in alert watchfulness as outriders of the small procession. Huldra and Valearn had left their high-wheeled carts; Dedrina, her huge crocodile. They, like the Merchant and the Duke, were mounted on stocky ponies and wore sensible traveling garments. The air of menace that accompanied them was as great as when they had entered the city, however, and it brought me alert among the underbrush, suddenly threatened and vigilant.

There was Valearn, the Ogress. All the fears aroused by nursery tales were made immediately manifest, swarming in the shadows, wakened more by this one danger than by the presence of others, equally perilous. In her lands of the High Demesne in the south she had walked the woods alone, garbed in ragged robes with the staff of an old mendicant, seizing children who wandered by themselves, leaving their bones half-gnawed for the were-owls to finish. She had not troubled adults, only children. Them she had sought relentlessly, the child from the cot by the window, the babe from the blanket by the fire, the toddler snatched from a mother's arms. But, only children. Only children. I told myself this, more than once, assuring Jinian the child that she was too deeply buried in Jinian the Wize-ard for Valearn to find her, ever. Jinian the child was not so deeply buried inside me that she did not doubt this. We all doubted it together.

I waited until the troop had moved almost out of sight, then laid a hiding spell, Egg in the Hollow, that I might not be seen by them, that I might most assuredly not be seen by Valearn. It was all very well to assure oneself that the child one had been was outgrown. Such children had a habit of coming back at odd moments, moments that might prove unpropitious indeed.

I did not think of Sylbie's baby, and Peter's. Sylbie and the baby should have been far on the southern road by then; why think of them in connection with Valearn?

The rest of the night was spent in scrambling down long dark roads the way I had come twice in recent days. A drift of krylobos feathers beneath a tree, a scatter of straw, confirmed the location. Here the sendings had come.

The allies were not so far ahead I couldn't hear them talking. 'Clever,' drawled Huldra, seeing these telltale signs by torchlight. 'Clever little bitch. She sent my creatures back to me full of straw and quills, them that cost good blood to send, back with nothing but trash in them. Save one which came back not at all.'

'You think it's that Jinian?' Bloster, sounding as bedraggled as he looked. 'The one the Backless Throne wanted killed, the one who destroyed Daggerhawk Demesne?'

'You don't know that she destroyed Daggerhawk,' said Dedrina Dreadeye. 'The Seers have not verified it.'

'I know it,' he said obstinately. 'Even if the Seers said she had not, I would know it.'

'What ith thith girl? Thome great Afrit full of mighty powerth? Thome twinned Talent or other?' The Merchant did not sound really interested.

'She's the cause of my losing my captive,' snarled the Duke, trying to ease himself in the saddle. 'You may lay money on that.' He was too fat to ride in comfort; he and the pony suffered equally upon the road.

'And why doeth the Backleth Throne take an interetht in her?' the Merchant asked.

'I was never told,' said Porvius, aggrieved. 'Only that the Throne wanted her dead. As do I. I had her in my hands, like an egg between my fists. I was only concerned with her brother then; him I hated. But if I'd killed her when I had the chance, we'd not be homeless, traveling on the charity of our friends.'

'Scarcely charity,' hissed Dedrina. 'We pay good coin for our keep, brother. Cease your whining. If you have energy to spare, remember you are a Tragamor and spend it smoothing this road. It is unpleasant to travel full of bumps as it is.'

'Talents don't work well this far north,' he said, in the petulant tone of a child. 'I have not the strength even to Move gravel.' Oh, how far Porvius had fallen, into this meekness, this whining infancy.

'Keep silent, then, lest you waste what little power you have!' They rode on, becoming less loquacious as the hours passed. Near dawn they paused; and I was ready enough that they do so. I was wearier than the distance would explain. Following, keeping quiet, finding the trail in the dark, worrying that I might be about to step into shadows, all had been an exhausting effort. The fact that I did not step into shadows, that none of us did, should have told me something. I was preoccupied with other thoughts, however, and did not learn from what was not there.

We had come to a small village. The Merchant called it Bleem. While the guards were left to camp in the forest as best they might, preparations had been made for the others to spend the night under roof. Someone's house had been vacated and made ready for the group with a supper laid upon the table and the beds prepared with fresh straw. So much I learned from the lean-to at the back, where an old wagon lay half against the warm chimney, making a nest for me to supper in. I could hear them through the wall.

Moreover, I could see out the open end of the shed well enough to observe the comings and goings of the people there. There was no rejoicing among them, certainly. I had seldom seen such a whipped-fustigar crew, their jaws dragging halfway to their bellies and more of the women crying into their neckerchiefs than not. I still had the hiding spell on me, so I left the cozy nest and went among them. Curiosity, I suppose. There was something about them that teased at me.

There were two men standing at the well, one a fairly well-set-up middle-aged fellow, the other slightly older. He was lecturing the younger man, beating his fist upon the well coping, tears running down his face like a river.

'I say we can't go on, Dolcher. We can't. You know that. First it was just a few zeller off to Morp. Then it was a few zeller plus a few old people. Now it's all the oldsters and most of the zeller and half our children. By all the old gods, they'll have your son next. This time it's my Zenina they've chosen to take, and your boy was to wed her this season. Next time him. The time after that, what? There's none of us left . . .'

131

'Servants,' whispered the other man. 'They want our young ones for servants, that's all. When they've served a few years, they'll be home again.' His gray face belied this.

'Man, are you blind? Why take our oldsters if they want servants? They took Granny Zeeble, and she so trembly the children had been calling her Feeble Zeeble for ten years. They took your own father, who hadn't walked a step without two canes for seven seasons. Hush. Here's the wife.'

A woman approached them, one of the weeping ones. 'You can't let her go, Vorge. You can't let Zenina go. The time's come to say no. We've given enough.'

'Well, well,' the younger man said, patting her clumsily on the shoulder. 'That's what we've said to them at Morp, Lina. We sent that message only yesterday.'

'But *he's* here. The Dream Merchant. They say *he's* their son. Talk to him. Beg him. Make him understand.'

'Now, Lina. We've sent the message already. I wouldn't want to get them upset.'

'If you won't, I will.'

The man called Vorge shook his head, wrung his hands. 'It would be better if you did, Dolcher. You're village chief. It would be more natural.' The old man shook his head. 'We've got to do something.'

Two of them went away. Dolcher stood at the well, one hand dragging into a bucket of water, lifting it to drip the water into the well, listening to the slow plop, plop. I examined his face; hopeless. Something was tugging at my memory about Morp. I'd heard the name somewhere.

I wandered through the village. There were empty houses, small places falling to ruin, empty stables. Of all the people left in the place, Vorge was about the oldest. So, the oldsters had been sent – where? And if not as servants, as what? Around the village stretched the small fields; between the houses were the gardens.

Ill tended. As though the people could not spare attention for them. It had the look of a settlement upon its last breath.

Dolcher still stood at the well. At last he shook his head and went to the house occupied by the Merchant and his group. I slipped back into the lean-to, my ear against the wall.

'Well, fellow, what do you want?'

'May I speak to you, Your Reverence?'

'Thpeak. You are thpeaking. Tho thpeak.'

'Your Reverence, they've come from Morp, from the Backless Throne again. They want our young people, sir.'

'Tho?'

'We can't send our young people, sir. They're needed for the crops. For raising the zeller. The Throne wants the zeller, too.'

'Let me underthtand thith. You are refuthing to do the Throne'th will?'

Silence. I could visualize what was going on. Groveling. Fumbling for words.

'No, sir. Not the Throne, sir. Just Morp. Morp isn't the Throne, and they don't understand . . .'

'I hope you have not thaid thith to anyone!'

'We did send a message, sir.'

'Fool. Then why are you thtanding here? Get under your roof. Pray you do not all die.'

The door slammed. I slipped out to watch Dolcher staggering away from that door, reeling from sorrow and apprehension. Over his head I could see the sky, boiling. It had an unhealthy look. Suddenly I remembered what I had heard about Morp. A charnel town. A town of butchers. Through the wall came exclamations from the group there.

'The idiot hath refuthed the Throne. Yethterday he did it. Morp will have complained to the Throne. Thtorm will come. We will be fortunate to ethcape with our liveth.'

Back outside I went. Yes, storm boiled over the

133

western horizon. Black cloud, drooping at the bottom like great pustulent udders. High-piled, running toward us with the inexorable flow of lava. I got myself back into the lean-to and under the wagon just as the first drops of rain hit.

It was a punishing storm. First rain and wind, tearing at the structures of the place, removing roofs and shutters, sending them flying like pennants into the east. Then hail, piercing what the rain had left. Then greater wind. And with it all, a screaming sound of fury. Time and another time, dark as night. Howling rage. The roof of the lean-to went, but I remained half-dry beneath the wagon. I had anchored it as best I could with stakes driven in during the first roaring moments.

I lay flat, empty, the storm driving out all thought. There was no village. There was no life. Only this horror of falling water, this terror of screaming wind. One might as well die. I knew they were dead, I was dead. No point in being alive in this.

And then, after a forever time had passed, it was over. They had given the best house in the place to the Merchant, and now it stood alone. From inside it I could hear snoring. The Merchant and his guests were asleep. Among the sodden ruins the people of Bleem struggled into the light. There were no fields left, no gardens left. I went out into the woods, took away the hiding spell, and came into the village from the other side. Dolcher was there, standing dazed in the midst of the ruin, staring with empty eyes at the punishing sky.

'Dolcher,' I said. He had been deafened. It was hard to make him aware of me. 'Dolcher. Listen to me. Take all your people, now. Right now. What little they can carry, nothing else. No wagons. Nothing else. Go. Go that way, back toward Fangel, *around the city, not through it,* and then south. You hear me?'

'Who are you?' He looked at me, not really seeing me. 'Who are you?'

'It does not matter who I am. I am here with a message for you, to help you. Storm Grower will kill you all. You cannot pacify Storm Grower. Only when you are all dead will she rest. So, you must leave here. Go quickly. Go far. Find caves to protect you from hail. Forests to protect you from sight. Go. And go before those in the house waken.' I used every persuasive trick of voice I could manage, setting several small compliance spells on him meantime. Not enough to draw interest, just little ones. When I went back toward the lean-to, he was in motion, staggering, bleeding, crying, but in motion.

It did not take them long. The longest time was spent simply in getting their attention. Once they understood, they moved quickly, as quickly as people can who are half-drowned and totally beaten. There were some dead. They laid them out in one of the wrecked houses and set fire to it. It bled smoke into the sky, smoldering. Then they went as I had suggested. Back toward Fangel, a sad, straggling procession. The last of them wended over the hill out of sight sometime before the Merchant woke.

He came to the door, opened it, stared out into the shambles. I had restored the hiding spell and was sitting on the well coping. He did not see me.

'Hey,' he shouted. 'We will have our breakfatht now!'

Needless to say, there was no response. He cursed for a time, which woke the others, and they came out of the place together.

'Storm Grower?' asked Betand. 'Did she not know we were here?'

'I doubt they thought of it,' sulked the Merchant. 'We will find no thuthtenance here. Let uth depart.'

'What was all this about?'

'The people objected to the levy from Morp. It ith Morp which provideth provender for Thtorm Grower and Dream Miner.'

Provender was one way of putting it.

Huldra came into the light, blinking, snarling. 'How much farther? You have been to That Place before, Betand. How much farther is it?'

'I haven't been there,' he said in astonishment. 'What made you think I had? No. I have been near there once or twice. The Merchant knows. He has been there.'

'I don't know,' the Merchant said. 'I have been there many timeth, but each time there hath been a guide.'

'Then how do we know where we are going?'

'There will be a guide thith time ath well.'

My ears pricked at this. What kind of creature could serve as guide to the Dream Miner? Premonition stirred, and the Dagger of Daggerhawk burned with sullen fire, as though it had ears of its own. I tried to ease it on my thigh and bit back a curse. I was wearing loose trousers with tight cuffs, almost a pantaloon, a very sensible garment for this kind of scrambling travel, but there was no slit in the pocket through which the Dagger could be reached. There was no time to remedy the situation. They were going off into the forest to find their guards.

The Tragamors had Moved themselves a cave large enough to protect them from the storm. They were unharmed, perhaps even slightly amused to have had a better night than those they guarded. This was my own conjecture, from the few words I overheard as we went downward in the early light, the horses' hooves making soft plopping noises in the dust of the narrow trail, the troop almost silent except for occasional exclamations when low-hanging branches buffeted them. The voice that greeted them startled them all, and me as well, though I realized I'd been half expecting it. My old friend the Oracle. I sneaked forward through the underbrush to get a clearer view of it. Somehow I had known it would be the Oracle.

It stood half-concealed behind a leafy branch, only its painted face and one hand clearly visible. 'Oh, my, isn't this a *fine* array of Talent and perspicacity to bring before the Backless Throne. How *marvelous* Dream Miner will find you all, how *intrigued* the Storm Grower will be. I have waited for you for simply *days*.'

'Nonsense,' grated Huldra. 'We are here on the day appointed.'

'One *anticipates* so! One cannot *wait*!'

In this sober light of early day, I was struck by the artificiality of the creature, by a certain surreal quality. I had been too ill in Chimmerdong to notice much, but I wondered at myself for not having seen this. It still wore the hooded robe of straps, bright-colored ribbons that moved and swayed, hiding its form. It turned its face away as it spoke, and I strained eyes to see it. Had its mouth moved when it spoke?

The question went unanswered as the Oracle swept away in a flurry of ribbons. It went through the trees, appearing now and then upon the trail, the ponies following from point to point. Within a few turns it led them aside from the main trail into a twisting path. Patches of shatter-grass and startle-flower grew across it, growing evidence it was seldom used.

'Do you bring us to the Throne by some servants entry?' the Duke demanded. 'Is this the honor done the Duke of Betand?'

'Oh, Duke, my love, be not *offended*. There are only three entries to the Backless Throne! One from the center of the Great Maze, and we have not the *time* to take that path. One from the charnel houses outside Morp, where *provender* for the Great Ones is prepared, and we have not the *stomach* for that one. And this one. Of the three' – the Oracle giggled in a shrill mockery of amusement – 'this is the safest.'

Morp? Again Morp. I thought the people of Bleem had done well to escape when they had. I doubted their young had been useful as servants. Morp had an evil reputation. There was an entrance there. So. And another entry from the center of the Great Maze. I made a mental note, hanging back at a turn of the narrow path, waiting for them to get farther ahead.

The way ended at a tunnel mouth, a gaping hole between two tumbled pillars that once had been carved in the likeness of some great beast. I identified claws, horns, a vast bell-shaped ear. Obviously this route had been more used in ancient times, and I wondered why it had fallen into such neglect, but this question, like others, had no time for consideration. The Oracle had plunged into the darkness.

'Leave the guards to guarding, good friends. Come *along*! We are no doubt *eagerly* awaited!'

Well, I had half anticipated some such problem when the hiding spell was set; now I reinforced it, binding it more closely about me. When I drifted from the trees and among the surly Tragamors and Armigers, they noticed me no more than they did the wind. Though I had taken little enough time, the others were far ahead, down distant turnings of the tunnel way.

Since that time I have often pondered over my heedlessness. I think it was the label set upon Huldra that did it. She was a Witch. Wize-ards had nothing to fear from Witches. They were a minor Talent, no more, and nothing to worry us. Never mind that sendings had come from her; never mind that Queynt had taken the trouble to point out she had more than mere Witch's Talent to her; still I thought of her as a Witch. This is the trouble with too much Schooling. One learns to manipulate the labels in a way that the Gamesmistresses approve, and one doesn't realize that things do not always act in accordance with the labels in the real world. One doesn't realize that the labels, come to that, are often wrong.

Be that as it may, and even though I knew better, I had taken no steps beyond a simple hiding spell – there are a dozen forms of Egg in the Hollow, and I had used the easiest – to protect myself. It worked well enough against the guards, and I didn't think beyond that. Ahead of me were the ones I followed, and that is all I was thinking about.

Fortunately, there were no side ways, no mazes to confuse. One way, one way only, the dust of the tunnel clearly marked by their footprints. I sped after them, risking a wize-art light from fingertips to show the way. I heard their voices, extinguished the light, slowed to their pace. Now they were dawdling, moving without haste.

'Is this the way guests of the Throne are greeted?' Huldra, more than merely annoyed. Sharply irritated; perhaps suspicious. 'Hauled through dusty tunnels, league on league?'

'Oh, lovely one, why say *guests*? Are there guests honored in the great audience hall? Do plenipotentiaries arrive with their steeds all caparisoned, bringing gifts from potentates afar? *Guests?* Did you imagine you were asked as *guests*?'

'What then?' Dedrina, stopping dead at the center of the tunnel. 'If not guests, what?'

'You should not imagine these are *my* words, dear friends, not my language at all – I, who am the perfect *fount* of diplomacy – but if asked – as indeed I have been – I would wager the word used by Storm Grower would be "lackey". Dream Miner might say more than that, though *both* grow laconic with the passing centuries. Still, "lackey" will do.'

'Lackey!' The Duke spat. 'I have long been a faithful friend of the Backless Throne!'

'You have long' – smiled the Oracle – 'been a well paid puppet. *Ath hath the Merchant here,*' in bitter mockery of the Merchant's lisp. 'Come now. It is not wise to linger. Should Storm Grower grow *impatient*, we all know what consequence might follow.'

This was sobering. For the first time, I began to worry. I had assumed what the Duke had assumed: he and his party were guests and would be treated with some degree of courtesy. If they were at risk, then so was I.

They wound deeper under the earth, down twisting ways. Above us, I later learned, the Great Maze stretched its illimitable hedges; around us worm holes opened into the tunnel, admitting odors of swamp and jungle, hill and moor. They had walked half a day away with me scurrying in their wake when I began to hear the sound, the susurrus of the sea, the ebb and flow of waves upon a shore.

Waves.

Not quite. Not quite that ebb and flow. Two rhythms, rather, running almost counter to one another. One slightly slower. And with the sound the movement of air, laden with that same sweetish-foul stench we had smelled too often upon the road. Dead things. Decaying things.

Huldra made some expression of disgust. The Merchant said something to her that made me shudder, something to the effect that it would be wisest not to notice the smell of anything she might soon see. They had fallen silent, so I slowed my pace, peering carefully around each corner before sliding around it into the next stretch of rocky corridor. Still that wave sound. The stench stronger. Still those ahead moving in the wake of the Oracle, now taking no notice of either smell or sound.

They came to an open area, perhaps two manheights from floor to roof, that roof supported by several dozen great, rough-hewn pillars, irregularly set, much as though the diggers had left a pillar whenever they felt like it rather than by any plan. Beyond this hall of pillars was a much larger space. There was light there, though not much, and the sound of vast emptiness swallowing up the footsteps of the troop. They moved to the left among the pillars, and I to the right, keeping a pillar between myself and them. By this time the sound was enormous, great heavings of air which I felt gust past me in first one direction, then another.

The hall of pillars ended in a gallery, a wide shelf

140

curving high around one side of the greater space. A low parapet of stones set in mortar edged it. The others were looking over this parapet at whatever was below. At one point the parapet was broken as though something had struck it; the stones were tumbled inward upon the shelf. It was here I stretched myself, hidden from the others both by my spell and by the stones, looking out into the cavern.

It was lit from above by a few worm holes piercing the stone. Dust swam in these beams of light, fugitive shining specks to speak of the day. At the center of the cavern a great pile hid the opposite wall, a monstrous, fantastic pile, twisted into organic forms; prodigious legs, monstrous warty arms, folded stone almost like gigantic faces; great jutting plinths of nose above twisted strata of lips. Wrinkled runnels of water-deposited stone above seemed to form gigantic cheeks and eyelids.

Which opened.

I was clinging for support to a block of stone while an enormous eye peered into my own. It did not blink or change expression. Only gradually, as my heart slowed, did I realize it didn't see me.

The others were at a point far to my left, somewhat around the curve. I could see them easily. The Merchant stood at the center of the group, his long face as impassive as the stones. On one hand were Valearn and Dedrina. Porvius stood somewhat behind them, his face down. The Oracle was some little distance from them, waving and bowing as it made introductions.

'Dream Miner. Honored sir. Storm Grower. Monstrous madam. I bring you once again your *servant*, Dream Merchant of Fangel. Also, those you have summoned. Betand. Valearn. Huldra. Dedrina. *Fop, cannibal, crone,* and *lizard*. An assortment, madam and sir.'

The huge stone lips writhed, revealing themselves as flesh capable of great, slow words, like rocks rolling together in avalanche. 'If you say "cannibal" as a term of derision, Oracle, you would be wise to say rather less. Some of us eat what we will. So far as we are concerned, Valearn may eat what she likes.'

'Come a little closer!' Another voice, one seeming to come from the opposite wall, enormously booming, higher in pitch. Hearing it, all those present squirmed, feeling the words as an assault. I saw them bend a little, twisting, trying to shed those words. 'Come a little closer so I can see.' The voice was full of wind, horrid and cold. 'Only a little closer.'

'Careful,' said the Oracle, laughing. 'I would not recommend that *any* of you leave this gallery. If you come within reach of the mighty madam or the honored sir, they may eat you. They *cannot* help it, poor dears. They are always hungry.'

They moved down the gallery, however. I didn't need to follow them. I could see the source of the other voice well enough from where I was, though it had its horrific head turned away from me. It was another giant, seated behind the first and faced in the opposite direction, a female, perhaps, though what I could see of the huge face had no delicacy to it and was as obdurate as the first. If they had been standing, they would have been ten manheights tall. They were about seven manheights tall, seated as they were back to back upon a colossal pillar.

'The Backless Throne,' I said, surprised into uttering it half-aloud.

Across the cavern on the gallery the Oracle turned in my direction. It had heard me! Through all that ebb and surge of mighty breathing, it had heard me. I lay quiet, not moving so much as an eyelid, letting the surge of air wash to and fro. With all the echoes in this chamber, it could not be sure. So I told myself. So I assured myself, sweating, swallowing, trying to get my heart back where it belonged. After a time, it turned back to the others, ribbons quivering as though in laughter, poised in its eternal mockery.

I slipped back into the hall of pillars and worked my way toward them, pillar by pillar, keeping stone between. The damned Oracle might see through my spells – I thought it might see whatever it pleased, quite frankly – but it was not likely to see through stone.

'Storm Grower, mighty madam, may I present your servants.' The Oracle bowed, gesturing to all those on the gallery. 'Your most *obedient* servants.'

'By all the gods,' said Huldra, amazed. 'What are you?'

'Oh, do not be *offensive*,' said the Oracle. '*Giant* madam may be *most* annoyed.'

'I am not offended,' said Storm Grower in that voice of horrible wind. Her left arm came up, slowly, like a tree rearing skyward, bent, straightened, its skin like a lava flow, cracked deep, soiled with the dirt of centuries, its huge fingers like scaly pillars with nails twisted and ragged, slowly, slowly, then snapping toward the parapet with lightning motion, missing the parapet by less than an arm's length so that Huldra stumbled back with a screaming curse, tripping over Bloster and falling full length upon the stones.

Laughter then, monstrous laughter, as though volcanoes amused themselves. The left hand did not fall but stayed where it was, twisting and twisting as though to wring a neck. 'I am always glad to educate lesser creatures. I am a giantess, sweet Huldra. Born with my brother many centuries ago in the monster labs of the humans. Reared there for a long, long time. Fled from there by my own courage and resourcefulness . . .'

'And mine,' rumbled Dream Miner. 'You were not alone.'

'Never alone.' The other laughed, shifting to display the obscene flaps of filthy flesh that bound them together, shoulder to shoulder, rib to rib, buttock to buttock. 'No, never alone.'

'Grown to great size and power over the centuries,' thundered Dream Miner. 'Grown to a size and power capable of revenge.'

'Handicapped *somewhat* in that their great size prohibits mobility,' chanted the Oracle. 'Otherwise, most puissant, most powerful.'

Storm Grower twisted her fingers once again, and a lightning bolt flicked from the air to the gallery where the Oracle stood, missing it by a finger's width. 'Subside, beribboned jester, painted riddler. You are useful, but you try our patience.'

'Try our patience,' agreed Dream Miner. 'Take those with you elsewhere for a time. We will tell them of our will later. Now we have other matters to see to. Besides, I am hungry.'

The Oracle led them away. There were a number of lighted tunnel openings from the gallery, and into one of these the troop went, shuffling, seeming both fearful and angry. There was no point in following them. They would be returning. There was a narrow crevice to one side of the hall of pillars, one about my size. I decided to explore it, finding that it climbed upward and outward toward the cavern and it had a window in it, a place where the stone had broken. From this vantage point, I could look over the parapet and down into the cavern. I could see Dream Miner's feet – not a sight to inspire confidence or good appetite – and a part of the floor of the cavern. To either side, right and left of the giants, low, long archways curved like bows led off into the darkness. From the archway at Dream Miner's right, several dozen long poles protruded into the cavern, their nether ends hidden in the darkness.

Dream Miner reached for one of these. His monstrous arm descended toward the rocky floor; the flesh between the two giants stretched, revealing its leprous, mottled surface, full of crusty sores and small, scurrying vermin; his hand grasped the pole and dragged it forth. Its end was burdened with the body of some large food beast, perhaps a giant zeller. This spitted beast was thrust into the giant's mouth and half bitten from the pole, the pole withdrawn

144

like the stem of some obscene fruit. It made two mouthfuls for Dream Miner, two huge, bloody mouthfuls gulped down with much gnashing and masticating.

I put my face into the stone, unable to watch it. Until this moment I had not seen his monstrous nakedness. He was so stonelike, so monumental, that one did not think of it as flesh. The act of eating, however, with all its gustatory noises, the stinking belch that filled the cavern, the rubbing of the behemothian stomach – all this, all at once, horrifying and sickening both.

Worse was to come.

'Pass me one,' blared Storm Grower. 'Pass me one as well.'

'You don't need it,' he bellowed. 'You live off my gut as well as me.'

'We live off our gut, monster. I have a tongue to taste food as well. Pass me one.'

'Get your own, Cloud Teaser.' He set himself, grunting, not giving way as the flesh between them stretched. A lightning bolt flicked him on the ear and he bellowed, jerking upright. Storm Grower took advantage of this to pull out a pole of her own, this one decked with the body of a man. I stuffed my hand into my mouth to keep from crying out, for the body was not dead.

'Not fresh,' she complained in her giant's rumble. Stones quivered from the roof far above, and a sprinkling of dust fell upon them. 'Not fresh enough.'

'Keep your voice down, idiot. You'll have us buried alive. And what do you mean, not fresh? I saw it squirm.'

'Barely. Been there too long. Mostly dead. I like 'em lively, Miner. Lively. So they tickle on the way down.'

'I'll tickle you if you don't keep your voice down. You're bringing rock on our heads.'

'Time this cavern was opened to the sky, brother. Time to get the moles in again.'

'Time enough for that when we've done with our plans for mankind, sister. Soon, now. Call the creatures back. Time to dispose of them. And keep your voice down.'

Still the caverns quivered at her call, a vasty bellowing as though some cataract rumbled far beneath them, summoning the Oracle's return. When it came, it brought the Merchant with it, but only him, to stand as they had before at the gallery edge.

'Well, my son,' bellowed Storm Grower. 'Have you done our will?'

'I put the powdered crythtalth in their wine at the rethepthion, if thatth what you mean.'

'All of them? Huldra? Valearn?'

'All of them. They didn't know it wath there. They thtill don't. Tho far ath they know, they follow you of their own free will. Jutht ath I do.'

'Ah. Well and good, my boy. Well and good.'

'Tho, now I've done it, I want you to tell me.'

'Tell our great boy what? What would he like to know?'

'When I'm going to grow. When will it be? I am no bigger than ten yearth ago.'

'Ah, well, when do you think it will be, Miner? When was it we began to grow?'

'Not much for the first hundred years. We were no bigger than he when we escaped. After that, sometime. And mostly in the last hundred. You'll be mobile a while yet.'

'I want to grow.'

'What's this? The power you have in Fangel isn't enough for you?'

'I want to grow. I want to bring down the thky, ath you do. You have no idea what impertinenth I mutht put up with. They do not fear me ath they ought.'

'Tush, my boy. Nothing. Mere nothing. You have your city, your servants, your hunters. You have your warehouses full of creatures ready to come out and do your bidding when we empty the world of men!

146

You have your army laid away for the coming day. You have a city full to come out and play at the sound of your gong. What more would a boy want? Ah?' And the monstrous face broke in a cavity of laughter, laughter that did bring rocks down upon their heads and made the Merchant dance back into the tunnels to escape being crushed. I was safe enough where I was, wondering if this madman was truly their son and, if so, how such a monstrous thing might have been accomplished.

'Enough,' snarled Storm Grower at last. 'Be on your way out, my boy. Wait for the others at the entrance, they'll not be long. We have one or two small items of business.'

The Oracle led him away, very silently for the Oracle, usually so full of quips and speeches. For a time the cavern was full of breathing noises, then the Oracle returned with the others. All of them.

'We have summoned you for a reason,' said Dream Miner in an insinuating whisper. 'The time has come for one of our most-hoped-for projects to reach fruition. We must depend upon you for the next stage, but we know we can do so, for the rewards are great.'

'Let us talk of those rewards,' drawled the Duke. He was standing well back from the parapet, well out of reach. 'They have not been inconsiderable in the past, but let us talk of them further.'

'Ahhh,' hissed Storm Grower. 'Let us rather talk of punishments when our will is not done, for those are severe. I was limited in my range at one time, Betand. At one time I could bring storm only upon those places near to me. Then I began to grow, greater and more great. Over eighty years ago I began to reach out, and out, beyond this very world. It was I who tumbled a moonlet from the sky onto the Wastes of Bleer, I who wrecked Dindindaroo and all the lands between, foiling the works of Wizards and men. I am no longer limited in any way. As the disobedient people of Morp have found to their dismay. And those of Thorpe and Woeful. So will those of Betand, or of the High Demesne.'

'Tsk,' said the Oracle. 'We need not speak of *punishments*, lady. These good people are *eager* to help you.'

'Hear us, then. In our caves here we have prepared a new crop of crystals. They are of a lovely amethyst color. Those who take them will be our slaves. They will find their way here, eager to do our will. It is our desire that they be widespread among the lands of the south. There are Demesnes there which we need to have under our sway. You will be our agents in this matter.'

'Where do you want them distributed?' The Duke, sulky, not liking this. His notion of the fitness of things was suffering. Punishments were not a proper thing to have discussed. Still, for some reason, he did not seem inclined to rebellion. I thought I understood this. They sought their own advancement through following the giants and were as much the lackeys of these great beings as the Oracle had said.

Storm Grower was continuing. 'Firstly in the Bright Demesne, to a Wizard called Himaggery and one called Barish. I have ended their works before, but they have had the luck of man and may yet bring something from it. They are contentious. Ambitious. So far, all they do is meet and plan and devise processes while time spins away, and it is likely they will not need my crystals to spoil their future. They may do it for themselves. Still, why should we risk, eh? Give one also to a Shifter there called Mavin. And in Schooltown to Mavin's brother, King Mertyn. Those first. Those most importantly. They are engaged in a project we do not wish to see fulfilled. They would raise the hundred thousand frozen Gamesmen, the great Gamesmen, those who lie in the ice caverns near the place we were born. We do not wish those great Gamesmen raised. Let them lie,

148

let them lie, until time spins out and the world cools. Let no man come near that place.

'Thus, when you have given crystals as well to all in Schooltown and the Bright Demesne and to those in Xammer, and Dragon's Fire, and the other Demesnes in that land, and particularly among the Immutables – they are governed by a man called Riddle. Him first, then all others, being sure to include a man named Quench – I say when this is done, then go to the caverns I have spoken of, destroy those who sleep there, and guard the place until we tell you a guard is needed no more.'

'We are your willing servants,' said the Duke.

'You are what you are, Betand. And what you are is not quite good enough. Do not fear. You will enjoy being our servant. Enjoyment is built in.' Dream Miner laughed, a hugely hideous laugh that shook the rock walls, causing me to tremble to the floor and lie there curled against the wall, hoping it would not fall. 'This, however, is a negotiable point. If you can do us a small service we have previously mentioned, you will earn your freedom of the crystals.'

'Any service is too small to convey our gratitude,' Huldra, bowing, smirking. 'The Oracle has told us what is needed. We will be glad to comply.'

'We won't discuss it here,' snapped Storm Grower. 'What we may discuss is the yellow crystals.'

I got up from the floor, pricked my ears, and listened. Yes, yes, the yellow crystals.

'They must be stopped!'

'Stopped! I thought they were yours?' The Duke, much surprised. 'I thought you had dug them.'

The cavern rumbled as the giants shifted upon the Backless Throne. Discomfort there, so I thought, some vast distress. What was it?

Dream Miner, rumbling like a forest fire. 'We have dug no crystals for fifty years. Until then there were many we could use, many we could change to suit ourselves. Our moles dug them in the deep mines

149

and brought them here.' He gestured to the low arch at his left. 'And here we changed them, corrupted them. We would look into the crystals to see what message they carried, and then we would corrupt that message. It is easy. Easy when one knows how. As we knew how.'

Storm Grower, flicking tiny bolts of lightning around the cavern, playing, fitful gusts of wind teasing at the garments of those on the gallery. 'As we knew how. Some we used to corrupt Pfarb Durim, ancient city of your kin, Oracle. And Hell's Maw, which lay at its feet. And those who dwelt there. Some we used to move Huld – this should interest you, Huldra – into bringing forth the great army of bones upon the Wastes. He would not have done it had we not moved him. That was a favourite project of ours.'

'He failed,' Huldra said, her voice dead. 'He died there.'

'He failed because someone opposed us. Some deep dweller brought forth by a girl, a creature called Jinian. A girl we were warned about in advance by our Seers. The girl you were supposed to have disposed of for us, Basilisk.'

Dedrina Dreadeye looked coldly into the giant's eyes. 'We attempted to do so. I sent my own daughter to take care of it.'

'It was not taken care of. You, Bloster, hiding there behind your sister. You had her in your hands.'

'That was before,' he mumbled. 'I didn't know you wanted her dead, not then.'

'Perhaps not. And let us speak of you, Ogress. We had another favorite project here in the northlands. We were using your son, Valdon—'

'Do not speak of my son,' she shrieked. 'My beautiful son. Valdon the glorious, the perfect boy. Do not speak of him.'

'Do not tell us not to speak.' The lightning played at Valearn's feet, making her dance. 'We speak of

150

whom we will. Valdon, for example, stupid Valdon, proud Valdon, sucked dry by the Faces his own servant had set in the Lake. Oh, we have seen it all, our Seers have seen it all. We know. We know. So Valdon failed us and we have you, Valearn. And Bloster and Dedrina-Lucir failed us, but we have both Bloster and Dedrina Dreadeye. And Huld failed us, but we have his sister, Huldra, as well. So. We will not fail again, will we? Though our strategy in these northlands has failed somewhat heretofore, it will not fail again. Not here. Not anywhere.'

Silence. The threat was palpable. Even where I crouched, far across the cavern, I could see the sheen of sweat on Betand's face, the sick slackness of Valearn's jaw.

'Never mind,' said Storm Grower. 'Past is past. But tomorrow is ours, and we cannot brook delay or opposition. And we cannot use crystals which are dug from the mines, for they are all yellow ones, and the yellow ones we cannot change. We are forced to grow our own, but that does not stop the yellow ones being spread about upon the earth.'

'What should they *do* about it, Great Ones? You have not told them how they can *serve* you.'

'Find where they are coming from. Find whatever Wizard or Magician is responsible for them. Come and tell us. Whoever is making these yellow crystals must be sought out, caught out, destroyed! See to it!'

The Oracle bowed. To me the gesture looked mocking, sinister, as though the Oracle, had it willed, could have answered many of the questions the giants were asking. Seemingly, however, the giants found no fault with it.

'Go, now. We are weary of you,' rumbled Dream Miner.

'Beware my lightning,' whispered Storm Grower. 'If you think of disobeying. Beware my hail.'

The troop I had followed came toward me along the gallery, moved into the hall of pillars. I crawled down to the entrance of my rock cleft, waiting until they had passed. The Oracle was still standing at the parapet, around the curving cavern. I heard the giant ask if all had been prepared and heard the Oracle say yes, it was all in readiness, these words almost in whispers, and then the Oracle swept by in a flutter of ribbons and all of them moved through the hall to the tunnel mouth from which we had come.

I did not think.

This is true. My head was full of giant talk, conjecture, ideas, theories. I wanted only to get out of there, out into the clean air once more. Behind me the great surge of breathing faded as we turned one corner, then another . . .

Into blinding light and a chanting voice and a smoke that sent me reeling. A fire, a caldron, Huldra there with the smoke pouring forth, the others half-hidden in it, and the Oracle somewhere nearby.

Huldra's voice. '*Disclose by the Deep Powers. Disclose by the Shadow's dark. Disclose by the Night's teeth. Smoke surround, dark betray, blood hold fast.*'

They saw me! All of them but one were turned toward me, eyes upon me, avid and victorious, not moving, not needing to move, for there were other things swarming around me, binding me, while the smoke held me fast and I could not move. Porvius Bloster lay upon the stone, a knife deep in his back. It was his blood that held me. His life.

The words came as though in a dream, from some distantly echoing place. 'Let me have her,' begged Dedrina.

'No,' the Oracle said, looking in my direction. 'Such is *not* what the Great Ones prefer.'

'Ah, but let me have her, Oracle. I will dispose of her well enough. For my daughter's sake, whom she killed, though we have never proved it. For my sisters' sake. This one did us great harm, took from us a great possession. Let me have her.'

'The Great Ones have their *own* ways. You have all done your part. Well done, I should say, particularly Huldra. You will all be rewarded for it.'

'I will have her as my reward. Her and what of mine she carries.' Dedrina was persistent.

'The Great Ones *intend* that you remain free as your reward. I *may*, of course, go back and ask them. If you would prefer.'

'Shut yourself, woman,' demanded the Duke. 'Leave well alone. You'll have your avengement. She'll not live long, and she'll not leave here, ever.'

'Ah.' The Basilisk seemed in agony, dimly perceived through the veils that were settling around me. 'So, so, let it be.' She seemed deep in thought, turning to the Witch as though for guidance.

Huldra turned her back, but not before I saw the gleam of triumph in her eyes, not before I heard the words, 'Vengeance is sweet, Jinian Footseer. So dies the killer of my brother and the beloved of my son's killer.'

I hadn't killed Huld, not really. Peter had. Still, I supposed I was responsible for it, in a way. 'You didn't give a damn about your brother,' I tried to say. I said nothing. Lips and tongue did not obey. No part of me would move.

They went away into darkness then, Jinian Footseer became someone else. I, the observer, floated in the air somewhere, uninvolved, yet unable to escape. Where Jinian went, I would have to go. Something was dragging her through the rocky corridors. They came through beams of light from above, and I saw they were Oracles, six, eight, a dozen of them. Surely not. The smoke must have disturbed my reason. Still, they looked very much like Oracles. The same shape, size, costume. The same painted faces. The same flapping ribbons. They slipped in and out of vision, finally fading into darkness.

There were creatures. Moles. Not gobblemoles with their clean velvet skins and little pink feet. No,

153

other moles, ragged creatures with fangs and hands and half-blind eyes, which dug and dragged and dropped Jinian in a corner, where her eyes stared, unable to shut. Creatures from Morp, Jinian thought. From the charnel house at Morp.

There were people in the place. Someone came to peer down at Jinian. 'This is the one,' she said. 'This is the one I have Seen.' I looked up into a gauze mask painted with moth wings. A Seer, leaning forward to finger the little star-eye pendant Tess Tinder-my-hand had given me when I was a child. A Seer in this place, speaking as though her gauze mask were thick as a curtain, sound-deadening. Though I did not seem to be present, still something within me heard and remembered. 'This one wears the star-eye, Riddler. Here on her breast. She has worn it since a child. It was given her by a Wize-ard. And it was given to the Wize-ards by those you know. It has power, Riddler. I would advise you to take it from her.' Even in my weakness, something within me rebelled at the thought they would take my star-eye from me.

'Why take it?' Laconic, a voice I knew. 'The old ones, *Ganver* and the rest, they pretend it has significance. Oh, I recall that pretense, Seer. In my youth I was shown many things. "Watch and learn," they said to me. "Bao," they said to me. So I watched, but it was only nonsense. They showed me this and showed me that, but it meant nothing. It was only pretense, done to *mystify* us young ones and keep us subservient. The sign has no power. It is nothing. A symbol only; a symbol of our degradation. If it had any power at all, it would be the power of our people, not hers. She could never learn to use it.'

'You've been playing with her, Riddler. Playing. Games. Oh, I can See, See what you've been doing. Games. Risky Games. You gave her the Dagger.'

'Why not?' it asked in a bleak, careless voice, full of malice and yet without emotion, as though its evil were an abstract thing, intended but not felt. 'I created

154

it out of my anger. I gave it to Daggerhawk Demesne, saying it came from *them*!' And he gestured back, toward that place where the giants were. 'In time I grew annoyed at Daggerhawk Demesne and wished to remove my gift from them. So I played with them, with her. Why not play with her, with any of them? A moment's amusement at least?

'Am I not protected by your Seeings, Seer? You looked into the future and Saw her fall into our hands. You Saw she could not use the Dagger against me. Now. Why should I not play with her? Why not, Seer? Are you saying now you did not See what you told me?'

'No,' the Seer mumbled. 'I Saw as I told you. And yet the place I Saw her was not like this. The time was not this time. Do you not fear, Riddler? Fear she may yet find the book and the light? Fear she may yet find the bell?'

The words held association for me. They circled into my dizzy fog and whirled there, like moths made of light, and I remembered Sorah the Seer upon the Wastes of Bleer saying, 'The Wizard holds the book, the light, the bell.' What Wizard was that? Was it Jinian?

The Oracle paid no attention, made no answer. She-I was dragged away again, seeing things at the edge of vision, as through a cloud. Glass jars, vats, tall vats full of the same silvery stuff that had filled the pool of the sevens. Crystal milk. Wires hanging down inside the vats, and on the wire crystals growing. Green ones. Amber. Red. Amethyst. All with that shading across them, dimming the color. From the tops of the vats the wires ran out along the walls. Where? Where do they go?

The moles have picked Jinian up again, tugging her along, head bumping on the stone. They are dragging her along the wall of the cavern, near the giants' feet, just out of reach. See the fingers reaching for her, just out of reach. High against the cavern roof are great

155

caps where the wires go. That's where the wires go, into the caps, and the caps on the giant heads and the thoughts of the giants flow down into the vats and crystals grow. There. In the crystal milk.

Darkness and pain.

Then only darkness.

I came to myself at last, knowing nothing except that a very long time had passed. All of me was present in one place. I wanted to giggle about that and couldn't. Someone had put a gag in my mouth.

Light.

Low, at the level of my eyes where I lay. Dim. A long, bow-shaped arch between the place where I was and some other place. Out there the dim light swam and blurred. Things were moving between me and the source of the light. I slipped away, faded into black, realizing how uncomfortable I was. Something hard and curved was pressed into my back.

When I came back, the light was a little brighter. I could see what lay to one side. A pole. A long pole, extending outward through the window into the light. There were a pair of hoofed feet in front of me. There was something tied to the pole. Something dead.

I could move, some. I twisted my head, trying to roll myself on the curved surface. It shifted, rolled. On the other side, another pole, something tied to it as well. This body was human. The feet were on a level with my eyes. I pressed a trembling hand to my mouth, realizing for the first time that my hands were free.

The gag first. It came loose after a time, some wad of filthy stuff. I spat it away, blacked out for a moment, then came back to begin a frantic exploration of the ropes that bound me to the pole I was on.

No knots. Two heavy ropes bound below my breasts. Two around my thighs. I could move my arms, my lower legs, but it did no good. I was lashed to the pole.

My pack! In it the things needed to lay some spell upon the ropes, some freeing magic. It had been a little pack. When Huldra's smokes had caught me, it had been on my back. I raised my head, twisted, trying to see, sorry I had looked. The poles stretched away on either side, each with its burden. Not many. Half a dozen or so. Against a far wall was a pack-shaped blot, put where I could see it, where I could know where it was without reaching it.

There was a fine cruelty in that. The Oracle, perhaps. It felt like a thing the Oracle would do.

I lay back, breathless, screams trembling at the edge of my throat. I could feel them gathering there, like birds, fluttering in panic. They were ready to come out, fly out, shriek their way into the cavern's quiet.

Quiet. Too quiet. An expectant quiet.

Perhaps that is what they were waiting for. To hear me scream. It was obvious they intended to eat me but had not done so at once. Why?

Vengeance, Jinian, I told myself. They want to hear you scream, girl. Want you to struggle. Cry out. Beg. They will eat Jinian then. But not until then. Perhaps. So she would not scream. Would not let herself make any sound.

Out of this frantic fear I heard an old voice, long remembered, harsh as a slap across the face. 'Enough, Jinian. Consider water.' Murzy's voice, coming clearly even through this hysteria and fear. So I took a deep breath and considered water. The dams had always suggested this as a way of recovering calm and good sense. I considered water in all its aspects, raging and still, bringing myself at last to a kind of quiet.

Outside the low archway, in the light, something moved from right to left. By raising my head from the pole I could see its shadow. There was something familiar in that shadow.

'Our vengeance approaches,' rumbled the voice of the Dream Miner. 'Are you content at that?'

'Who can say?' the answer came, a whisper, something familiar about that voice. 'Who can say if we will be content?'

'You have planned it. These hundreds of years, you've worked at it, as we have. It was you who began it.'

'And yet, who can say we will be content? Some of us think not.'

'Faugh. Some of you are witless fools, hiding in your graves like rotten nuts in their shells.'

'Still, they are some of us. We feel their absence, Giant One. As you might feel Storm Grower's absence if she were reft from you.'

'In which I would delight,' came the other giant's voice. 'I would walk the world in joy.'

'You could not walk the world at all,' said the Miner. 'Nor could I. We have grown too great for our bones to carry us. Never mind.' The great voice paused, then continued speaking to the smaller creature, whatever it was. 'No, never mind. Vengeance will come from here, at last, as it was begun a thousand years ago when you gathered up all the blue crystals and brought them here.'

'Which some of us have since regretted.'

'Fools. Hadn't you suffered enough at men's presence?'

'We thought so, then.'

'And now?'

'Some of us still think so. Though we may find our vengeance bitter.' There was a titter then. High-pitched; the sound a bird makes in the night when it only dreams of singing.

'It wearies me,' whined Storm Grower. 'Send it away. Then give me one. I'm hungry.'

There was a great huffing sound, as of lungs compressed. Into the light came great groping fingers. One of the poles was pulled outward into that light and the munching sound began. Another pole followed. And then two more. Chewing, swallowing noises, a

158

scream. One of the poles had carried live meat. Now there were only three left. The ones on either side of me and the one I was lashed upon.

I began to rip at my clothing. Perhaps they had left me the Dagger. If I could get to the Dagger, I could cut the ropes. It took only a moment to find what a vain hope that was. The scabbard lay at the back of my thigh, tight between my leg and the pole, bound there.

The Seer. She had seen me falling to the Oracle. She had seen the Dagger being of no help to me. Of course they had left it. As they had left my pack, out of reach. Out of hope.

I fumbled at my waist, trying to find the cord on which my pouch was hung. It was tangled deep in the fabric of the pantaloons, lost in them, which was probably why I had it still on me. If they had seen it or felt it, they would have taken it.

I worried it out at last, opening it to pour the contents onto my chest. The amethyst crystal in which Huldra's sending was trapped. The yellow crystal from the mines outside Fangel. The blue one Beedie had given me. A few restorative herbs. A tiny bottle of scent, shaped like a frog. A lock of Peter's hair. My fragment from the well of the sevens. I lay, head up, looking down at these few things. After a time I returned all but two of them to the pouch, shoving it inside my shirt.

The munching had stopped and the breathing sounds from the cavern had become louder, slower, as though the giants slept. Soon this breathing was succeeded by snoring, great rumbling sounds, rhythmic as tides.

I braced my feet and arms against the rock on either side of the pole and pushed, trying to drag it back, out of the light. It moved a finger's width. Again. Again a tiny movement. I timed the pushes to coincide with great snores. Once again. And again. Over and over, endlessly, exhaustingly. I was wet, even in the clammy cold of the cavern, soaked with the sweat of this effort. Push, and push again. The creature on my left was almost even with me now. I reached out to touch it. My fingers were a hand's width from the thing's mouth. I needed its mouth.

Push again. The snores stopped. A giant mumbled in his sleep. A giantess answered in hers. Again the breathing of sleep. Push, and push again. My legs felt as though they had been dipped in fire. I could reach the thing's mouth.

I took the amethyst crystal in one hand, reaching out. I was trembling. My hand was slick with sweat. I dropped it, dropped it, rolling about on the stony floor.

Tears then, silent and bitter and exhausted. And after the tears some measure of resolution. I rolled as far to my left as I could, explored the floor with my hand. It could not have gone far.

Fragments of rock. Bits of bone. Things filthier than these. And then the hard, faceted shape of it in my fingers. I brought it back to my chest, wiped the fingers dry, tried again.

I reached out and thrust it into the mouth of the dead thing next to me.

Push, push again. The human corpse on the other side was farther back. Twice I had to stop to rest, the second time using some of the restorative herbs from the pouch, which left a bitter taste in my mouth but a painful clarity of mind. Then push and push again, and the yellow crystal in the corpse's mouth. It was a corpse. It was dead. I wept at this, too. I had been wondering what I would do if it were alive.

I peered down between my feet. The end of my pole still lay outside the window, in the light. With the last of my strength I pushed once more, seized a rock behind me over my head and pulled as well, seeing the end of the pole slide under the arch, into the shadow, into the room where I lay. So much for that.

I let the swirling darkness swallow me up. Just for a time, just for a bit of rest, to wake thinking of the Oracle, perhaps having dreamed of the Oracle. Oh, I knew the creature now for what it was. Not a simpering, harmless creature. No. No. Full of malice and ancient guile. The true source of the evil in the north. The Oracle, not the giants. They were too simple. All their cleverness came from the Oracle. I prayed it had gone away. I prayed it had not stayed to see my end.

'Aaaangh,' came a whining rumble from the other room. 'Aaangh. Give me one. I'm hungry.'

'Get it yourself. I'm tired of giving you. Get it yourself.'

The sound of lightning. A frying noise. Complaint, monstrous hairy fingers groping at the window. 'There's only two here.' Voice like thunder. 'Where's the other one? The fun one? The one that was supposed to be here. You there, minions. You from Morp. Provender!'

Chewing, masticating noises. At the far side of the low room, a scurrying as some large furry creatures moved in and out of the light, moving poles, tying bodies to them. They did not come near me. I made not a sound. This had an air of calculation about it. The giants would not eat me until they had wrung the last shred of agony and apprehension from me. I played dead. Let them think I had fainted, or slept.

Then an anguished howl, the howl of a tornado, of a hurricane. 'Ouuuuugh, pain. Brother. Ouuuuugh, pain. I have got a pain in my gut.'

I caught my breath. Across the dim room the furry shapes stopped what they were doing, froze in place. The howl was immobilizing, terrifying. It rang through the cavern, blasting at the stones. Dust fell. Gravel rolled.

Oh, she should have a bellyache indeed, should Storm Grower. She had Huldra's sending in her belly, dissolved out of the crystal that had held it, a voracious sending ready to eat its way out of its fleshy prison. It should find enough in Storm Grower to fill it. I wondered briefly what Huldra would think when it returned. This made me want to giggle hysterically, and it was all I could do to bite down hard on a finger and keep silent.

'Hush,' breathed Dream Miner. 'You are disturbing me. I want to . . . want to . . . sleep. Peace. Contentment. How sweet. I did not know how sweet . . . '

She had the amethyst crystal. But he had the yellow one. He desired sleep. Peace. Contentment. I hoped it would last for some time. This would solve the problem of being eaten, but I was still firmly lashed to the pole.

'Ooooogh, pain.' A sizzle of lightning ricocheted from the floor into the room where I lay. In the flash I saw one side of the room disappear in a sapphire glow. In the after-image I thought I saw a small form leaping there. Perhaps more than one.

Wind began to blow. Wet wind, clammy with fetid smells in it. The pain the giantess felt was being translated into storm. 'Ouuuugh, pain. Dream Miner. Wake. How can you sleep? Wake. I'm dying.' There was disbelief in that voice, horror and anguish. 'I'm dying and you sleep!'

'Lolly lolly alum baff?' sang a quiet voice. '*Is the Wizard girl in here?*'

'*Here!*' I cried half-hysterically. '*Who's there?*'

'*Proom,*' answered the small voice, approaching. '*Come to help you if you need help in return for the help you gave our people in the town.*'

He was not alone. Others of the small people had joined him; still others were gathered at the far wall in an excited horde, busy with something.

'*What did you do to the giants?*' He seemed to know I had done it, though that was far from obvious, given my condition.

'*I fed them something bad for them. She may die of it, maybe not. He may die of it, maybe not. They are very big and what I gave them was quite small.*'

162

'*Then we had best hurry.*' He knelt at my side, busy with teeth and knife. I felt the rope loosen, then give, as I struggled to sit up while he worked on the ropes around my thighs. When he had done, I stood up, wavering on my feet, almost falling.

'*We will lead you out!*'

'*In a moment. First . . . first I should be sure they do not recover.*' I stumbled to the pack where it lay against the wall, falling over bodies of men and beasts, to stand over it panting. What could I use? No missile I could control would be large enough. There were two or three very complicated spells that might be useful. End and Beginning. That would take all day, and in the other room Storm Grower was summoning up such a storm as might kill us all. Lightning flashed around us, in and out of the room. No time for that. No, no, not that. No window magic usable in such circumstances. Gamelords, what? Rain splashed wildly around us. Water.

'*Proom, is there a river near? Any water? Anywhere near?*'

'*Under us, yes. I can hear it.*'

Of course. There had to be a river there to carry away the filth of the giants, else they would have long since drowned in their own excretions. That was it.

I burrowed into the pack, laying out the few things needful. I did the gestures twice and didn't get them right either time. My shoulders kept going into spasms. Oh, gods and Gamelords, but I prayed the one I was about to call upon would remember. A boon a d'bor wife had offered me. *The* d'bor wife, rather. One of the old gods, perhaps. At least some thought so. A boon. Call on me, she had said. Call on me. I bowed my head, thought of water for a few moments, got myself together, and then tried it again.

'*All things of the sea are yours, great and small, of river and lake, of pond and stream. I call upon you, d'bor wife, for the boon you promised me.*'

Nothing. Only the raging of Storm Grower from

the outer cavern, the stertorous breathing of Dream Miner. Nothing.

And then a rivulet running beside my feet, coming from a gap in the wall. Rock breaking free to make it larger. A moist echoing space full of the sound of waters. Salt. The smell of tidal flats. The cry of gulls and the crash of waves in my ears. And with all this the harsh music of a well-remembered voice.

'What would you have, Jinian Footseer?'

'I would have this cavern flooded, d'bor wife. Filled from top to bottom so that those creatures within may be drowned.'

'So be it, Jinian. I will fulfill the boon I promised you.'

The Shadowperson had been standing beside me, watching me, seemingly unafraid. Well, this was Proom, Mavin's friend. Proom, Peter's guide. He had seen strange and mighty things before, this one. '*Out,*' I said to him. '*We've got to get out, and all your people as well.*'

'*No,*' he cried, anguished. '*There are things here we must take.*'

Things he must take? What? There were no victims left. He pointed to the far wall, where his people were dashing about, calling to one another.

'*Too late!*' I pointed at the roof. A stream had broken through and was flooding down onto the sapphire heap where the Shadowpeople were at work. In the intermittent flashes, I saw what it was. A pile of blue crystals, a hill of them, millions. A shout of dismay was all I had time for, echoed by the little people. Then we were all running up the twisty stone corridors toward the light. Behind us the storm raged and the water rose.

When we came into the light, it was into the heart of the storm. Hail fell around us in great, white boulders, and the wind raged against the night, throwing huge trees across the sky like arrows. We crouched in the entrance to the cavern, me, Proom, a

164

dozen of his people bent protectively over their sacks of crystals, all staring with disbelief into the night.

Storm Grower did not die easily. For hours the storm raged. Toward morning it began to wane. Then, as we watched in fear, a fog spewed from the hill above us and took the form of the sending; screaming with laughter, it dwindled into the east.

'Is she drowned?' asked Proom. 'Is the great giant Deviless drowned for all?'

'I think so. Drowned or eaten. One or both.'

'Then perhaps it is a good trade. Long and long ago did great Ganver send me seeking these things. Blue, he said, as a summer sky. A great thing of Lom, of the land our parent, a great thing misused and betrayed and hidden away.

' "Find them, Proom," he told me. "Go into the world and find them where they have hidden that we may undo the wrong which had been done." So I sought, long and long but fruitlessly, and returned to my people to find they had been abducted by Blourbast the Ghoul. Then was the song of Mavin made. She was a young girl then. And now you come. And you are the friend of Peter, Mavin's son.'

I apologized to him, wearily, sincerely. 'I'm sorry. I didn't see the crystals were there until after I'd called for the boon. I didn't know you were looking for them.'

'Who would have thought to look in the lair of the giants? Who would have thought the evil ones would have brought them there?' He sighed, calling to his people. The storm had almost abated. 'I must take these to Ganver. Farewell, Jinian, Peter's friend.'

'A moment, Proom,' I begged him. 'Will you leave a few of the crystals with me?' He assented, pouring a small heap of them into my hands. Then he and his people ran off into the morning, leaping over the fallen trees, flitting like birds into the shelter of the forests – that of it which was still standing. There were a thousand questions I could have asked. A thousand answers he could have given me. I could talk to them. Mavin couldn't. Queynt couldn't. But I could. A thousand questions, Jinian, I told myself. At least that. But those I should have asked them of were gone.

CHAPTER NINE

I had no need to choose which way to go. The Duke's party had gone back to Fangel, obedient to the instructions of the giants. Those instructions, once set in motion, would not have been stopped by the giants' deaths. So, one must go to Fangel once more, brave that strange city once more, see what could be done to stop the amethyst crystals going south.

I wished for some way of getting there more quickly. If I had only been a Shifter. Or if Peter were with me.

'If wishes were geese, we would all have feather-beds,' I told myself sternly. 'Come, girl, what is the matter with you?'

The matter was I was exhausted, hungry, battered, worn. I knew the feeling well. I had felt it before in Chimmerdong and was too experienced in it to give it houseroom. I will eat as I go, I told myself. I will rest when I must. My body did not believe these promises, but the rest of me calmed down somewhat. I took time to fish out the Dagger of Daggerhawk and slit a seam from the pocket with it, returning it to a more sensible location, cursing all the leagues I had not needed the thing and could have had it in my hand, only to have needed it the one time it could not be reached.

I climbed upward from the entrance to the cavern, over tortuous drifts of fallen timber, through slides of mud and rock, around piles of hail so high they looked like snowdrifts, wondering how long I had spent in that underground warren. How far ahead of me were the Duke and Valearn and Huldra? Huldra?

Huldra. A shiver down the spine. A hard clutch at the stomach, pain behind the throat. It was Huldra who had caught me in the cavern. Huldra who had been ready for me, expecting me. How?

There had been a Seer, of course. I vaguely remembered seeing a Seer. A Seer in the employ of the giants. Somewhere down in that underground warren right now there was a Seer, perhaps more than one, alive or dead, who had seen Jinian's part in the battle on the Wastes of Bleer. And likely that same Seer had seen Jinian following the Duke of Betand into the cavern of the giants?

Likely, yes. And once seen, the vision had been used to trap me. When the Oracle had taken them aside, he had told Huldra of it, told her to make herself ready. Those spells had been rehearsed beforetime. The ingredients had been laid ready to make the paralyzing smoke. Certain creatures had been posted in readiness to bind me.

I dimly remembered Dedrina demanding to have me for her own. The Oracle had said no. No. The giants had wanted me for another purpose. To feel fear, panic, pain, humiliation. Was it indeed the giants who wanted me for that? Or had they been led to that thought by the Oracle itself?

I reflected on this. How they must have hated mankind, mankind who had created them so monstrously, no less monstrously than the pig I had met in Chimmerdong. How they must have fumed and plotted through the centuries; how they must have welcomed the power that came to them, slowly, the hateful destruction moving out from them like a cancer. What did they desire in the end? That all men should be enslaved? That, at least. That all men be made as horrified, as panic-stricken, as humiliated as they themselves had once been? Oh, yes. They would have left me tied to a pole a long time. Long enough to wring every drop of agonized apprehension from me. But, as it happened, they had left me a little too long.

Huldra believed I was dead.

Still, Huldra was more than a Witch.

And I had seen Huldra's sending go screaming back to her, out of that dripping cavern. What might Huldra learn from that?

'I hope it drops a washtub full of blood on her,' I muttered, too tired to ill wish more usefully. 'She'll be there in Fangel. Likely she is able to unspell any spell I set. Unless I can come up with something she'd have no knowledge of at all. Oh, Jinian, why did you decide to be a Wize-ard?'

There was no answer to this. The Jinian who might have answered had crawled between two sheltering trees and had fallen asleep.

I woke some hours later, feeling more hopeful, able to go on. I went past the place Bleem had been. There was nothing left of it but trash, and the remnants were awash in shadow. Where did it come from? Where had it come from so recently? Where had it lain, waiting? At least those poor unfortunates had had a chance to escape. I wondered if they had made it to safety. If any place could be called safe in these days. The farther I went, the fewer trees were fallen, the fewer landslides in the path. Storm Grower had not reached far with her destruction; she had probably been unconscious much of the time. I tried to feel some pity, could not.

The way became easier, drier. I passed a scattering of krylobos feathers.

'Back and forth,' I groaned aloud. 'Back and forth. Like some backlewheep, bat, bat, bat.'

'Jinian?' The voice was disbelieving.

'Who?' I demanded, putting my back to a tree. 'Who is it?'

'Jinian?' No mistaking the joy in it this time. 'It's Peter!'

Something large and furry slid down the tree, encompassed me in an enormous embrace, half smothered me before beginning to Shift into a Peter

169

shape. 'I thought you were lost forever.' He kissed me; I so surprised I could do nothing about it. He shook me. I did nothing about that, either.

'What are you doing here?' I demanded. 'You're supposed to be on your way south, taking the blue crystals to Mavin!'

'They're going. Queynt and Chance are taking them, with those two from oversea and their monster in the basket.'

'But you . . . '

'But I wasn't about to lose you, stupid girl. I love you, Jinian Footseer. After we found you were gone, I sat there for hours trying to convince myself it was all for the best. You're not easy to get along with, you know . . . '

'*I'm* not easy! *I'm* not!'

'That's what I said, you're not. Neither am I, but we both knew that to start with. It doesn't matter, though. I love you, and that's all. I'll just have to make the best of it.'

'But . . . but . . . '

'I know. It would have been easier to just let you go. I know why you went. At least partly. It was my fault. Some of it. But what decided me was thinking about Mavin and Himaggery, you know. They love each other and always have. The first time I ever heard my mother say his name, I knew she loved him. The first time I ever saw him look at her, I knew he loved her. She risked her life to save him, you know. Risked mine, too, come to that, though I was a bit too undeveloped to know anything about it. But he never really said the right things to her. And she never said the right things to him. And so they spent most of their lives apart and the time they spent together they spent fighting with each other. So, I said no. I wouldn't do that. I wouldn't just let you go, and when I found you I wouldn't sit around saying nothing. Even if I said all the wrong things and had to take them back.'

170

'Sylbie,' I said stuttering. 'The baby.'

'Oh, well, yes. There is that. Stupid girl left the wagon and followed me. I didn't catch her at it until it was too late to send her back. Then the first time I Shifted she went all hysterical.'

'But she . . . it's your baby.'

'Yes. It's my baby. Which was begot, you might say, in pursuance of duty. Now I'm not going to do what Mavin would, which is not talk about it. And I'm not going to do what Himaggery would, which is talk about something else. You've got to understand this . . .

'It was in Betand. They called it "the City That Fears the Unborn". Some Necromancer had come there, got drunk, and summoned up a ghost. Instead of being a ghost of something dead, though, it was the ghost of someone unborn. So, every visitor to the city had to beget if at all possible in order to get the unborn born as soon as possible. You understand?'

'I don't understand what an unborn could do to send a whole city so silly.'

'Well, Jinny, you're going to have to take my word for it. The howling alone would have driven you crazy. It was a real haunting, no mistake about it. Half the people in the town had lost their minds. Well, so there I was, riding up to Betand, all innocence, trying to find out something about where Mavin was, and the next thing I knew I was in this room with Sylbie, having been instructed to beget. She was crying and carrying on, and I was scared to death. See, I'm being honest. If you don't like that, tough.

'It was more Trandilar who did it than me. I didn't know anything about sex at all, Jinian. Not a shred. I knew it would be awful, so I summoned up Trandilar, and she actually did all the lovemaking and so forth. Of course Sylbie fell for that. Who wouldn't? I would have myself. Trandilar is — well, you know what Trandilar is. So, we begot a baby, which was what we were supposed to do. As it happens, it's likely the

171

very baby who was haunting Betand. At least, so Dorn said when we put the haunting down. He's turned out to be a very nice baby, but I don't love Sylbie, I never did. It would be very easy to love the baby, and that would be pleasant, but not if it means giving up Jinian. If we can work out something including Jinian *and* the baby, very good. What I got to thinking was, suppose the baby turns out Shifter? Sylbie will fall apart.'

'She really had hysterics when you Shifted?'

'Full-fledged, whooping and screaming hysterics. All I did was a snakey little thing to get to the top of a tree, and it set her off.'

I had seen some of Peter's snakey little things and was not entirely unsympathetic with Sylbie. 'Where is she now?'

'She's up this trail, a league or so. In a cave which I dug for her – took pombi shape to do that, and she didn't like that, either – until I could get back. She's got food and water.'

I sighed, sagging back into his arms. It would be nice just to stay here, close held. Spend the night, perhaps, cuddled in furry arms in the hollow of a tree. Too much had happened. Too much was going on.

Too much was going on. Exactly. I drew him down beside me and told him the tale.

'Giants? I never dreamed there were real giants. And Proom?' he whispered when I had done. 'Really, Proom? He's like some kind of fairy godmother following my family around. Mavin, then me, then you. Gods, those amethyst crystals. We've got to warn them. They have no idea.'

'None of them have any inkling at all. Not Himaggery, nor Mavin, nor any of the rest of them. But there's more to it than that.'

I told him then what I suspected. What I'd been worrying over in my head ever since we saw the little crystal mine outside Fangel and talked to old Buttufor.

'I'm afraid it's true, Peter. Everything the giants said only confirmed it. Up until then, I thought they might be responsible for those yellow crystals, but they're not. They were as frightened by them as I am.'

His face was as drawn and hopeless as I'm sure mine had been many times in recent days. 'What can we do?'

'I don't know. It may be too late to do anything, but we have to try. That was the lesson I learned in Chimmerdong, Peter. No matter how hopeless it looks, you still have to try. I got a few more of the blue crystals from Proom. You'll have to take them south with you. Warn Himaggery and Mavin and all the rest. Then suggest to them in the *strongest possible way* that they stop arguing and get the hundred thousand out of the cavern. And when each one wakes, he or she must have a sliver of this crystal in his mouth. If the ones I have here aren't enough, then more must be found in Beedie's land. Perhaps Mavin can get them, and perhaps some of her kindred would help.'

'You're going with me.'

'It would slow you down. I hope you can take some shape that flies, for that's what's needed now. You've got to go south. Gamelords, how I prayed for a Shifter outside that cavern.'

'I can't leave you.'

'You have to leave me. The warning must be brought to our people, Peter. As soon as possible, delaying for nothing at all. I'll meet you when you return. Ah. Where? Listen, if you follow this trail down to the northwest, past where the village of Bleem was, you'll come to a trail leading north. The trail forks. The right-hand one goes to the giants, and the left-hand one goes up over the mountain by a huge red pillar of stone. I'll meet you there, by the red stone, with or without Sylbie. I'll go get her. Maybe I can find someone to take care of her and the baby, bring them south to Mavin. If not, I'll keep them with me, but they should be taken farther from Fangel. I don't like the idea of the baby that close to Valearn.'

He wasn't listening. But then, he hadn't been reared on nursery stories of Valearn. 'I don't want to leave you! I'll carry you with me.'

'I don't want you to leave me. But you can't carry me *and* Sylbie *and* the baby without wasting time, and we can't just leave them here alone.' Briefly I let myself melt against him, let all the turbulent feelings I had quelled for season after season burgeon between us until a new kind of storm began to batter at me, melting me. 'I don't want you to leave me. And whichever of us gets to the pillar first is to wait for the other one – forever, if need be. I don't want you to leave me, but I have to ask you to.'

'Jinian, I swear by all the gods and most of the new ones, if we get out of this . . .'

'Yes. Now go.'

I didn't watch him, not out of any sense of dismay at the changes, but simply because I was crying and didn't want him to see. I heard odd sounds, a strangled cursing, and then the irregular beat of wings. When I turned at last it was to see a black-winged form staggering across the sky. Evidently Peter had not recently practiced wings. The thing looked more like a dragon than a bird, and it was not built for speed. Even as I watched, however, the black silhouette elongated, became more slender, more streamlined. It plunged out of sight against the southern clouds.

So much for that. I dried my face, noticing in passing that all my hermitish notions seemed to have left me. So much for the lonely life, then. If there were any future, I would spend it with Peter.

If there were any.

I plodded a league away, seeking the cave, calling softly when I should have been near it, and only after wreathing the area with Inward Is Quiet, a pacifying spell when done in the passive mode, to be sure no one lurked there with evil intent. No response. I walked another league, repeating the call. Nothing.

Now seriously worried, I returned the way I had come, this time casting back and forth either side of the trail. Halfway to the place I'd met Peter, I found it, a cave well dug in sandy soil, half-hidden behind a fallen tree. And tracks around it. Boots. More than one pair. Two parallel lines, where someone's feet had been dragged. The soil still moist. It had not happened long before. A baby nappy drying on a branch. It, too, still damp. Half-hidden under a stone, the baby trousers Roges had sewn, their bright checks showing up against the dun earth.

I didn't need window magic to peer into the past and learn what had happened. Huldra had been watching, through a Seer, perhaps. Through a sending, perhaps. Or perhaps Valearn herself had hired some Rancelman to help her find the food she yearned for. It did not matter which. More than one person had come here to drag Sylbie and the baby away. Up the hill a way were the tracks of horses, not on the trail. That's why I hadn't seen them as I searched. They did not join the trail to Fangel for another league beyond.

Weariness left me. I went at speed through the waning day, forgetting the ache in my legs. At sunset the trail left the forest, sloped downward along the meadow toward the walls of Fangel. When dark came, the city would lie in a cataleptic sleep; watchers would watch, but they would not be the people of Fangel. Huldra? Valearn? Perhaps the Duke of Betand?

There was no spell I could cast that Huldra might not be able to counter. Worse, if I used any spell at all, anyone competent in the wize-arts could smell it out. My use of the arts would say 'Jinian' as loudly as the Fangel curfew gong. The only advantage I had was that they all thought I was dead.

I sat, arms wrapped around knees. Shortly it would

be night. If Sylbie was to be saved, it could not be put off until the morrow. On the morrow there might be no Sylbie, no child. The walls of Fangel loomed, the gates still open but shortly to close. I dared not use a spell, not the least one in my art, for Huldra was there and watching, there and waiting. Huldra might have learned much from the return of her sending. Full of Storm Grower's blood and d'bor wife's water, it might have had much to tell her.

So. Get in. Without a spell. Without being seen.

There were wains moving in and out of the north gate when I arrived, hay wains, others that had been loaded with meat and vegetables for the markets and were now returning empty. My hair was thrust up under a cap, my face dirtied, my clothes stained. I walked beside a horse, talking to it, it obligingly hiding me from the wagoner who drove, my face further hidden behind a sheaf of fodder I had picked up along the way. The team hid me not only from the driver but from the guards as well, troubled enough by this great load of hay arriving so late.

'Business?'

'Oh, come down from it, Gorbel. You know my business. I've got a load of hay for the residence stables, and I'm late enough without all this.'

'You're almost too late. Word runs there's a hunt tonight. Get in and get out.'

'I'd 'a been in and out except for a broken wheel. Don't shut the gate 'til I'm through. Won't be long.'

When the wain turned into a side street, out of sight of the gate, I slipped away into an alley. The late afternoon light made cold blocks of shadow in the streets. People were leaving the park, the alleys. Doors were shutting. A food cart still plied along one alley; I hid my face behind a meat pie, working my way toward the center of the town.

From there one could see in all directions down radiating avenues, almost to the wall.

I ensconced myself in a deep doorway, black with

176

shadow. After a time I heard the distant creaking of wheels as the last wagon went out through the gate. The gate closed with a metallic, clamoring echo.

Nearby, at the residence, the great gong rang its tremorous demand upon hearing, shattering into silence.

The streets were empty. On the western horizon the sun sank in a swollen ball, leaving a stripe of red like a bloody sword upon the horizon. Dusk came, then the rushing dark, then the first light of the full moon setting alternating blocks of gray luminescence and ebon shadow, long diagonal lines of black slanting down the sides of walls and into the street to make hard-edged crevasses of dark. I walked from light to dark to light again, no less conscious of being watched in the darkness than I was in the light. And yet, it was almost an impersonal watching. A machine kind of watching.

High on the walls the twined letters of the Dream Merchant's monogram glittered and twinkled, little gems gleaming with a light of their own. It was a machine watching! Up there on the walls were eyes. But who observed what the watchers saw? Was there some deep den in this place where human observers crouched, seeing through these glittering eyes? I thought not, sensed not. The city of Fangel watched for itself, but what it watched for or why it cared, I did not know. There was undoubtedly some action that would bring out the denizens of this place. Briefly I wondered what would happen if one rang the great gong now, in the middle of the night. The idea sent horrid premonitory shivers down my spine, a kind of visionary grue, as though a door had opened into some unpleasant future.

I shut down the thought, crept around a corner, paused within sight of the residence, its serpentine gates now opened wide.

Somewhere in the city a pombi roared and was answered by another, a howling, grumbling tumult that waxed for a time, then waned into silence. There were beasts loose in the city. And hunters. What had the guard at the gate said about a hunt tonight? For whom? By whom?

Somewhere a baby cried, shockingly close, and a woman's voice hushed it. Echoes from this, from one side, from the other. No direction. I sought the location frantically, running back the way I had come. Nothing. Nothing but the sound of my own steps magnified. Nothing but the sound of laughter. Laughter. Somewhere. Nasty, chuckling laughter, a sound that reveled in its hunt, in its prey.

Valearn?

Footsteps, not my own. I shrank against the wall, into a hollow there where a heavy door barred entry to the courtyard beyond. Out in the street a skulking figure walked from shadow to shadow, its long staff tickling the stones with a small clicking, barely audible.

Again a pombi roared, closer this time, perhaps only a street away. The skulker turned, mouth stretched wide in a gape of surprise, Ogress fangs exposed to the moon. Yes. Valearn!

She moved too fast for me to follow her. One moment she was there, the next moment gone. Again the baby cried, was silent.

So. The Ogress was hunting the baby. Sylbie was fleeing from the Ogress. The pombis would eat either the Ogress or Sylbie, though it seemed the Ogress might not have known of their presence. And Jinian . . . What are you doing? I asked myself. You're not being useful here!

Light and shadow. A sound of something panting, a massive body running, scratch of claws upon the stone, heavy lungs heaving as the thing went past. I expelled my breath, tried to melt into the stones, thanking whatever gods there were that I smelled only of greens and hay. That had been something larger than a pombi. I remembered the caged gnarlibar in the procession and cursed silently. What kind of zoo was loose in the streets? How many hunters were there?

Now a horn. A horn and the sound of hooves, far away. An echoing clatter in the hard streets. It was to be a drive. The game was to be driven into the hunter's claws. Or the hunters upon the game? Or both against the wall for the amusement of whoever was coming?

Enough of this. Risk or no risk, I had to find Sylbie and the baby. Huldra or no Huldra, I had to use the art. I fled along the streets, seeking. Somewhere should be something besides blank, closed walls. A window that could be used for window magic, to make a summons. Even a room, an enclosure, a corner of a courtyard.

Everything closed tight, obdurate walls towering over my head, stone streets, black and gray, the moon swimming in silence, far off the horn and nearer than that the howling of things abroad in the night. A chuckle again, echoes, how near? Valearn.

The distant hunt was circling the walls. The sound had come at first from the south, but now it extended east and west from there, a circle growing. As soon as I realized this, I knew what they were doing. They would circle the walls, then drive in along each street, ending at the residence, with all driven before them to a bloody conclusion there. Valearn could merely have waited to have Sylbie driven into her hands.

Again the chuckle. Waiting was not Valearn's way.

I ran quick footed down that street, around the corner. I thought the baby noises had come from this direction. Nothing. Gamelords. I was planning what of the art to use. Assuming that Valearn had none. Assuming that Huldra was elsewhere, with the hunt, perhaps, not hanging around the next corner waiting to sniff me out.

Abruptly, I saw it. There in the wall next to me was

a grill, a rare, narrow window in the wall that separated courtyard from street. I grabbed the bars with both hands and went up it like a thrisbat, up and over the wall and down the other side. Unseen, one hoped. Unseen. I was in a barren little court, barred door at my back, barred gate to one side, grill before my face, blank wall to the other side.

I could not lay a hiding spell on Sylbie if I didn't know where she was. Or, truth to say, I could, but it would have taken too long. Each uncertainty one added into a spell made it take that much longer. All I could use was her name and the baby's name, very important, true, but without knowing where she was, a hiding spell wouldn't do. Besides, Egg in the Hollow wouldn't cover the baby's crying. There was another one I should have learned, one Cat was going to teach me. Damn. Too late. No point thinking about it now. It had to be something else. With the grill before me, I could do window magic. Summoning. Them to me. Or something else to Fangel, to confuse the issue.

Which made me think of what Queynt had said about not being pregnant when one did summons. Which made me remember what he had said about summons resulting in mermaids and dryads. Which made me remember the deep dwellers.

Mischievous. Pesky. And childlike.

Valearn sought children.

So. There were only two things I needed that I did not have in my pack, and I found both in that barren little courtyard. Luck? Perhaps. I set them out on the sill, where the iron bars were anchored in the stone, starting the summons silently. Music and Meadow. The bars were perfect for this window magic because it established that those summoned were barred from me. If the window had been an open one, I would have hesitated to try it.

I called them up, those near, those far, those within sound of my voice, those within the intent of my action. Deep dwellers. By Bintomar. By Favian. By Shielsas. By Eutras. By the scent of this herb, by the sound of this bell, by the color of this stone. By the flame I flicked from a fingertip, by the winding of a hair. Dwellers of the deep, all you childlike creatures of the depths, come up, come up and into Fangel, where Valearn who loves children awaits you.

The first sign I had that something had heard me was the rattle of a cobble in the street. I peered between the bars, quickly brushing the necessaries of the spell into my pack. I didn't want the dwellers even looking for me. I had used Valearn's name, and that was where they should be going.

The cobble rattled again, heaved up, banged upon another to reveal a cavity below out of which a pair of luminous eyes stared at the walls of Fangel. What came out of the hole did look childlike. Short. Slender. Large headed. Arms and legs nicely proportioned. There were not children anywhere with such teeth as those the dweller had, however. When the thing smiled, the grin split its head in two and both halves of the grin were fang-fringed and eager.

Now, quickly, protection from these specific creatures for the baby and Sylbie. That was a simple distraint, done in a moment. It wouldn't keep the dwellers away from the girl, but it would keep them from harming her. And they would find her. I was certain of that.

Up and over the wall once more. Follow the trail of forms pouring out of the earth where they went sniffing, seeking, like hounds upon the trail. They called to one another, chuckling, a pleasant chuckle, not like Valearn's. I remembered hearing them, long ago, when Murzy first did bridge magic over Stonybrook. Almost, one would like to pat them on the head. One did not, wary of those teeth.

A calling from this one to that one, running feet, taloned toes scraping upon the stones. I looked back. They were still coming up out of the hole. I frowned, reviewing what I'd done. It had been a rather unlimited summons.

Chatter of voices; baby cry again, fretful. I went toward it, through the crowded dweller forms to find Sylbie crouched against a wall, baby tight held against her, just getting ready to scream. They weren't menacing her, just looking at her, but she was ready to scream anyhow.

'Don't,' I said. 'Get up from there and follow me.'

I turned on the dwellers. 'Valearn,' I hissed. 'By the stone, by the hair, by the bell, by the flame, by the scent of the herb, find Valearn.' They chittered at me, mockingly, knowing well enough what they were here to do and that it suited them marvelously, but still taking time to make a bit of deviltry over it. Pesky, as Queynt had said.

'What are they?' shrilled Sylbie, barely able to stand.

'Never mind what they are. You and I have to get out of this city. Away.'

'They're hunting me. With horses, the Duke said. And with strange creatures he wakened up, like people only not. Like lizards. Like frogs. And when they catch me, they'll kill me.'

'Very probably. Which they will do if you insist on standing here talking. There's worse than the Duke abroad. The Ogress is looking for Bryan, there. She wants to eat him.'

This was perhaps the only thing I could have said to get her moving. Threats to herself paralyzed her. Threats to Bryan mobilized her. Ah, motherhood. Nature is quite wonderful.

We went back the way I had come, back to the grilled courtyard. I found it by following the line of dwellers, who were still coming out of the hole in the cobbles, single file, seemingly in endless numbers. One or two of them said 'boo' at me as we went past, but I spat a spark at them and they let us be. I went over the wall, unbarred the gate, and let Sylbie in, barring the gate behind her. With any luck at all, the hunt would go by us. Sylbie sank to the floor, sagging there like a bundle of laundry. The baby seemed to have gone to sleep, and I fervently hoped he stayed that way.

I hung in the grill, watching the dwellers pop out of the hole, one after another like so many corks. Far off something screamed. Pombi, I think. There was an avalanche of laughter, dweller laughter, so they'd found some mischief to get up to.

Horns again. Hooves at the end of the street I was watching. I pulled a scarf to hide my face, leaving one eye to peer with.

There at the end of the street came a mounted man, the Duke of Betand, perhaps, or even the Merchant himself. And to either side walked big men in remnants of Gamesmen garb, Tragamors without their helms, with only arms telling what they were. Elators. Armigers. Blind-eyed, marching as in sleep. And scaly creatures out of nightmare, armed with whips. The whips were being dragged, slithering on the stones. It sounded like a convention of serpents. I dropped to the floor, crawled over beside Sylbie, and put my arms around her. Whatever else happened, I didn't want her to yell.

I needn't have worried. No one could have heard her if she had screamed her head off. The dwellers had discovered the hunter. The scaly creatures had discovered the dwellers. What had begun in black, mysterious silence under the swimming moon went on in a tumult of sound such as I had never heard and do not wish to hear again.

Laughter, screams, curses, whip cracks, snarls, shouts, horses neighing and screaming, hooves clattering on stone, growling, more mocking laughter, shrieks, howls, and all the time more dwellers popping out of the hole in the ground. Queynt had said they were not common. I think Queynt must have been mistaken.

None of which was helping us escape from Fangel. I had hoped the dwellers would keep Valearn busy and the hunt would pass by. Neither had happened. They all met in a general confusion, much of it outside the grill, and there was no possibility of getting through that mess. Moreover, the noise had wakened the baby.

So, I said to myself, on the verge of hysteria, why don't we make it a really good mess? I fixed Sylbie with a hard, hypnotic eye and said, 'Can I depend upon you to stay right here until I return for you?' She nodded fearfully and I took it (the more fool I) for agreement. 'Don't move,' I said. 'I'll be back shortly.'

Up the wall once more, this time to perch upon the top, well above the melee below. The wall stretched for a long block toward the residence, and I ran along its top, unnoticed by any of the participants in the brouhaha. At the corner, two dwellers were strangling a lizard man, and I thanked them for the courtesy as I jumped off the wall and went past. The next street was fairly empty. A pombi was trying to play bakklewheep with two dwellers in the middle of the block, they evading him and he getting angrier about it by the minute. He was too busy to notice me.

Next block was the residence itself, still dark and silent. The great gong hung in its usual place, the striker beside it, and I put every measure of strength I had ever possessed into hitting it, not once or twice but three horrendous times.

Lights came on. Doors opened. People poured out, just as they had done on that morning we had arrived in Fangel. Food carts, guardsmen, populace, more of the lizard warriors, more of other kinds of things, too. Though their responses were fairly limited by the crystals they had been given, the populace had not been prepared for lizard men or any of the other creatures that swarmed from the Merchant's warehouses. They ran screaming through the streets, their voices betraying terror even as their words did honors to Betand, to Huldra, to Dedrina Dreadeye. They had no other words to scream with and were forbidden the safety of their houses by the tyranny of the gong.

Better than I had hoped, great mobs of them made for the gates. Of course. When the gong rang, the gates were always open. Good. Now back to Sylbie.

I ran openly in the street. There were so many creatures running, people and monsters both, that I was merely one of a throng that spread in every direction, like an anthill that had been overturned. One block, two, down toward the grilled window . . .

To stop, horrified. No. Furious. The gate into the little courtyard was open. Sylbie had unbarred the gate and left.

I found her two streets down, toward the gates. Unfortunately, Valearn had found her first.

Valearn had the baby. Sylbie had Valearn by one leg. There were a dozen deep dwellers fastened onto Valearn at various points. Valearn was paying no attention. Her fangs were bared and she lowered them to Bryan's throat . . .

And all that had gone before became as nothing. There was no baby in her hands. There was a boiling, formless, gorbling cloud, a keening scream of rage and hatred battering her with its sound, its horrible sound, driving her before it like some farm zeller while she screamed in genuine horror, Valearn the Ogress, victim of what she had sought.

I sagged on the stones beside Sylbie, trying to hold my splitting head together against that sound, mouthing, 'What in the name of all old gods? . . . ' There was a break in the howling.

'The unborn,' she whimpered. 'It's the unborn. It's Bryan. He went back to being what he was before. He was frightened. I told her not to frighten him.'

'You knew he would do that?'

'He does that. Whenever he gets angry. Or doesn't get fed on time. Or gets too wet.'

'You hadn't seen fit to mention it.'

She arranged her dress and looked at me with honest-seeming eyes. 'I didn't think it was important.' Little liar.

'How long will he stay that way?'

'I imagine until he kills Valearn. She bit him.'

'And then?'

'And then he'll find me, wherever I am.' Was there a note of satisfaction in that?

'Outside the walls?'

'Of course. He may be very temperamental, as my mother would say, but he's quite bright. He'll find me.'

'Then let's go, Sylbie. Let's leave Fangel to its own mighty troubles.'

Which we did. On the south side of the city there were wagons parked that had been waiting to enter Fangel on the morrow. I made arrangements with a wagoner and his wife to take Sylbie south, all the way to Zinter. 'From there,' I told her, no longer worrying about her safety. 'From there, keep going south. Here are enough coins to pay your way. Don't waste them. Get to the Bright Demesne, south of Schooltown, on Lake Yost. Once there, ask for Mavin. That's Peter's mother. I think she'll want to meet her grandson.' Two of a kind, I thought.

'I was waiting for Peter.' Shyness personified, sweet little look out of the corner of her eye.

'Don't, Sylbie. Peter's a Shifter. I think it probable that Byran is, too. This manifestation of his is strange, but it fits with being Shifter. Shifter young need to be reared by their own. I know Bryan comes back to you now, but when he begins to change into snakey things' – why did I enjoy seeing her shudder at the thought? – 'he'll need some older Shifter to control him and teach him. I'm sure if we put our heads together, we can come up with a better plan for you than just waiting for Peter. I hope that doesn't make you too unhappy.'

'He was different once,' she said, a dreamy look in those violet eyes. 'In Betand, he was wonderful.'

'That wasn't really Peter,' I said brutally, telling her who it really was.

'Trandilar! But she's . . . she's . . . '

'Trandilar is the great Queen of Beguilement. She's female, and who would understand better what some young female would enjoy? It wasn't Peter. Now, can I rely on you to go with these people, or will you do something stupid again?'

She nodded. It was a real nod, I think. 'I'll do what you say, Jinian. Tell Peter . . . tell him I decided it wouldn't work.'

'I'll do that.'

I trusted that little nod not at all. I watched from the forest until the wagon left in the morning. Both Bryan and Sylbie were aboard.

CHAPTER TEN

There were many dead in Fangel. The Merchant was one, the Duke of Betand another. The pombis and the gnarlibar had been less successfully hunted than they had planned. I found Valearn's body just down the street from the place she had bitten the baby. Her neck was broken, it appeared. There was no sign of Huldra. Nor of Dedrina Dreadeye. On reflection, I thought it likely they had left Fangel before the confusion started and were on their way south with the crystals they had been told to distribute. Of all in that group, those two were the most dangerous, and I regretted that they still lived.

There was great disorder in Fangel. The dwellers had gone back to their depths, but there were bodies everywhere, and roaming beasts, and those strange creatures that had come out of the Merchant's warehouses. The city was not likely to survive. It had no real reason for being. Already the wagons that had been assembled to enter the gates were turning away. They would find other customers.

I went to the residence. It was luxurious and spacious and empty. I knew which room Huldra had occupied by seeing how it was littered with bits and pieces from her spell casting and from the great flood of mixed blood and water on the floors. Her sending had returned, but Huldra had been gone. She did not know, then, that the giants were dead.

Looking the rooms over, I shuddered. I knew what some of the litter was for, and it was the kind of stuff that the seven would repudiate, always. Still, it was best to know how deeply into the art she was. The answer: deeply indeed. She knew things I did not. Of that I was sure. I picked up what food was available in the place and went out the northern gate. It stood open and unguarded.

A day traveling once again the same old way. Around ever-deepening masses of shadow, down toward Bleem. I didn't go into the village, though I did speak to a herdsman on the road to tell him Storm Grower was dead. If there were any left there or any who had returned, let them enjoy that news. The next day I got to the red pillar of stone. I had seen it from the valley before. Up close it was even more imposing, an obelisk that pointed a long black finger of shadow down into a little valley, much damaged by storm but with a small lake sparkling at its bottom.

The evening was spent thinking before the fire, pulling the shreds of evidence together. I stared for a long time at the blue crystal. I didn't taste it, just stared at it. There was no one near to make demands upon me. No rescuing to be done, no sneaking or slying. No great white roads to be repaired. Merely quiet in the evening with the fire making small scrolls of smoke, ephemeral writing upon the slate of the sky, meaning flowing into meaning and mystery into mystery.

And, on thinking it over, I decided I had been right. Right all along. Everything I had told Peter was true. All the evidence pointed in one way and one way only. I felt as I had felt so long ago, traveling toward Bleer with Peter, when he put the clues to a mystery in my hands and asked me to make sense of it. Now, as then, all the pieces were in my hands, or in my head. The great flitchhawk who had granted me a boon in Chimmerdong, and the d'bor wife, and the gobblemole. The story of Little Star and the Daylight Bell. The Oracle. The Eesties. Yellow crystals and blue, separated by a thousand years of time, more or less. What was a thousand years, after all? Even to Vitior Vulpas Queynt it was a mere lifetime. My illness in Chimmerdong. The diagnoses of Bartelmy of the Ban, the Dervish, my mother. All these. And they did make a kind of horrible sense. No matter how I turned them, there was no other explanation. Only this one.

So. Could anything be done?

If anything could be done, who would do it? Not one young Wize-ard alone, surely. It was all very well for Bartelmy of the Ban, my mother, to set me a gigantic task in Chimmerdong, saying it was mine and none other's. No one's life had hung on that. Had *seemed* to hang on that, I amended. If I had failed, things were no worse. Though I had succeeded, were they any better?

But this. This meant an ending. For all of us. For everything. Tree and flower, hill and road, sea and shore, man, woman, child, all beasts, all birds, all fishes.

And though I might do what I could alone, surely it would be better if a disciplined body of persons were to work at it as well.

So. I thought about that for some time. Finally, I resolved upon a sending. Not an eater of blood, like Huldra's, but a seeker of persons. It did not take a blood sacrifice, at least not much of one. A few drops of my own, was all. I sent it out into the world to seek Bartelmy of the Ban. She had said we would meet again. Why not now? Now, when I needed her. The sending pulled at me. I was like the reel on a fishing pole; it was the line with the hook; and it pulled at me, reeling out and out and out until there was nothing left of me at all. Only the line, spun into the world, far, far beyond any place I could see. I lay upon the ground, close-wrapped in my cloak, and let the line spin out.

For a very long time, I knew nothing. Then the line reeled in, restoring me to myself. The hook had caught something. I lay on a long bank above a length of flat that could only be a buried stretch of road. Down this flat the Dervish came, a whirling silver cone balanced on its tip, blurring with motion, settling before me into a still column of fringed quiet.

'Jinian, Dervish daughter,' it said.

'Bartelmy?' I replied from the ground. It had not sounded exactly like Bartelmy and yet almost like.

'No. She is not far from here. I was closer, however. I am one of her near kindred, alerted to expect your coming.'

'Even I did not know I would be coming this way.'

'Still, Bartelmy had thought it likely. When your sending came, we were not surprised. A Seer's vision, perhaps.'

Murzemire Hornloss, I thought. Who had not been distressed at my going into the north. Was it because she had known what would happen? Had she known why I would leave the others?

'You say you expected my coming. Have you plans concerning me?'

'Not plans precisely, since we do not know why you have come. Provisions, certainly, for one not exactly a Dervish. A rare thing among us to provide for one outside our company.' The Dervish gestured off down the flat stretch. 'If you are strong enough to rise and walk?'

I struggled to my feet. The line had been reeled in, but I was still weak enough to stagger.

'Heat food for yourself. I can wait.'

The Dervish not only waited, but helped me by gathering sticks for the fire and talking gently about trees and clouds while I ate. Much refreshed, I buried the fire and stood ready to walk beside the Dervish, who surprised me by walking beside me, stride on stride. It noticed my surprise. 'We walk, sometimes. Sometimes we eat, drink. Rarely, we sleep.' It made a sound, almost like a chuckle.

'You astonish me,' I murmured. 'That sounded almost like laughter.'

'We even laugh, sometimes. Bartelmy is among the most serious of us. She finds little to laugh about. I can find it amusing to walk beside a Dervish daughter who is no Dervish, who is a Beast-talker, so I am told. Speak to that owl yonder and tell me what it says.' The Dervish gestured and I saw a tiny dot upon a branch, so far at the limit of vision it could scarcely be seen at all.

It was too far to speak in its language, so I spoke to it silently and it replied in muted tones which floated toward us on the wind. 'It says, "Good day,"' I said. 'As would any polite and sensible beast.'

The Dervish laughed again, a very small sound, but unmistakably amusement.

'Where are we going?'

'The pervasion of the Dervishes is nearby.'

'What is your name?'

'Cernaby of the Soul.'

'What do they mean, your names? Bartelmy of the Ban? What is that? Of the Soul? What sense does it make?'

'If you have ever lain beneath Bartelmy's Ban, you would know. As for me, I can see souls, Dervish daughter. As you would see a flame burning. I see yours now, hot and red with angry pity. It must itch you, burning like that.'

This surprised me, sure as I was I had achieved a kind of balance. 'I suppose yours are never like that.'

Cernaby did not answer, merely turned to lay her hands upon my eyes, like a mask. I could see through them to the flames that surrounded her, blue as the noon sky, cool and limpid as water. I looked down at myself to see my hands and arms, blossoming with heat. 'You can dim it,' the Dervish whispered. 'Watch it, concentrate upon it, think of it turning orange, then yellow, then green. Finally blue, blue as water.' She laughed a little. 'As your dams of the seven would say, "Consider water."'

With Cernaby's hands across my eyes, I could do nothing else. The flames upon me leapt and danced as I watched them, thinking them faded, thinking them cooled. At last they were green as grass upon me, only an occasional flicker of yellow lighting the edges of the flames. I could cool them no further than that. Cernaby took her hands away and I blinked up at the evening stars. I had not been conscious of the time passing. 'It will come easier next time,' said Cernaby. I felt a little calmer, that was all, together with a little core of anger at her having wasted so much time.

We walked farther then, along the winding flat among the jungle trees, then up a rising trail that wound above the trees toward two pillars of stone high upon the ridge. We looked down to our left to see mighty hedges, solid as walls, twisting, turning, winding upon themselves as far as I could see.

'The Great Maze lies below us,' said Cernaby, 'league upon league of it, from the mountains to the sea. When last the band marched here, it spent ten years marching through the edges of the Maze. It is said there are cities in the Maze lost from all outside contact for millennia. It is said no man knows the extent of it or the way to its center.' She pointed to this impenetrable wall of foliage below the trail we were on. 'That is the edge of it.'

'What is it, exactly? I had always thought it was roads with walls or hedges, full of misleading turnings.'

Cernaby again made the sound of quiet amusement. 'More than that, Jinian. Men can climb walls, cut through hedges. We will go a little way in and I will show you.' Along our trail several little paths went down the slope into openings in the hedges. She spun down one of these. I followed.

A narrow door was cut into the solid green. A narrow path stretched inward. Cernaby stood upon it at some small distance, where it made a turning. 'Here,' she called. 'Come to me here.'

I took a step.

Onto the rim rock of a high cliff, so near the edge I staggered back in fear. Below me lay a shadowed bowl of green. The dawn, or sunset, was on my face and on the rock at my feet. From above came a shrieking, a banshee howl, mightier than any number of voices. I looked up to see a dart of silver falling, bellowing as it came, downward and downward, the sound shivering the rocks on which I stood so that I fell to my knees, hands over ears, watching in amazement as the thing landed in the bowl, as a door opened in it and something strange came out. Strange? So I felt, and yet it was obviously human. Nothing strange about it? Why this feeling of intense curiosity, this thought of weirdness?

'Jinian,' I heard the voice. 'Turn to your left and walk toward that midnight tree, the first one. Go behind it.' Cernaby's voice. 'Jinian!' Commanding now. Obediently, I turned and made my way to the midnight tree, outpost of a grove. I moved behind it . . .

Onto the Wastes of Bleer. It was as I had seen it last, barren and cold and dry. Full of thorn and devil's spear. Heaped with wind's bones, which were not wind's bones at all but the bones of the ancient creatures of this place. Coming toward me out of the eastern sky was a glowing ball of flame. No sound, only this ball, hurtling toward me. 'Jinian. Quickly, to your right, and down into that little empty crevasse.' I did not like the look of the doom approaching so made quick work of the directions; half a dozen steps to my right and down . . .

Into a hall, vast and gray, where my footsteps echoed whispering down corridors of pillars. From a high window came a crowd roar so threatening I turned instinctively to flee. 'No!' cried the voice in warning. 'Turn again. The other way! Beside the pool.'

Resolutely I turned back, stumbling across a fallen pedestal, kicking a silvery lamp that lay there in my path. I caught myself. Another pedestal lay across the way, the book it had held flung against the far wall. I walked beside the low coping of a pool, coughing as a fitful draft blew smoke into my eyes, so that I stepped blindly . . .

Onto a road. Cernaby was beside me. 'Here,' Cernaby said, stepping in a certain direction. I followed. We stood outside the Maze on the path we had left only moments before. High on the ridge the tall stones brooded above us.

'What is it?' I asked. 'I can't believe it!'

'Who can? One time long since, Mind Healer Talley came here to confer with the Dervish paramounts. She spent long hours within the edge of the Great Maze and left at last, saying the places within it were memories.'

'Memories?'

'She did not explain. We did not ask, for at that time we were greatly concerned with another thing. The Maze, we then felt, was not the greatest mystery of Lom. There are many things about Lom we do not understand.'

'Lom, Cernaby? Is that what this district is called?'

'Lom. The world. This world. We took it from the language of the Shadowpeople, whose word for the soil is "lom".'

I realized suddenly it was so. What had the little people called to me when I'd released them in Fangel? 'Lolly duro balta lus lom.' *Walk well upon the lovely land.* I turned to examine the leafy walls of the Maze behind me. 'You say the band marched through that? How could they?'

'They hired a guide. The only guide. They put on blindfolds and marched to the music. They didn't turn. At night, the guide would stop them in some relatively safe place until the morning, when they were blindfolded again. It's the only way.'

'But you . . .'

'But I know a few short ways in and out. Not to the center. No one does, except the guide. Perhaps not even the guide. No, I know only a few short ways.'

'How did you learn them?'

'Oh, step on step. One step in, turn and take one step, take that step back. Turn and take another. Take that step back. And again. Each time returning to the same place, building the chain longer with each try. In that first short chain you walked, there are many other ways out to other places.' Cernaby made the amused sound once again. 'I don't know what good it does to know that. Except to show a Dervish daughter what to be wary of.'

'Who is the guide?' I already knew but wanted it verified. Who else could it be?

'Bartelmy tells me you have met it. It calls itself the Oracle.'

'The Oracle!' I spat. 'It has probably had no time for guiding recently. It is too busy giving comfort to giants and distributing death crystals to the unwary!'

'We know of the death crystals. One more reason why we are gathered in the pervasion now, to talk of this.' We went up the last little way to the ridge. At either side the great stones peered down at us, an electric tingle between them. Had I been alone, I don't think they would have let me pass. Cernaby stopped, looking downward. 'And we have arrived at the pervasion.'

We looked down on a long clearing through which the road ran, bulging at the center into a wide oval, then narrowing once more to continue over the next rise. To either side were small houses. No, I thought after a moment, not really large enough to be houses. Small, one-room places perhaps two manheights square, neatly made, but little more than sheds. They reminded me of the small outbuildings in which domestic zeller are shut at night to protect them from prowlers.

Outside each of these stood a Dervish, still as a tree.

'What are they doing?' I asked.

'Thinking. Practicing. Becoming.'

'How long will they stand like that?'

'Some days, perhaps. Some for a season. Or until the next obligatory takes place in which they must join. There is an obligatory going on now in the next node.' The Dervish led on, between the rows of silent figures. I sensed that the very air around her was under tension. It vibrated like the string of an instrument, full of silent harmonics. I could hear them, could have sung them had I the voice for it, and it seemed that the soil sang in this same way. Soil. Trees. Air. We moved over the next small rise.

Again the road bulged into an oval, paved space, this time occupied with silent ranks of Dervishes, all moving together like a wind-waved field of grain.

'An obligatory,' whispered Cernaby.

Below us the Dervishes spun and stilled, advanced, retreated, twisted with outstretched arms, then fell into pillar quiet. From somewhere music came, at times insistent, at others almost lost among the sounds of the trees. It was the previous music made manifest, and it was some time before I realized it came from the Dervishes themselves.

'They dance their dedication,' whispered Cernaby. She laid her hands over my eyes, revealing the pure blue flames in which the Dervishes moved. It reminded me of something, an elusive thought that came and slipped away.

'Shhh,' whispered Cernaby. 'They are almost at an end. We will wait until they finish.'

The dance went on for some time, making me wonder when it had begun that so long a time was considered 'almost at an end'. Still, my impatience faded as I watched. The surging movement was hypnotic, relaxing, like watching waves move around rocks on a quiet shore. This relaxation troubled me. Deep inside, I chafed against it.

At last the music faded into silence, the dance into immobility. This, too, was part of the obligatory, for they stood still in silence for some time before the Dervishes moved away toward their huts.

'It is likely Bartelmy has arrived,' said Cernaby. 'We will go to her cell. We have arranged it so that you may stay there as well, though this is never done once a child is past babyhood.' That sound of amusement. 'We are a solitary people. Perhaps we have carried our reclusion too far.'

Bartelmy was waiting for us beside one of the white-painted huts, a silver pillar beside the weathered gray of the door. She said, 'I said I would come to you, and you to me. So we have come. Welcome, Jinian Footseer.'

'Call her rather Dervish daughter,' said Cernaby, a note of admonition in her voice. 'She calmed herself into the green, Bartelmy, and stood for half a day of the obligatory.'

'Would we have expected less?'

'Yes, considering how she was reared. I was doubtful, Bartelmy.'

'I was not.' The pillar turned a little, as though to examine me more closely. I heated a bit at this, at their talking of me as though I could not hear them.

I smiled nonetheless. 'Is this to be another game without a name, Bartelmy? Like the one in Chimmerdong?'

The pillar shook itself, a negation. 'No, Jinian. Except that you are one always eager for answers, and there are not always answers. If we have an answer, we will give it to you. If we do not give it, you will know we do not have it to give.'

They did not know I had come to give them answers. Not yet, though. 'You expected me!' It was half a challenge.

'Murzemire Hornloss told me long since you would come here at this time. Yes. We expected you.'

'But you do not know why I came?'

'No. Murzemire saw you. She saw Storm Grower. She saw Dream Miner. She saw shadow. She saw the Daylight Bell, broken. And when she had seen all this, she told us it might mean nothing much.'

Cernaby laughed. 'Nothing much.' I realized the laughter had grief in it. Perhaps they had seen something of the truth. 'Nothing much.'

The words spun among us in the quiet clearing, without reverberation, without echo, and yet without end. 'Nothing much.' Said humorously. Said without consequence. Said without anger. Said in the blue, my heart said; said in the blue they so much cultivated. In me fury bloomed like red flowers. 'Nothing much.' This calm interchange had the very flavor of Dervishes in it. I shook away the spell the dance had put me under, demanding concentration from myself. It would not do to fall under their sway, their patience,

198

their strangeness. There was too much patience among Dervishes. The time for patience had passed.

I had not planned what I did next. I had never done it before. It came out of my belly, out of my lungs, my heart, all at once full blown. Before I knew what I was doing, my hands were out and I was making that gesture which the seven called 'Eye of the Star'. It was an Imperative. It allowed no choice. Though I did not know its meaning – might never, so the seven had said – I put all my fury behind it, all my red flame. I felt it going out of me like a shout, a summons, a demand. They stared at me from behind their fringes. Had anyone ever evoked the Eye of the Star upon them before? There was only one spell stronger than this; one I would probably never know enough to use.

'Nothing much?' I said. 'A little more than that, I think. Storm Grower sat in a cavern making moonlets fall upon this world, destroying cities. Dream Miner sat there as well, corrupting the messages of the world into filthy intent and evil consequence. Hell's Maw was his doing, and the corruption of Pfarb Durim, and they only a few among many. Even now his will speeds south to be spread among our kindred there. The giants are dead, but their evil lives.

'Knowing nothing of this, I came north. I came, to be with Peter. Nothing seemed as important as that. As we traveled, we began to find dead people, men, women, children, even babies, all along the roads, all with yellow crystals hung upon them or sucked away to shards. Peter saw it, but it did not seem to tell him anything. Queynt saw it. Him, it troubled, but he did not see in it what I did.

'We came to Bloome, and Bloome led us to Fangel, where the Dream Merchant was – with guests. Huldra. Valearn. Dedrina Dreadeye. And with captives. Sylbie, a girl Peter had known in Betand, and Sylbie's baby, Peter's baby. And two people from far over the Western Sea, people Mavin Manyshaped had known years

199

ago. Beedie. Roges. And with them a creature so strange I can scarcely believe it . . .'

'Come inside,' said Bartelmy with enormous effort. It took much for her to break the Eye, but she did it. 'Cernaby also. We will forget the eremitic laws. We will sit together, drink together, talk together . . .'

The pillar that was Bartelmy was shivering in the effort of control. I knew why. Dervishes were not constrained by others. I had evoked the star-eye upon her. I was being allowed this presumption only because I was Bartelmy's daughter, but if we went inside, all urgency would be set aside. Oh, I longed to be patient, quiet, to put decision aside, to take time . . .

I made the gesture again, even stronger. 'There is no time,' I said in my Dervish voice, cold and demanding. From the edges of my eyes I saw a multitude gathering about us, a thousand silver pillars upon the hillside, turned toward me. There was fury there, barely withheld. They had felt my summons. Their resentment was a palpable menace. Bartelmy wanted to save me. Too late. I could not be saved.

I said, 'All the time we might have spent talking has been wasted away. Listen to me, Dervishes! The piss-yellow crystals come out of this world – this Lom, as you call it. A kind of milk secreted in pockets of stone, and out of this milk a crystal grows. Little tubes run from the crystal pockets down into the earth, deep into the rock. The giants beneath the earth sent their messengers out to find who made these things. We have traveled league upon league wondering who made these things. You have gathered here to discuss who it is who makes these things.

'They are not made!

'They are not made by man or by any other creature. They come from the world itself. The woman from over the sea calls them message crystals. The little old man at the crystal mine says there are no more blue ones, no more green ones, only these yellow ones, only these death ones.'

200

'We know.' Bartelmy's voice, hushed hesitant, plaintive, beating my will away. Was she begging for my life from her kin? 'We would talk of this matter, Jinian. Consider it.'

'*There is no time to consider it!* When Beedie told me what the crystals are called over the sea, I knew then. These are not dreams which the world dreams. These are messages which the world sends. To itself. To all parts of itself. To bunwit and tree rat, to gobble-mole and d'bor wife. To Shadowman and gnarlibar, krylobos and pombi. To Eesties. To mankind. And there is only one message now. Death. Peace and a final contentment and death.'

She cried at me with the last of her strength. 'Why does the world want its creatures dead? We have known this for some time. But we do not know why.'

'*Listen to me!*' I stamped my foot in my frenzy then, knowing I must be blazing red to their perception, seeing them shiver in an agony of what? Anger? 'Listen. You're not understanding me. The messages are not to the *creatures.* The messages are to *all parts of itself.*

'*Do not ask me why the world wants its creatures dead! Ask why it wants itself dead!*'

Stillness then. A thousand Dervish pillars standing around me, not moving. The fringes did not shiver but merely hung, still, as though extruded of some hard metal. The anger was gone as suddenly as it had come. Nothing moved, and yet I felt something go out from them, a hard blow, a wave of . . . something. Pain? No. More a question. I looked up to see them there in their thousands. I stood at the center of an ominous circle, so silent, so utterly silent.

I made the gesture of release.

'Itself,' said Bartelmy at last. 'Sisters. Dervishes. Could we have been mistaken?'

'Mistaken?' A breath. A sigh.

'Mistaken?' I demanded. 'Mistaken in what? What have you done?'

'Not done,' breathed Cernaby. 'Been.'

'Long ago,' said Bartelmy, 'far in the past, there were creatures who ran the roads of Lom. Looking deep into the past, we have seen them.'

'I saw them, too,' I said impatiently. 'When I looked into the past in Chimmerdong.'

'But those creatures run the roads no longer. Not since we came. Lom cries for this journey to be made, this endless journey.'

'The blind runners do it,' I said. 'All the time. Every year.'

'Not correctly. Not as it should be done. They cannot. The roads are broken. And they are still too near to . . . to humanity.'

'And you are not?'

'We have bred ourselves for centuries to run the roads of Lom as we believed another creature did before us. We have believed this to be Lom's will. But if this is Lom's will, then Lom would not will to die. If Lom wills to die, then what does Lom will for us?'

'To die also,' I said flatly. 'I don't know what you Dervishes have been up to all these centuries, Bartelmy of the Ban. I don't know what Barish thought he was doing fooling around with that hundred thousand Gamesmen under the mountain. I don't know what any of us thought we were doing. All I know is that every sign points to this world wishing *itself* dead.'

'But this must be recent . . .'

'Not all that recent, no. Within old Buttufor's lifetime, certainly. He can remember the crystals coming out blue and green when he was young. He is over a hundred now. But it has not been long.'

'Why? Why?'

'Listen to me,' I said again. 'I'm not going to waste my time asking why. I've been thinking about this for days now. In Bloome I thought about it. Outside Fangel, it seemed sure. After leaving the others, I did nothing but think about it. If a person wished himself dead, we would assume he was sick. Injured, perhaps. Well, we know well enough this world is injured. You told me that, Bartelmy. It was you told me to fix the roads in Chimmerdong. Was that only an exercise? Some kind of lesson you wished me to learn? Or did it mean something?

'And if it meant something, then why are you here? Why are you doing your dances when there are roads broken everywhere? Why are we wondering why the world wishes itself dead when we are doing nothing to heal it?'

'How do you know this?' A sigh again. Was there a hint of anguish in it? Of injured pride?

'I know it because I am Dervish born, Gamesman reared, wize-art trained. I know it because I am Jinian Footseer and have run those roads while you all were studying to do so. I know it because I have seen all its signs and portents across all the lands, seen the clues to it where I have walked and ridden, heard its voice in the quiet reaches of the night. I know it because I know it.

'I know it because logic tells me it must have happened. A world, this one, Lom, which has existed for untold time, which is in balance with itself, which is healthy, which sends messages to all parts of itself in order to stay in balance, to stay healthy. Messages to groles and Shadowmen and Eesties. And into this world comes man, the destroyer, for whom no message has been made.

'What then? What does logic say must have happened? It says that Lom must have made a message for men and about men. A blue crystal, telling men their place in this world. Showing them the balance. And the message was sent.

'But evil walked upon the roads of the world, evil and envy and pride. Evil which did not want man in this world at all. Evil which believed man would die if deprived of the message meant for him. Not knowing Lom would die, instead. So the message meant for man was stolen away, taken into deep caverns and hidden there, where *no* creature might receive it.

'Except Queynt, who was given the message by the Shadowpeople in the long ago.

'Except a few, here and there, who found it without knowing what they found.

'Except the people of a chasm far over the sea, who found it, knew what they had found, and brought it to Mavin Manyshaped, their friend.

'Except for Jinian, who took that message and carried it with her and carries it now!'

I staggered. Suddenly my legs wouldn't hold me and I plopped to my knees, shaking. 'A message meant for me. And you. And every human person here. And for all other creatures as well.'

I had given almost all of them to Peter, retaining only eight or ten. I took one of the small blue crystals out of my pouch, almost dropping it from trembling fingers. I passed it first to Bartelmy. 'There isn't much of it. Make it go as far as you can . . .'

'Hold!' The voice hummed from the back of the throng, a reverberating, gonglike sound. 'Hold, Bartelmy of the Ban! I, Marno of the Morning, speak. You hold a crystal in your hand. Has Jinian Footseer tasted it?'

'I have not.'

'Then why should we?' The voice was cold and scornful. My heart sank beneath the weight of it.

'I will if you wish. I have not.'

'Why have you not?'

'Because I know what it says. And I am vain and proud and would do the message's will of my own will, knowing I do it of my own sense and intelligence, without compulsion. But if I cannot gain your understanding in any other way, I will taste it.'

'Taste it, then!'

'No!' This was Bartelmy, in a voice that ached. 'This is a Dervish daughter. My daughter. If she would do a thing of her own will, is there any Dervish would say her nay? And if I would do a thing of my will, is there any Dervish who will deny me? So, what I do, I do of my own will.' The crystal disappeared beneath the

204

fringes of her veil and in a moment reappeared to be thrust into Cernaby's hand.

It passed from there beneath the concealing fringes, here and there, mouth to hand to hand to mouth, from one silver pillar to another. Some refused it. Most tasted it. I gave them all the others but three. Fringes shook, quivered, bodies turned. One reeled into another. Some cried out. Then stillness. The Dervishes were there in their thousands, assembled rank on rank, and the rear ranks quivered now as the remnant of the crystal passed.

'How long?' asked Bartelmy. 'How long, Jinian?'

'How long? How long ago did this world send us that message? You guess, Bartelmy. Soon after we came here, I would suppose. If we came here a thousand years ago, perhaps a few hundred less than that. More or less.'

'And who robbed us of it?'

'I don't know. I suspect, but I don't know. A race of creatures, ambitious, proud, who did not want this man on this world. A race of beings who sought to drive me away, who gathered the message crystals up, every one, and who took them to the cavern where the giants dwelt. Some creature which hated man.' I could not identify that creature. I suspected. Only suspected.

'Is it too late?'

'It may be. I suppose we could give up with good grace. Lie down and die. Disport ourselves for a time, like lice on a corpse. Or go on dancing while the shadow comes. The shadow is part of this, I'm sure. You've seen it Bartelmy. I've seen it. Perhaps all you Dervishes have seen it. It flows now, from somewhere, like a flood. Where is it coming from?' Silence greeted this, but they did not disagree. 'Of one thing I am very sure. If this world dies, we will not survive it long, but we might play while there is time.

'Or we might try, whether it is too late or not. Try to get the roads fixed. Try to get some runners on them. Yourselves, since that's what you've been breeding for. What race ran these roads before we came?'

'Eesties. We have seen so with the deep look.'

'Eesties? Really?' This did surprise me. 'I thought it might be Shadowpeople.'

'No. Eesties. We look into the past and see them spinning upon the roads, spinning into the ancient cites. They spin. As we do. Those odd doors in Pfarb Durim? Larger at the top? They are Eesty doors. It was an Eesty city. All across the world there are ruins with those doors.'

'That's why you're Dervishes. You copied them.'

'We tried. It is said one of them helped us originally.'

'You copied them, but then just sat about waiting?'

'We thought . . . we thought the day would come. We were holding ourselves in readiness for the day.'

'The day when someone else would fix things?'

'The day things would be fixed, somehow. Yes.' A collective sigh. Then, 'Jinian, why was it you who saw this?'

I considered this. How had I known it? How did anyone know things? 'I don't know, Bartelmy. There always has to be someone to see things first. By the time Queynt gets to Himaggery in the south, others may have seen. Surely – oh, surely you will not merely stay here in your pervasion and let it happen.'

'What can we do?'

'Mavin told me you have powers. You changed Himaggery into a beast one time.'

'We made him think he was.'

'Then you can make Tragamors and Sorcerers think they are road builders. You can make Demons think they are hunting fustigars to seek out whoever robbed us of the message. You can make Healers think they are Lom fixers. I don't know. You can do *something*!'

'If there are more of these crystals across the sea,' said Cernaby, 'they must be brought here. Shared out.'

'Better late than not at all,' came a voice from the ranked multitude. 'Better a tardy lover than a lonely bed.' A quiver of what could have been laughter ran through the ranks. Laughter? I was shocked at this, realizing only later that it was the laughter of despair.

'You can help Himaggery decide how to get west over the sea and back again. It took Beedie and Roges three years, and we don't have three years to spend. Mavin flew there, Beedie said. Which means Shifters can fly there and bring crystals back. Oh, Dervishes, I beg you . . .'

'You need not beg,' said Bartelmy. 'I told you once to stop crying and get to work. I will not wait for you to say the same to me . . .'

'Mother,' I said, shivering at the sound of the word in my mouth. 'Mother. Do not take time to confer. Can you truly set your patience aside?'

'When we must. Yes, Jinian. When we must.'

They went. I was not sure which way they went, except that in a few moments all were gone. Beside me the door to the hut stood open. Within were two narrow beds, a table with two chairs. A cupboard. They had indeed set their laws aside and prepared for my visit. I sat at the table, laid my head upon her arms, and wept as I had not wept since Chimmerdong, weariness mostly. Sadness, perhaps. And after weeping I lay upon the narrow cot and slept.

When I woke Cernaby was standing in the doorway.

'I waited,' said the Dervish. 'We wanted to know what you were going to do next, and Bartelmy thought you might need one of us to carry a message somewhere, to someone.'

'Where are the others?'

'Some have gone south to others of our race. Some to find Queynt and the rest and be sure they reach the south safely. Some into the Shadowmarches in search of the Shadowpeople, though it may be we will need Mavin to help in that search. Some to the caves where the hundred thousand lie. A few to the giants' cavern to see whether any of the blue crystals remain there when the waters drain away. Some to carry messages among those others, to keep us all informed.'

I stared at her incredulously. 'So quickly! I did not think it possible.'

'We are not benighted, Jinian. If we have had any fault, it has been too much pride. We had a revelation from our founder. We had Seers' visions which we misinterpreted. We had what we thought was the answer and we troubled to look no further. Who ever believes that time will end before one's solution can be put into place?'

I laughed, coughing. 'Give me a moment, Cernaby. You have moved faster than I can.'

I rose, walked around the room, found bread in the cupboard, ate some of it with a cup of water from the pitcher on the table. 'It seems I am part of this matter. Not of my own doing, but merely because Murzemire Hornloss saw me involved in it. If for no other reason than that, I must play out that part.'

I thought long on this. Then, 'Cernaby, my thanks. No. This is one of those games without a name and which I keep getting involved in. Let me play it out, I do not think your presence will matter. Though I would welcome your company, perhaps your company is not what is most needed. I would rather you carry a message for me. To Murzy – Murzemire Hornloss. Tell her what we found. Tell her to raise the sevens. In all my dreams I can think of only three forces in this land unified enough to do anything sensible: the sevens, the Immutables, and the Dervishes. Himaggery and Barish will argue. Mavin will go kiting off on her own wild way. The pawns? Well, what powers have we left them that would make them useful now? Peter has destroyed the Magicians. Beedie's people are far away. So. Go to the Immutables, and carry the word to Murzemire with my love.'

Cernaby did not linger. There was no sentimentality among the Dervishes, there was little enough sentiment. When she was gone, I was alone in the pervasion with only my thoughts for company. I went through a number of the huts, packing what food I found. There was not much. Evidently the Dervishes lived on air, or sunlight. It would not have surprised me much to learn this was true. When I had repacked everything, as tightly and neatly as possible, I went back the way I had come. Wherever I was going next, I wanted Peter with me.

CHAPTER ELEVEN

I arrived at the pillar of red stone. Peter wasn't there. I didn't really expect him. It would have taken some time for him to get to the Bright Demesne – assuming that's where everyone was, which might not be the case – and convincing them of anything might take longer. Unless he'd simply put the crystals in their soup. Which I abhorred philosophically but thought might be pragmatically justified. As long as it wasn't me it was done to.

Since it was possible I might have a long wait, I made a good camp, summoning up a few flood-chucks to help me with it. They explained they were very busy cleaning up the storm damage, and I explained that I understood all that, but I needed a camp nonetheless. We bowed to one another and said it all once again. Finally we compromised on a tightly woven hut thatched with reeds on the shore of a nearby lake. They threw in a latrine as lagniappe. We bowed again, satisfying one another with our mutual respect, and then I gave them one of the blue crystals, which they shared before moving away very thoughtfully into the woods. I had not even taken time to consider before giving them the crystal. It seemed right they should have it.

I needed the hut to keep the shadow out as I had needed a house long ago in Chimmerdong. Shadow had lain deep on Chimmerdong, and I'd learned of its evil ways at first hand, getting myself shadow bit in the process. It lay thickly now in these northlands, flowing from somewhere in an unending flood.

Even if there had been no shadow, a hut would have been a comfortable thing to have. Though Storm

Grower was dead, it might rain. There were pombis rambling about in the wood. I might have to wait a very long time. Forever, if necessary, I think we had said. So. I would wait. And watch.

Each day was spent wandering, looking, finding different lookouts from which one might spy upon the world. Each vantage point was more depressing than the last, for there were great swatches of forest dying, strange stinking smokes rising from far valleys. One day I thought of going back to the cavern of the giants but did not. Funk, I think. I couldn't face it. My imagination told me too vividly what I would find there.

Having rejected that idea, I decided to visit the ridge above the Great Maze. Since it was a high point, I could see a long way from there. It occurred to me I might see Peter returning.

It wasn't far, actually. Less than a half day's scramble. It was saddening to look down into the empty pervasion, and the hill wasn't as lofty as I remembered it. Still, it gave a good view out over the Great Maze and the lands sloping down to the sea. I scouted around in the pervasion, robbing a few huts of their stale bread – it wasn't bad dipped in tea – and a pot to boil water in. Somewhere between Storm Grower and Fangel, I'd lost mine.

I built a small fire at the foot of one of the stone pillars, brewed some tea, and set myself to watch the southern sky.

Birds. Clouds. Nice white ones, for a change. Sitting there with the fragrant breeze in my face, it was hard to believe that the world was dying beneath me. Grasses nodded; small things crept about making nests. It didn't feel dead or dying, and yet I knew it was. The more I thought about it, the more I wanted Peter, and the less likely it seemed he was going to come. The sky was empty.

I looked down for a while, to rest my eyes.

I saw it coming out of the Great Maze.

It came from the Maze itself. There was a movement

at the edge of the Maze, a puzzling kind of change. I stared at it. The hedge of the Maze was no different. Nothing was entering or leaving it. And yet . . .

Something had changed. There was a new configuration of light. Something shifted. For a time I gazed at it, uncertain, and then it moved. The shadow. Flooding out of the Maze and flowing downward, along the trail. An endless gray tide, covering the world.

From the Maze? Why from the Maze?

I spent a few minutes in futile cursing, then headed back for my camp. I'd have to find out as much as possible, before Peter came. He might drop directly into it. Be frozen, as Himaggery had been before Bartelmy had rescued him. Oh, by the Hundred Rotten Devils, I sighed, why now?

Finding out anything would be like playing with an avalanche, rather. Toying with an angry dragon. I had talked long with Mavin. I knew what the shadow could do. Still, one had to know, as Queynt would say. One had to know.

Back at the hut I considered the matter. What was there around me that still retained some integrity? The forest was smashed, riven, and storm-wrecked. The very mountains were torn. About the only thing around that looked whole was the lake we had built the hut beside, a charming little oval of shallow water, set in reeds, decked with lilies, full of fish and small plopping things. Though the forested banks were reduced to rubbish and the lake itself muddied from landslides upstream, still it had a certain immaculate charm left about it.

The hut had one window, which I used for the window magic. As in Chimmerdong, I hung my blanket before it to serve as a curtain. Then I called up the lake.

I don't know quite what I expected. Some bubbly shape, perhaps, with fish for eyes. Some reedy thing with lilies in its hair. What came was a rounded silver dart, not unfishlike in shape, curved on every side and reflecting the interior of the hut like a mirror so that I saw a hundred Jinians in its sides. It did not bubble; it did not splash. It spoke as running water speaks, a quiet burble, a ruminative sibilance. 'What would you, Jinian Star-eye?' it asked me as I was shutting the curtain.

'The giants are dead,' I told it. 'I expect you already knew that.'

'We did. Yes.' Expressionless. That fact meant little to it, I thought.

It made me dizzy to look at it. I stared into the fire, instead. It kept shifting, never alike for two instants. 'I have seen the shadow flowing from the Maze. I thought it might come from there for some reason.'

'You thought your being here might evoke it? That your summons might interest it?' It still seemed very little concerned. Instead it was detached, remote. 'No. It does not concern itself with you now, Jinian Star-eye. It grows as the algae grows when lakes and rivers have died. It grows without thought, without care, and will die in its time without grief. When everything dies, so then will the shadow die as well.'

'I am told,' I said carefully, 'that the shadow can seek a certain person.'

'It can be sent to do so,' sighed the lake. 'Of itself, it does not seek. It grows in the Maze and flows from there. Whenever the destruction is remembered, more shadow flows . . .'

'Destruction?'

'Of the Daylight Bell.'

I thought about that. At the moment it didn't make much sense to me, but I didn't pursue it. 'Then the only reason it's flowing out of the Maze now is that the Maze is full of it? No other reason?'

'No other reason. We are too near, too small, to concern those who sometimes send it.'

'Chimmerdong concerned it.'

'Chimmerdong was mighty, once. Boughbound was mighty, once. And the Glistening Sea and the Southern

Sea and the River Ramberlon, which you call Stony-brook. If we live, call us up again, Jinian Footseer, and we will tell you the names of all the mighty who once gloried in the world.'

'If we live. If the shadow does not catch me.'

'You know,' it whispered to me. 'You know. They may send it after you, human-girl, but they have not done so. Yet.'

It left me then. I had not had the foresight to realize the hut would be very wet when it left. That night I slept beneath the stars, nervously.

Peter returned in the morning. He woke me where I slept, rolled in my cloak.

'There was a flood in your hut?' he asked in a despondent voice. 'I thought maybe you'd drowned.'

'Peter, what's the matter?'

He hugged me sadly, almost absentmindedly. 'Oh, Jinian, from worse to worse yet. Himaggery and Barish were arguing when we left there two years ago. While we've been away it went from argument to open animosity, and from that to a split at the Bright Demesne. Barish is for raising all the hundred thousand at once to make what he calls "massive changes", not that he's raised even one of them yet. Himaggery wants them raised a few at a time to make what he calls, "balanced programs". Mavin got disgusted with them both and left. No one knows where she is. Mertyn went back to Schooltown.' He seemed about to weep.

'Shh, shh,' I hushed him. 'Bad enough, my love. But I know you. I know my sly, snakey Peter. What did you get done?'

'I talked to Barish and demanded that the old Wind-low part of him listen to me. He heard the warning. I said it over and over until he really seemed to have heard it. Then I put a blue crystal in his tea.'

'I thought you would.' I wanted him to know I did not disapprove. Himaggery and Barish were stubborn, pombi-proud idiots. Heaven save me from male Wize-ards who want to play politics. 'And then?'

'Then I told Himaggery he owed it to me as his son to listen to me. Which he agreed to. I warned him. Then I put a blue crystal in his wine.'

'Ah.'

'Then I left. I made a stop in Schooltown. Mertyn did believe me and he will send word to Mavin – somewhere, somehow, if he ever figures out where she is and though no one knows how long it will be before she gets the message, if she gets it at all. The two of us together went to see Riddle and Quench in the land of the Immutables. I gave crystals to each of them. I was sure the Immutables would be immune, just as they are to Talent, but they weren't. None of them doubted me.'

I cursed. 'Doesn't it prove what I said, Peter? Only three disciplined forces in the world. The Immutables; the Dervishes; the sevens.'

'Well, we've got three alerted. A Dervish arrived about the time I left Schooltown. Don't ask me how she got there that fast, because I flew the whole way. She said her name was Cernaby and to tell you your message had gone to the sevens.' He sighed, stretched out beside me, and pulled half my blanket over him. I didn't even worry about his closeness. Oath or no oath. It just wasn't that important anymore.

'What did you do with the other crystals? You had several dozens of them?'

'Gave them to Riddle and Quench and Mertyn. One for Mavin, when they find her. Six to be sent by trusted messenger to the others of your seven in Xammer – if they are still there . . .'

This astonished me. I had not thought of it myself, but Peter had. He continually surprised me by being more thoughtful and intelligent than I expected him to be. He didn't notice my surprise but went on.

'The others they will use as they see fit. I told them what you said about the hundred thousand good Gamesmen who are still frozen under the mountain. When I left them, Quench was talking with Cernaby about starting the resurrection, Barish or no Barish. Quench has the resurrection machine, you know. It's his people who fixed it, and they were the ones who were going to do the work anyhow, if Barish ever got around to it. The problem is, of course, that Quench hasn't enough of the crystals to be sure all of the resurrectees are given them, and you said that was important.'

'I think it's important. Why bring them back at all if not to help? Otherwise, they only return to die with the rest of us. I would have thought Barish would have started bringing them back to life by now, Himaggery or no Himaggery.'

He turned toward me, laying an arm across me, tugging me close. 'He'd rather argue than do. I think the mixture of Windlow into him has immobilized him. He still remembers what he planned to do once, but with Windlow inside his head he sees all the flaws in his original plan. I felt sorry for him.' He breathed very deeply in my ear. I lay very quietly, not discouraging him. If something was going to happen between us, I was not going to talk about my oath. What did happen between us was a gentle snore. So much for breaking my oath to make love beside the limpid waters. I laughed at myself and fell asleep.

When he wakened, I told him what I had learned about the shadow. Peter had heard Mavin's story of the shadow. 'It lives in the Great Maze?'

'So the lake creature said. It lives in the Great Maze, among the memories of the world.' I did not realize what I had said until I had said it. Cernaby had told me that.

'Among the memories of the world? Jinian. We store our memories in our minds.'

'In our brains,' I corrected him. 'The mind is something else. It, too, lives in the brain, but it is something else. So I was told long ago by a Healer who saved my life. Peter, if the shadow lives in the brain of Lom, of the world, then is the shadow part of this world, or is it something else? Something from outside? As we were from outside? As mankind was from outside? Did we really bring some plague with us? Queynt talked with Eesties who alleged so. Were they right?'

'We could go in the Maze and find out,' he offered. I laughed, then told him only a little about my short journey through a shallow edge of the Maze. He gave me disbelieving looks. 'Wasn't there a guide?'

'The Oracle. The Oracle who almost got me killed at Daggerhawk. The Oracle who trapped me and gave me to the giants. That Oracle?'

'We could tie it up. You could put distraints on it.'

'We could tie it up. I don't think that would work, but we could try. Distraints, however? I don't think so, Peter. I think anything I know, the Oracle knows something stronger. It's a kind of evil Devil. A kind of dancing mischief maker. All full of – puffed-up anger and pride and envy. Some kind of trouble-god. And there isn't only one of it. I thought I was dreaming in the cavern, but the more I think about it, the more sure I become that it was all true. I saw many of them in there. Oracles and Oracles. One, perhaps, as the leader, but followers without number. And oh, Peter, but I am afraid of them.'

He was listening to me, concentrated upon me, looking deep into my eyes. 'You know what you're implying, Jinian. You don't say it, but you must know it.'

'That they're the ones who hid the blue crystals. The ones who took them all instead of seeing they were distributed all around the world. Yes, I'm sure they did it. The Oracles.'

It was out. Said. It rang true. Who else would have assembled them in the cavern of the giants? Who else would have taken them? Who else would have displayed such warped hatred for mankind? Oracles. Who never told the whole truth. 'Oracles The very father and mother of liars,' I said. 'Not trustworthy as guides, Peter. Truly not.'

217

'I can see you thinking, Jinian Footseer. You're thinking about going into that Maze, guide or no guide. No matter what it's like.'

I couldn't deny it. I'd been thinking about it for days. How to get in. How to find my way in. How to test whether my art worked there, and if so, how. How to use it, then. How to find the place the shadow lived. If Lom was dying, wasn't it possible the shadow was killing it, no matter what the lake had told me? Oh, I thought about it. At various times I had thought about a whole seven going in. Or maybe a group of Dervishes. Each time, something within me said, No. Not great armies, just one or two people. That's all.

'Yes,' I admitted. 'It seems someone will have to. Everything that can be done on the outside is being done, except one thing.'

'And that is?'

'Going to Beedie's land and getting the crystals that are there. Mercald-Mirtylon said there were many. They only brought out a few. Since I made that mistake at the cavern, calling up the boon too quickly, the ones in Beedie's chasm may be the only ones left. I was dependng on Mavin to do that.'

'Mavin will, when they find her.'

'*If* they find her. *If* they find her in time. If she agrees to go. If she gets there. If she gets back.'

'I see. You want me to go.'

'Someone has to. I can't. I'm no Shifter.'

'Jinian. Oh, Jinian, I'm not nearly the Shifter Mavin is, either. You may not know that, but in Shiftery, experience counts. Mavin was much older than I when she flew the Western Sea. Stronger. She had more experience with the forms, with the quick changes. My pride suffers to have me say it, Jinian, love. But I'm not sure I'd make it, Jinian Footseer.'

I hadn't known. He always seemed so confident. Then I remembered that clumsily staggering form that had left me a few days before, wobbling across the sky, and I wanted to cry. Wings, I suppose it took years to really get accustomed to wings.

And it dropped into my head like a stone into a pool. Wings. The great flitchhawk of Chimmerdong owed me a boon. The last one of the three great boons I had earned in Chimmerdong. And if any creature alive in this world had wings, it was he.

There was no reason to wait, so I didn't. Peter and I sat beside the fire, and I called him. I let Peter see me do it; that was against the rules, but I did it anyway.

'The ways of the sky are yours, treetop and cloud, sunlight and starlight, wind and rain. I have need of these and call for a boon.'

We sat quietly for a time until he arrived. On all previous arrivals, I had been buffeted by the huge feathers. This time Peter was in the way. He stood up to it no better than I ever had. It sent him sprawling.

'Your eyes are like moons, flitchhawk,' I said. 'Have you seen much of the world in the last two years?'

He perched on the ground, a monumental thing, his beak like the curved roof of a tower, his legs like obelisks, wings out like the boughs of mighty trees, shading us against the sun. When he looked down at me, I felt very small, and yet that gaze was no less friendly than it had ever been. He answered me. 'Destruction and wrack, Jinian Dervish daughter. High winds and low. Chimmerdong lives yet a while, but elsewhere the green of life dims to gray. I have swum in clouds, waiting for your call.'

'I want you to take my love over the sea, flitchhawk. Far over the sea to a great chasm, where he must gather crystals as blue as your skies and bring them to Mertyn and Riddle and Quench.'

'Is this the boon you would ask?'

'It is,' I said.

'No,' said Peter. He strode from beneath the great wing to stand facing the flitchhawk, unafraid of it, his face quite calm and adamantly strong.

'No?' The great bird flexed its feathers, letting the light shine through them. We stood in its dappled shade.

'When I said no, I meant that it wasn't quite right,' Peter said. 'Not quite what was wanted. You see, I must stay here. Otherwise Jinian will go into the Great Maze without me, and if I cannot be with her to help her and protect her, then I do not care if Lom dies. If I do not care, I could not do the job well over the Western Sea.'

'So you don't want me to take you,' the flitchhawk murmured, raising those wings.

'No. We want you to go instead. The crystals are blue. They lie at the bottom of the great chasm. The Stickies will bring them to you if you ask. Beedie's people will help you if you ask. Birds are holy to that people. Messengers, so they say, of the Boundless. If you will go now to the south where Beedie and Roges are, they will direct you.' He said this all in a rush, never taking his eyes off the flitchhawk, and I could not stop him.

'And is this your wish, Jinian Star-eye?' The wings were fully raised, high.

I didn't even take time to think. 'Yes,' I cried.

The wings came down, a huge buffet of air knocked us to the ground, the flitchhawk lifted away, circled, higher and higher, and we saw him turn away south, in the direction Beedie and Roges and Queynt and Chance had gone.

I was crying. Not sadly. Not happily, either, come to that, but out of a certain fullness inside me. 'We may never come out of the Maze, you know,' I said to him.

'I know,' he said. 'That's why I couldn't let you go alone.'

We stayed there that day. Resting a little. Talking of things long gone. Not that we had lived so long as to have many such things, but those we had were precious. I talked about the girl in the window of Schooltown who called up her love and gave him a slice of hot nut pie. He told me of seeing a girl at a banquet in Xammer

220

and never being able to forget her after that. We were not even tempted to make love. Something sadder and higher had us by the throats, and we slept in one another's arms, needing nothing more than that.

And in the morning we left the little hut by the lake and went up the trail to the Great Maze. Somewhere inside it lay all the answers to all the questions we had ever asked. We stood a long time hand in hand above it, readying ourselves. I knew what we must look for in that Maze. A book. A light. A bell. Twice now, Seers had Seen those things as having meaning for me, for us, and if they existed in this world, then Lom should remember them.

The little path Cernaby had shown me lay below us. Beyond those first few rooms? Cells? I did not know what we would find.

And there were no answers where we were. Peter kissed me. I heard him sigh, two sighs, both of us.

Then we went in.

THE END

Sheri Stewart Tepper was born, reared, and educated in Colorado, U.S.A. She worked for many years for various non-profit organizations including the international relief organization, CARE, and Planned Parenthood, the American family planning organization. As executive director of Rocky Mountain Planned Parenthood, she was responsible for the administration of some thirty medical clinics in Colorado, Wyoming, and New Mexico.

A longtime writer of children's stories, she sold her first book for adults in 1982. Other sales encouraged her to leave her job and retire to the family ranch in Larkspur, Colorado to write full time. She lives there with her husband, Gene, and an assortment of wild and domesticated animals including a small pack of Norwegian Elkhounds to keep the coyotes at bay, a herd of Belted Galloway cattle, and a family of shorthaired silver tabbies.

She is the mother of two children, one son, a scientist with the National Laboratories at Los Alamos, and one daughter, who is also a writer. She has one grandchild.

Jinian Footseer
by Sheri S. Tepper

I began to write this account upon the Wastes of Bleer, by firelight as others slept, sure I would die upon the morning . . .

I had come to that place with Peter — and with Silkhands and King Kelver of the Dragon's Fire Demesne, with Chance and Vitior Vulpas Queynt. Six of us. Upon that barren height Peter had raised up the Gamesmen of Barish — he had carried them in his pocket for several years — embodying them once more in their own flesh. Eleven of them, plus Barish himself. We were eighteen. And against us was coming a horde, a multitude, a vast army of living and dead, live flesh and dead bone, which none among us thought we could withstand.

So — I took pen and paper and began to write, thinking perhaps that someone might find the pages, long afterward, and remember me for a moment. A tenuous kind of immortality, but the best I could hope for then . . .

I am called Jinian Footseer by some. By some, Jinian Star-Eye. And by some, the Wizard Jinian. One or two call me Dervish Daughter. But I think of myself most often still as merely Jinian, an unloved daughter of Stoneflight Demesne, who found love later in a strange way. It is that Jinian I wrote of first, there in that horrid night, and that Jinian I must write of at last.

0552 13189 X

Coming soon — JINIAN STAR-EYE

SELECTED LIST OF TITLES
AVAILABLE FROM CORGI BOOKS

THE PRICES SHOWN BELOW WERE CORRECT AT THE TIME OF GOING
TO PRESS. HOWEVER TRANSWORLD PUBLISHERS RESERVE THE
RIGHT TO SHOW NEW RETAIL PRICES ON COVERS WHICH MAY
DIFFER FROM THOSE PREVIOUSLY ADVERTISED IN THE TEXT OR
ELSEWHERE.

*All Corgi/Bantam Books are available at your bookshop or newsagent, or can be ordered from
the following address:*

Corgi/Bantam Books,
Cash Sales Department,
P.O. Box 11, Falmouth, Cornwall TR10 9EN

Please send a cheque or postal order (no currency) and allow 60p for postage and packing for
the first book plus 25p for the second book and 15p for each additional book ordered up to a
maximum charge of £1.90 in UK.

B.F.P.O. customers please allow 60p for the first book, 25p for the second book plus 15p per
copy for the next 7 books, thereafter 9p per book.

Overseas customers, including Eire, please allow £1.25 for postage and packing for the first
book, 75p for the second book, and 28p for each subsequent title ordered.